KYRON

The K9 Files, Book 15

Dale Mayer

KYRON: THE K9 FILES, BOOK 15
Dale Mayer
Valley Publishing Ltd.

ISBN-13: 978-1-773365-48-0
Print Edition

Books in This Series:

Ethan, Book 1

Pierce, Book 2

Zane, Book 3

Blaze, Book 4

Lucas, Book 5

Parker, Book 6

Carter, Book 7

Weston, Book 8

Greyson, Book 9

Rowan, Book 10

Caleb, Book 11

Kurt, Book 12

Tucker, Book 13

Harley, Book 14

Kyron, Book 15

Jenner, Book 16

The K9 Files, Books 1–2

The K9 Files, Books 3–4

The K9 Files, Books 5–6

The K9 Files, Books 7–8

The K9 Files, Books 9–10

The K9 Files, Books 11–12

About This Book

Welcome to the all new K9 Files series reconnecting readers with the unforgettable men from SEALs of Steel in a new series of action packed, page turning romantic suspense that fans have come to expect from USA TODAY Bestselling author Dale Mayer. Pssst… you'll meet other favorite characters from SEALs of Honor and Heroes for Hire too!

Kyron swore he wouldn't work with dogs anymore, but, when Badger asks him to go home to Aspen and to track a missing War Dog, who is missing her left leg—as he is—Kyron can't refuse. Even if it means seeing his brother and his wife again. Not that he had anything against them. Kyron just couldn't deal with his parents. Finding the dog seems like the easiest part of returning to Aspen, until Kyron realizes a rescue run by a fascinating woman is the one that's spotted the missing dog, … only the dog isn't alone …

Miranda spends every waking moment working to keep her animals safe. Two jobs keeps them in food and shelter but not much more. Considering her miserable neighbor is always making complaints about her, she has considered moving, but it is too expensive to make that happen. She has seen a three-legged canine hanging around the back perimeter of her property and had been feeding it, quietly knowing it resembled the dog the neighbor had brought home, until it ran away.

She had no intention of letting her neighbor or anyone

else know about the dog, hoping to coax it onto her property, where she could look after it properly. However, then Kyron showed up, searching for the animal, and things got really ugly …

Sign up to be notified of all Dale's releases here!

https://smarturl.it/DaleNews

PROLOGUE

BADGER SAT AT his desk across from Kyron Edgewater, who stared at him, somewhat angered.

"You want me to go after a dog? Did you hear me say that I didn't want to do K9 anymore?"

"I did. And her name is Beth." Badger looked over at Erick, who sat beside him.

Erick picked up the argument. "We figured it's one of the reasons that you probably need to do this. We know how much you love dogs. We know how much you love that part of your life. And we figure some trauma's still there that you might need to heal."

"But you're not shrinks." Kyron felt his temper spike. "And I didn't sign up for therapy."

"Maybe not, but, at the same time, I'd like to think that there's room in your heart to help out another animal."

"What's wrong with it?"

"She's missing a leg, was injured, and retired out in Colorado."

"So that sounds like what all of us are dealing with." He made a hand motion at the three of them. He had two fake knee joints, a missing lower leg, some ribs, and a kidney. Well, bits and pieces were left of the kidney. "It is what it is."

"Sure, and then somebody went to do a welfare check on Beth to make sure she was okay. At which point, the new owners admitted that she had gone missing sometime in the night a few months ago."

He stopped and stared. "Why the hell would somebody steal the dog?"

"We're not exactly sure," Badger admitted. "They were having trouble with the dog. It was a little more aggressive than anticipated, and they didn't know why. So, when she went missing, they weren't too upset. They weren't planning on telling anybody either. Nobody would have known except for the dog welfare check."

"And so now what?"

"We want to make sure Beth is okay."

"Obviously it's not okay. It's gone missing. If it was getting aggressive, you also know there's a damn good chance that somebody took it out back and shot it."

Badger winced at that. "I hope not. We've had really good luck finding these animals and giving them a much better life. But if Colorado isn't a place you want to go and if Beth is one you can walk away from …"

Kyron frowned at Badger. "That's a low blow."

"Of course it is." Badger half smiled. "We're a little desperate here. We need people who can handle dogs."

"Of course I can handle dogs. The reason I didn't want to go back in the K9 unit is, I couldn't handle the death."

"And that's justified," Badger admitted. "Not to mention that you're not the first person to bring up that point. I'm just looking for somebody to take a quick trip and to see if they can find Beth."

"But it went missing months ago. You know there'll be no sign of it."

"Maybe not but we have to take a look, don't we?"

He groaned. "And of course this isn't a paid job, is it?"

"Would it make a difference to you if it was?"

"No." He sighed. "Just that you want somebody who can find this dog and make sure she's okay." And yes the dog was already a she – a warm and precious female life.

"Yes, and we'll cover the trip, and we'll cover the hotels and any equipment you might need." Badger studied him closely. "Are you okay with Colorado?"

"Sure. Why wouldn't I be okay with Colorado?" he asked in exasperation. "Aspen was my winter playground."

"And how will you handle returning there in the wintertime, when you only have one leg?"

He glared at him. "Maybe I'll pick up snowboarding and see how that works."

"Maybe you should. For all we know, Beth's been taken into Search and Rescue and is just fine."

At that, Kyron shrugged. "You know that actually wouldn't be a bad field for her."

"Except for the missing leg."

"Possibly." He stared off in the distance. "Maybe a prosthetic could be made for her too."

"Why don't you go find Beth, then talk to Kat about that," Badger suggested, "but only if you're interested."

He glared at him. "You know I'm interested. You also know there's no way in hell I'll leave that dog in trouble."

"That's what we figured," Badger noted in satisfaction. "Still, it's your choice."

"Meaning, you know I would go." Kyron got up and walked outside. He stopped, took a deep breath, and he knew that he was in for headache and heartache.

Every time it seemed like he got around dogs, it was just bad news. They either got killed, taken away, injured, or something bad happened.

But this one was already injured, the other part of his brain argued. *Maybe, this time, it'll go better for both of you.*

He doubted it. But he was a sucker for anyone in trouble. Especially a dog. "Hang on, Beth. I'm on my way."

CHAPTER 1

KYRON STEPPED OUT of the airport, shouldered his bag to a different position that didn't press on some of the scar tissue around his ribs, then turned to look around. He'd left a message but hadn't heard back from Allen. Absolutely no guarantee his brother would even be here. Kyron hadn't talked to his brother in, well, let's just say a long time. A vehicle drove up, honking its horn. They used to be good friends, but Allen hadn't agreed with Kyron's decision to go into the navy so long ago.

Allen had gone into local law enforcement, and that was something that Kyron didn't have a problem with at all, but that wasn't what Kyron wanted for himself. They kept in touch at first but had drifted apart. After a couple bouts of brotherly rivalry had hit, they never seemed to really talk after that.

He looked over at the vehicle honking again and realized it was Allen. Kyron walked forward, threw his duffel bag in the back of the pickup, and hopped up into the front seat.

Allen shot him a hard look and then pulled out into the traffic.

"What's that look for?" Kyron asked.

"I was just assessing your walk."

"I'm walking just fine," he replied in a calm voice.

"You'd be walking better if you had both legs."

"Well, that won't change," he murmured, "so it's a dead conversation."

His brother shrugged. "Considering my partner just lost his leg on the job, I guess that's a fair assessment."

Kyron looked over at him. "Conrad?"

"Yeah, car accident, high-speed chase. Conrad ended up whipped out and pinned behind a power pole, and the leg couldn't be saved."

"I'm sorry to hear that," Kyron said sincerely.

"Me too. I think his wife is more torn up about it than Conrad is. Although I'm not sure reality has set in for him."

"It takes a long time," Kyron stated. "You put on this good front and a happy face and say, 'Hey, it's only one leg.' Then you believe it'll all be better—until you wake up in the morning and try to go to the bathroom and end up flat on your face because you forgot you are missing a leg."

Allen looked at him, startled. "Never thought about things like that."

"He'll adjust, the same as I did."

The two brothers didn't say anything for a long time.

"So, in that very short text of yours, you didn't mention why you were coming to Aspen," Allen stated. "It would be lovely to think it was to see me and Sandra, but I highly doubt that's what is on your mind."

"Let's just say, it's good timing for a chance to combine two things with one," he replied.

"Which also means that you wouldn't be coming for a visit if you didn't have this other purpose."

"Well, I didn't have a whole lot of purpose otherwise," he shared. "Don't worry. I'm not planning on sticking around as a deadbeat brother, and the visit would have happened eventually either way," he admitted finally to himself and to his brother. "I just wasn't sure when or how."

"You pick up a phone, and you book a ticket, and you make it happen," Allen stated. "You know that we would have come to you anytime over the last couple years."

"Yeah, you probably would have," he agreed. "But it's only now that I'm really somebody worth talking to." Allen didn't say anything for a long moment. And Kyron appreciated that.

"I gather the anger was pretty rough."

"You could say that." Kyron paused. "I lost my career, along with my leg and my best friend," he noted, his voice low. "You tend to either get over it really easily, or it takes you a hell of a long time to let it go."

"I think you got over it just fine," Allen added briefly. "You're at least talking to us now, so I take that as a positive sign. I do know some guys, some veterans, who have a huge hate for the world around them."

"And a lot of guys don't," Kyron countered quietly. "I needed to get to the point where I became one of the ones who don't have that hate." He knew his brother would understand, especially being in law enforcement. They took risks every day of their lives, and sometimes the risks were just a little bit worse than others.

"I'm sorry about your career."

"Well, I could have had a desk job, if I wanted it."

At that, Allen snorted. "You and me both would have the same attitude about that."

"Well, that's the thing." Kyron sent a brief smile in his brother's direction. "It's been pretty tough, and I just couldn't see myself at a desk job. Some guys can adapt and do well, but I couldn't see myself in that role."

"And yet," Allen noted, "you used to be in a K9 unit."

"I was, and I walked away from that just before the accident."

His brother looked startled. "You didn't tell us that."

"No."

"And why didn't you?"

"Because we had four dogs die," Kyron snapped. "One mission went bad, real bad, and I just decided that I'd had enough of the deaths."

"And yet you didn't retire."

"No, I didn't, but I probably should have. *Hindsight.* It's awesome if hindsight actually had the ability to change anything," he stated. "But when you can't change things, it just makes you feel like an idiot for not having seen the signs ahead of time."

"That's terrible." Allen shook his head. "I hadn't ever considered it that way."

"And, honest to God, it could be so much worse," Kyron added.

"It could be, yes," Allen agreed. "I could be driving to your funeral right now, instead of driving you back home."

"I appreciate the lift, by the way."

"And I hope you're staying with us." When Kyron hesitated at that, Allen shook his head. "Don't be stubborn. We haven't had a chance to see you in a couple years. You damn near died on us, and you know how much we want to see you." He looked over at him. "By the way, Sandra's pregnant."

He looked at his brother in shock. "Seriously?"

Allen gave him a pleased smile. "Yeah, I know. We didn't think it would happen. The doctors even told us it wasn't likely to happen, but, hey, it did. So, what we're trying to do is keep her calm, quiet, and not have anything go wrong. It's considered a high-risk pregnancy, and we all know how that can go. I'd appreciate it if you'd keep that part of the conversation out of the house though." Allen shot a glance at his brother. "We always have too much of that worry in the back of our minds."

"How far along is she?"

"She's seven months already."

"Wow, but that also means, if something did go wrong now, you're at the point where the baby could survive, right?"

"That's what we're counting on. She's been off work since we found out, just trying to be as careful as she can," he noted quietly.

"How is she doing mentally?"

His brother nodded. "Much better now. The miscarriage a couple years ago hit her really badly, and she was in a really depressed state. I had trouble getting her to eat. She didn't care about anything, and she lost weight, too much weight."

"She doesn't have any to lose to begin with."

"No, and it's been a struggle to get her to put on enough to make it through the pregnancy. Honestly, we're pretty stoked that she's at seven months and that things are still looking solid."

"I'm sure you are," he replied. "Any idea what it is?"

"It's a boy." Allen grinned.

"Holy cow." Kyron sat back, staring at his brother. "You'll actually have a son."

"I know. I know. I'm pretty excited."

And he was; Kyron could tell from the proud look on his face. "Well, let's hope everything goes well for these last couple months."

"We're doing our best to keep everything calm and quiet."

"Then it's better if I go to a hotel, isn't it?" Kyron asked. "The last thing I want to do is upset the apple cart."

"And how would having you home upset the apple cart?" Allen asked, frowning. "If you went to a hotel, it would make her all worried that she'd done something wrong."

"Yeah, that's a Sandra thing, isn't it?" Kyron rubbed his temples. He didn't know what to do. He thought that maybe he could stay with his brother, although Badger had specifically said they would cover the expenses. Yet hotels here were really expensive, and there wasn't any need for it, as Kyron had family here. Also, if he didn't have to spend as much money, then Badger could use it to help other dogs, which was always part of his thought process.

"Yeah, to some degree. Listen," his brother continued. "I would appreciate it if you did stay, and, hey, if it looks like it'll be stressful, I'd have no problem asking you to leave."

Kyron snorted at that. "Bro, you've never had a problem telling me exactly what you thought." An awkward silence followed for a moment.

Then Allen finally spoke. "I've wondered if you still held that against me."

"Trying not to." Kyron shrugged. "It was great that you got to make your life choices and have everybody's support, but I just couldn't go that route."

"Yeah." Allen nodded. "I've thought about that a lot over the years, and I have to admit that is something I regret. Your parents do too."

"You mean, *our* parents?" he corrected, with a wry tone.

He winced at that. "Yeah. Listen. I know they supported me becoming a cop because that's what our father was as well. So, to them, I was following in his footsteps."

"And I was following in Granddad's footsteps, but, because they were on outs with him, they chose to be on the outs with me," Kyron replied quietly.

"Have you talked to them?"

"Nope, I sure haven't. They told me that I'd get hurt and to not come back to them when I was all crippled up and in need of financial support," he shared, his voice hard. "So, no, I haven't reached out."

A shocked silence came from Allen's side of the vehicle. "Jesus, I didn't know that."

"Yeah, and they were pretty specific. So I've not had anything to do with them since then, now that, of course, I am injured and what they would think of as 'in need of financial support.' Therefore, you can damn well bet I won't have anything to do with them now either."

"That's a little harsh, isn't it?"

"Nope, it sure isn't," he snapped. "Not if you're me. Not if, like Sandra, you're protecting your health or your sanity, by keeping cynical and hateful people out of your life."

"They were trying to stop you from running away and dying in a far-off land."

"Maybe so, but you're just as likely to get killed in law enforcement here in Aspen as I was in the military."

At that, Allen nodded. "Unfortunately it happens, but one was a little more honorable to them than the other."

"Of course. One kept you close, and I left to pursue the other," Kyron replied. "I also think it had an awful lot to do with Granddad."

"You were always really close to Granddad too," Allen murmured.

"Always."

"It was just something they hated, but I never quite understood that either," Allen murmured.

"No, and I sure never got the reasons for it either, but, because they were mad at Granddad, they considered my friendship with him to be choosing sides."

"Maybe." Allen pulled out of the traffic and headed down a side street.

"No *maybe* about it. They were supposed to be the adults back then, and now." With a huge sigh, Kyron asked, "Have things in town changed much?"

"Nope, still big money, still big problems, and most of it under the counter, until something brings it to light, you know?" he replied. "We are getting two more patrol positions in the department, but, with tourist season on, it's pretty rough sometimes. I do enjoy my days off, when I get them."

"Any thoughts on retiring, now that you have a family?"

"Haven't got enough years in for that," he stated. "I'm looking for my twenty, and then we'll discuss it."

"You still doing search and rescue?"

"I am, indeed." He looked over at his brother. "Are you interested in doing that again?" Then he frowned and added, "Jeez, sorry."

"Sorry why?" Kyron asked. "Because I'd have to learn how to ski and all that all over again? That's true, but people do it all the time, so I won't say I can't."

"Me either," Allen replied. "The last time I told you that you couldn't do something, as I recall, you knocked me down a few times and broke my nose."

"That was your fault." Kyron laughed. "I'd forgotten all about that."

"Well, you can bet I haven't." Allen chuckled. "And, yes,

you're probably right. I deserved it. I was being that nasty older brother who didn't want the younger kid tagging along."

"Hey, that was my life." Kyron sighed. "I didn't want to tag along behind you in law enforcement either."

"No, and I think sometimes that you deliberately went into the military to get away from us all."

"Not so much to get away from all of you but away from being part of that whole clone system that you guys seemed to have down pat."

"You're really into being the second son, aren't you?"

"I struggled because the first son was obviously the favorite, because the person I was closest to in all the world was Granddad, who was well and truly hated. I mean, I had to sneak off to see him after work and after school and not tell Mom and Dad about it. And then, if they did find out, I'd get grounded," he snapped. "So, yeah, definitely hard feelings existed, which undoubtedly pushed me into enlisting."

"I mentioned that to them in the ensuing years, and they really didn't like me pointing it out," Allen noted.

"Of course not." Kyron stared out the window, streets passing by in an endless stream. "Not a whole lot they like about anything to do with me." He looked over at his brother, frowning. "But I want you to know that I'm not bitter. I was at one time, but I just don't have the time or energy for it now."

"Good, and I am glad to hear that because life is too damn short." And, with that, he navigated around several sharp corners, then pulled up in front of a house.

"Look at that," Kyron said. "You're also the only one of us who owns property. Jeez, you did all the right things. You married your high school sweetheart, and you got a job locally in a career your family approves of, and look at this. You have your own house, even though property prices are out of this world."

"And you also know that I only got the house because Mom and Dad helped me."

"Oh, yeah, don't worry. I heard all about that too," he confirmed.

Kyron was surprised that he really wasn't bitter about it. It had been made very clear to him a long time ago that his brother was the favorite son, and, if Kyron wanted to come anywhere close to measuring up, he needed to toe the line, but toeing the line wasn't something Kyron did well. It just wasn't him. Instead he'd chosen to be a bit of a maverick, and he'd hightailed it out of here, knowing that he would never compete and certain that he didn't want to. What he and his brother had shared at one time hadn't survived while they had gotten older. As his brother became more and more the favorite, Kyron had willingly chosen a different pathway.

"I'm really sorry about a lot of things," his brother said, as he pulled into the driveway and turned off the engine. "And that's one of them."

"Yeah, but I'm not sure it's worth wasting time and energy on now." Kyron looked at the house, shook his head. "You know what? I won't stay. I'll grab a rental vehicle and a hotel close by—or maybe a bed-and-breakfast. I don't know."

At that, his brother opened his mouth and argued, "Come on. Don't be a fool. You know you don't have to do that."

"Maybe I don't have to," he agreed, "but you know what will happen the minute Mom and Dad find out I'm here."

"Well, I would hope"—Allen stared at him—"that maybe you guys could mend the rift."

"The rift of me officially being the black sheep who went into the service instead of law enforcement, even though we all know those are two sides of the same coin?"

His brother winced at that. "I never really saw it from your point of view before. But, even as I look at my house from your perspective, I can see that it's also a result of my relationship with them. I guess there are a lot of reasons for hard feelings. I hadn't really seen it before."

"Hey, they wouldn't even talk to me, so at least one of us has a better deal with the parents." With that, Kyron got out of the vehicle and slammed the door shut. Just then the front door opened, and Sandra stepped out. She took one look at him and burst into tears. He walked to her, his arms out, and he immediately held her close.

"Why the tears?" he asked against her hair. She was round and obviously emotional, but then what did he expect from somebody who was pregnant and trying so hard for a successful pregnancy after struggling with the issue for the whole of her married life?

She leaned back and looked up at him. "Because it's good to see you," she stated firmly. Then she reached up, kissed him on his cheek, and whispered, "You have no idea how much Allen wanted you to come. Thank you." And, with that, he knew his plans of escaping to a hotel were about to crumble into dust around him.

SOMETIMES MIRANDA GALLOWAY thought she'd somehow taken a vow of poverty. Except she wasn't religious, and she certainly hadn't gone down that pathway deliberately, scraping by just to get food for all the animals. But somehow she'd ended up with an animal rescue that wasn't on anybody's radar, so she worked a full-time paying position, plus a Saturday job, just to keep the food flowing at her rescue.

Her family had often told her that she needed to stop that "foolishness," and either get animal control in to put them down or to find "real" rescue organizations for these animals to go to. And she had done some of the latter—never the former—as she farmed out as many as she could on an ongoing basis, and she'd adopted out as many as she possibly could too.

Yet she always seemed to have more mouths to feed. It drove her crazy that so much big corporate money was here in this town, and yet it seemed like so little help was available. She didn't even know for sure if that was true; it's just that she couldn't seem to find a way to access the people with the money, much less get them to loosen up and to spend it on the animals in her care.

She also worked part-time at the local vet's office to pay off the bills she constantly incurred, when the animals needed shots, surgeries, and the like. It was an agreement between them that worked well, but, at the same time, she also had that full-time hourly job as well. And she needed both jobs just to keep the animals cared for.

She'd heard about animal rescues with a steady income, and, for her, at least right now, that was just not a possibility. Getting some of the animal numbers under control would help. She'd just found new homes for twelve of her fostered animals, and that had helped, but she still had fourteen cats, three horses, a goat, and a llama.

And then there were the dogs. It seemed like the incoming dogs never ended. However, they were also often the easiest to move to better homes. She did have a network of animal-loving people from her two jobs, although most people would hold up their hands and cry uncle, saying they couldn't take any more home, even to foster.

Miranda had talked several out of money as well, but she'd pushed that as far as she could, for now at least. At the same time, she still needed to find a way to tap into more money, so that some of these animals—unlikely to do well in other settings—could live out their days in better conditions than she could provide for them now.

She posted newsletters around town; she tapped the local charities, and she regularly worked with one of the cat coalitions because it always seemed that cats were the first to get dumped. And, in a place like Aspen, Colorado, that was a death sentence in the winter. Which was one of the reasons Miranda kept a supply of cat food outside for feral cats.

Plus, she kept bundles of hay in the shed, with multiple pet doors for the feral or skittish cats to come and go, so they could at least get in out of the cold. For some of them that was all she could do, as they were too wild to domesticate. Yet she knew, if she had the time and the money, then she could rehabilitate quite a few of them and potentially bring them in from the cold on a permanent basis.

As it was, when she could get close enough to trap them, she took them in to get spayed or neutered, which would keep their numbers down, but it was still an ongoing problem here. So many people just didn't give a crap about any animals, whereas Miranda seemed to care far too much.

She walked back inside, her breath finally warming, as she took off her boots and her gloves and her big heavy coat and scarf. She wasn't always so cold, but, this last year or two, it seemed like she was always freezing. Then she'd also been on a tight budget, had cut down the house heat, diverting those savings in a desperate attempt to make ends meet.

She sat down at the kitchen table and hugged her cup of coffee, wondering what her next option was. She knew more animals out there needed help, but she was kind of tapped out. Yet she could do nothing but continue on this pathway, until something imploded. Of course what she was afraid of was that the inevitable implosion would be way more than she could handle.

If it wasn't for her grandmother, Miranda didn't know what she'd do. Her grandmother had been a life force, even when Miranda's parents got angry and fed up with her. But then her parents didn't seem to give a crap about animals. They only cared about people. Whereas Miranda could have happily left people behind and would do anything to save the animals.

People at least had choices; these animals did not. A lot of them had been dumped here, knowing she would care for them. Some were severely injured or sick, and many had been living in the nearby woods on their own, trying to do the best that they could. Sometimes they did well; and sometimes, well, they didn't.

She'd seen a dog that her neighbor, Old Man Brant Macintyre, had picked up somewhere along the road. It had been injured and was missing a leg, and the neighbor apparently thought it was a great talking point, but, when it had run away on him in the middle of the night, he'd been pissed. He'd told her that, if the dog had come around her place, it was his, and she was not to feed it.

Regardless she'd been trying to get a hold of the dog and had caught a glimpse of it in the woods every once in a while. She thought that it might be eating the cat food she put out in the shed, but she couldn't get anywhere near the three-legged dog. She also knew that, if she got close to it, she wasn't bringing him back for her asshole of a neighbor to shoot. She could only wish he'd sell his house and disappear from her life. Wouldn't that be nice?

Just then her phone rang. She looked down and smiled. "Hey, Grandma," she answered. "Yes, I'm doing fine."

Her grandmother gave a boisterous laugh. "You always say that. And you never give me a chance to actually ask if you're really okay."

"That's because it doesn't matter. I'll be fine," Miranda stated firmly.

Her grandmother sighed. "If only I could believe that. You're running yourself ragged, burning a candle from both ends, like you are."

"It doesn't matter if I am or not," she muttered. "I can't do anything less for the animals."

"I know that, dear. I really do. Oh, I did want to tell you that I got some money out of your great-uncle," she shared. "I told him what you were doing, what you are working toward, and you know that he's been a great animal lover all his life. Now that he's back in the US, I decided to contact him and see if he was interested in helping out. He wants to come by and take a look at your place."

"Oh, crap. When?"

"I don't really know," she murmured. "And I don't know how serious he is about that aspect of it, but he is interested in helping." Miranda wasn't sure exactly how she felt about her grandma contacting people like that, though the sweet old dear had only the best of intentions. But people who wanted to exert control over Miranda's life were precisely the ones she wanted to keep out.

So, if her uncle, great-granduncle at that, wanted to see the place, he likely wouldn't be happy because it was run-down and desperately in need of repairs. But still, how could she say no if he was willing to help?

"Anyway," her grandmother continued on cheerfully, "he cut me a check for you … for ten thousand dollars."

At that, she gasped in shock. "Seriously?" She bolted upright. "Don't you find that strange?" she asked immediately.

"Oh dear," Grandma replied. "We really have to do something with your attitude toward humanity."

"Most people don't give that kind of money without wanting something in return," she stated immediately. "And you know how I feel about people wanting to be in control."

"I don't think it's a control issue," she explained. "I think it's just wanting to make sure that the animals will be cared for."

"Well, the animals are loved. There's no problem with that, but their accommodations are a whole different story." Miranda sat back down again with a heavy *thud.* Ten thousand dollars would be a huge help. "And do you actually have that check?"

"Not only do I have it," she said, "but I'm walking toward the bank right now. I'll put it in your account. So, if you need food, dog food, cat food, whatever, go ahead and use the money," she urged.

"Wow, I will," she agreed, "but now I need to sit down and make a priority list."

At that, her grandmother paused. "I guess it's never

quite enough, is it?"

"It's huge, Grandma, thank you," she hurriedly reassured her. "It's really huge," she repeated. "I might get enough food to last through the winter on this."

Her grandmother sighed. "Well, could you make sure you buy a little food for yourself while you're at it?"

"I'm eating," she replied defensively.

"Sure you are, and how much weight have you lost this last year?"

Miranda shrugged. "I don't know, but I definitely had some to lose."

"No more," her grandmother said shortly. "You might have had it to lose, but you don't anymore. You are as lean as you ever should be, if not too lean. I'd feel much happier if you had an extra ten pounds on you."

"Hey, two jobs, mending outside fences, scrubbing buckets, and working outside in the cold all the time," she argued, "I don't know that I could put back on ten pounds if I wanted to. And I'm really not worried about it. You know I'm doing what I love."

"Sure, but do you sleep?"

"I try," she answered, "but money has been a huge nightmare, so trying to get sleep is a different story."

"Well, hopefully this check will help."

"Are you kidding? It's massive. Like seriously massive."

"He also has acreage in town, did you know that?"

"Who?"

"My brother," her grandmother replied. "I hadn't realized that he owned it, but he's apparently had it for a very long time. Now that he's getting on in years, he's looking at what he wants to do with his life. I told him that he was a little late, but he just told me to shove it." And then she pealed off with laughter.

"I like him already," Miranda shared.

"Well, it's been decades since you've seen him. You were little, so you may not remember him at all," her grandmother admitted. "We'll meet up for lunch again next week, and we'll talk some more."

"Well, I need to contact him to thank him," she said immediately.

"I told him that you would say that, and he mentioned that he wants to come by. So you can tell him then. I don't know what else to tell you about that, except that he's likely to just pop up out of the blue at some point."

"Good enough," she replied because how could she say anything different? She did want to thank this benefactor, who had made what was a massive donation in her world. And, if he allowed her to get more supplies and medications and to fix the back fence, not to mention a few other things that needed to be done around here, then his participation was even more of a big deal.

She sat here, with a cup of coffee in her hand, long after her grandmother had hung up. And, for the first time in a long time, Miranda knew she could sleep tonight. Something she desperately needed. As she stared out into the flurry of the cold bitter winds outside, she thought she saw a dark shepherd-looking animal shift in the wind.

It was the neighbor's dog.

Miranda bolted to her feet, stepped into her boots, walked outside, and called it softly. She sensed more than saw it, which was the way with injured and weary animals. She didn't know if this dog knew who was friend or foe. She didn't know anything about it, other than the neighbor hadn't treated it right, and this dog was desperately in need of care and comfort.

She walked out without her coat, wincing at that folly, but, rather than rushing back inside, she grabbed a big scoop of dog food and headed out to where she thought she saw the shepherd. She cleared a spot of snow off the ground and piled up the dog food as best she could. If nothing else, one of the other animals would find it. Then calling out softly to the dog, Miranda headed back inside.

There, she poured herself the last of the coffee and moved into the living room to curl up. For the first time in a long time, she intentionally relaxed, as she worked on a list of where that money most needed to go.

Such a list would always be longer than the money, but now she could see her way through the winter.

And she smiled.

CHAPTER 2

THE NEXT MORNING was Saturday. Miranda woke up with a cozy sense of well-being, and almost immediately the memory of the money being deposited to her account rushed into her head. Checking the time, she gasped and immediately jumped into the shower and only a few minutes later raced from the house. No time for coffee. She'd have to get it at the office. Dressed warmly, she would have normally walked, but she didn't have time today. She quickly jumped into her truck, backed out, and headed into work.

As soon as she got in the building, the vet showed up. He frowned at her, but she shook her head before he could speak. "I'm not late," she stated.

He smiled. "Actually I wasn't going to remark about you being late," he explained. "You somehow look like you're feeling better."

"I am a little bit," she agreed but didn't bother to explain. She quickly put on a pot of coffee, happy that at least she was right on time, instead of being ever-so-slightly late, because one was acceptable, and the other was definitely not.

He walked off to handle his patients, while Miranda did whatever was needed. She changed the bedding, cleaned the kitty litter boxes, fed and watered all the animals, as well as answering the phones and filing paperwork. Some days it was boring, but she relished the barter system she had set up here.

As she finished up her half-day's work, the vet walked up behind her.

"Miranda, I have another cat here." He held the little thing gently.

Her heart sank, but she nodded immediately. "How bad is it?"

"It's diabetic and will need insulin."

"*Great.*" She blew at the tendrils of her hair, as she accepted the frail-looking feline. "Oh, she's a sweetheart," she murmured.

"I know, and a lot of people would say to just put her down because she's a diabetic."

"I know. I've heard it all before," she murmured.

"We both have, haven't we? Maybe we can work together on this cat. I am willing to supply the insulin, if you can handle the care."

"Done," she replied immediately, so very relieved that she wouldn't have to bear the expense of the medicine.

As it was noon and time for Miranda to leave, she packed up the medicine, took one of the pet carrier cages that she always left here, put the cat in it, and took her carefully out to her truck. The interior of the vehicle was cold, and she kicked herself for not warming it up first, though she wasn't going far. As soon as she pulled out of the parking lot and headed home, the cat started yowling.

"I know," she murmured to her. "Let's call you Sophie." The cat had just been fixed and was looking decent, except for the need for insulin. Miranda had dealt with several cats like this though. As soon as she got her home, she put her in a room all on her own to start the transition, before getting her accustomed to the other cats. Miranda also wanted to monitor this cat's food, water, and medication for a bit, since she was diabetic.

With that done, and the pretty little thing now tucked up on a cat bed all on her own, Miranda headed outside to deal with the rest of the animals. She had tried to work on sorting her priorities for the money she'd just been gifted, but she had so many legitimate needs that she hadn't yet put them into any true order of importance because they were all important needs. She'd get there; she knew it. There was just no way not to, and it was a gift, a huge gift.

At the same time, she'd been worried about telling the vet about it, just in case he decided that he'd need to now be paid for the vet work he did on her animals. But, as long as they had a workable back-and-forth relationship, where she kept taking animals from him that needed homes, where he kept healing her sick and injured animals, then she hoped that their situation continued.

She headed out to the far corner of her property, a little too close to town for her, but she was glad for the moment that she had two acres, though she really could have used about fourteen. The house was a ramshackle old mess and probably needed way more money than she could handle putting into upgrading her home. But she didn't care about the house. Her focus was always on the animals and getting them the care they needed.

As soon as she'd fed the outdoor animals and taken a look to make sure everybody was doing okay and had fresh water, she headed over to where she'd seen the three-legged dog last night. At least she thought it was a dog, though she'd certainly had more than her share of coyotes come through. They were well-known for eating any and all food available to them because some winters were hard to get through.

As much as she sympathized with their survival plight, she also didn't want them looking at her animals as their next meal. That had happened a time or two, but sometimes there was just no way to stop the predators. It was one of the reasons she would be grateful to find a rescue that would take the rabbits. Although all of them were fixed, and they didn't have a very long lifespan to begin with, rabbits were special in her world. Miranda adored that certain splendor in their cuddliness. But Colorado was not necessarily the easiest place to raise them.

Back in the house, she took inventory of the dog food that she had left. There was certainly some, but she was easily going through twenty pounds a week and had only about twice that. She, as usual, was running low and needed to resolve that. She also needed hay for the horses, which was a little more challenging. She immediately placed a call to her supplier and put enough on order for the entire winter.

On the other end of the phone, Rhine laughed at her. "Hey, you must be doing well if you're ordering the whole amount."

"Well, I've got enough to get it at the moment, so I have to ensure the animals are fed."

"I got you." Rhine hesitated. "You know what? I can give you a better deal, since you're making a bulk purchase and all."

"I'll take any deals coming," she replied. "You know how many I've got here to feed."

"I know," he agreed. "With the amount of your order, I can pass on a discount to you." And the figure he gave her for the whole amount—that should get her through the winter—brought a smile to her face.

"Thank you," she said. It would be a major dent to her bank account, but, as dents went, it would be well spent. To know that the animals would have care and food, regardless of how rotten it got outside, would bring her a lot of peace of mind. Hay was not cheap, and neither was grain. Yet no way could she avoid this purchase.

Plus, she also needed to have the farrier come out. Sometimes she did barter deals with him as well. She called and left him a message, then went to work on the rest of her inventory. As long as bulk sales were happening, and she could take advantage of occasional deals offered through the suppliers at the veterinary office, she might get enough food for the dogs and maybe the cats too.

As she sat here wondering, she heard a bark. She ignored it at first because barks were common in her world. She currently had three dogs tucked up at her feet, and two were old seniors that she couldn't house anywhere else. They just needed a place to spend the rest of their lives, which probably wouldn't be all that long, but they still needed care.

When she heard a bark again, she raised her head and looked outside. She didn't see anything, but frowning and hearing more barking, she got up and headed out. Maybe a couple dogs had gone into their pens, which they accessed through a huge doggie door, but now couldn't get back through that same doggie door, as sometimes it stuck. That was a problem on its own but also led to another problem in terms of heating the house.

As she headed toward the barking, she saw two of her dogs, tails wagging madly, barking toward something off in the distance.

She checked to see if it was the shepherd that she had seen the night before. No sign of it, but she definitely saw some movement out there. Moving cautiously, not knowing if she was heading toward a predator—which definitely happened in her world—she headed in the direction of the movement. One of her dogs came right to her side, much more of a watchdog than the others.

She put her hand on the back of the big Great Dane. Although Dobbie was responsible for more than his fair share of the food bill, and he had a bad back, he was also the most protective of the lot. He had been with her for a very long time, and she had zero interest in moving him to another home. As she looked down on him, she smiled.

"You're one of the reasons why I can't feed everybody some days," she scolded lightheartedly. Of course she always fed everybody regardless. Other things, like the roof on her house, suffered, while she was busy feeding the animals. Her family always managed to get quite angry about that superficial stuff, worried about what the neighbors would think, totally ignoring the things that truly mattered. But, hey, Miranda had lived with their anger for a very long time, so what else was new?

As she and Dobbie got closer, she noted that the dog food she had checked on earlier was gone, and she saw no sign of anybody out here. She frowned at that, then looked around at the Great Dane, sniffing the air off to the west. She followed slowly, moving through the brush, calling out, "Hey, pup. You're hungry. You're cold, and you need somebody. Come indoors. I know it's pretty rough out here, isn't it?"

She kept calling to the animal, yet feeling a bit on the foolish side because she couldn't see anything. Still, she figured that the more the dog got used to her voice, the less frightened it would be. Maybe eventually the poor thing would see her not as a threat but as somebody who would help when things got tough. And no doubt that things would get tough. The worst of the Aspen winter hadn't hit yet, and that was another thing that she had to think about, regarding that gift of money. She didn't have enough firewood for the winter, and, with that thought, she headed back inside to add it to her list.

She had a lot of animals inside that needed to be kept warm too, and that was something she wouldn't cut back on. In addition to the added cost of heat in the winter, she also had to factor in things like broken water lines, which meant big bills. The minute any kind of plumbing issue happened, it became an immediate problem. Even though her brother was a plumber, and he helped her out as much as he could, he also usually tattled to her family, and that was something she didn't want to listen to, if she didn't have to. But, hey, when push came to shove, she'd listen to it, if that's what it took to keep everything going here and the animals safe inside.

As soon as she put firewood on her list and made a couple phone calls to see what she could get for deals, she heard the dogs barking again. Frowning, she got up and headed back outside. There was Dobbie, her Great Dane, still loping around in the backyard. But he wasn't barking. He acted as though he were greeting a friend. She frowned as she watched his behavior. "What is it, Dobbie?"

He looked at her and barked. She walked over to him. "Well, whoever it is isn't showing themselves, sweetheart," she murmured, "so that's making it a little hard for me to do anything."

Just then, she caught sight of something dark in the shrubbery. She immediately froze and called out to it. She stayed there for a good twenty minutes, until she got so cold that she would have to go inside herself. And, with that, she headed back to the house, got more dog food, and brought it back out, placing it on the other side of her rear fence, where the dog wouldn't have to get into her backyard, with all her critters, in order to get the food. She didn't know who or what this animal was. However, even if it were a coyote, she wouldn't see any animal starve, though that would make a lot of people angry with her.

With a final glance in that direction, she shrugged, then headed back inside to get warmed up again.

EVERY TIME KYRON got up, his sister in-law ran to get another hug. Finally he stopped, then held her close for a moment. "I won't leave."

She looked up at him, tears in her eyes. "Promise?"

He sighed. "Not for a while, okay?"

She nodded and brushed away the tears.

"You didn't used to be quite so teary," he teased.

"I didn't used to be pregnant either," she replied, with a bubble of laughter.

He grinned at her. "I don't know if I told you, but congratulations."

"You did tell me." She smiled, hugging herself now. "Over and over again. And thank you. You know how much it means to us."

"I do." He returned her smile. "I'm not sure I would want to go down the same pathway, but, hey, I know it's important to you."

She smiled. "You know what? I think, deep down, every

man wants a son."

"Maybe," Kyron agreed, "but that doesn't mean that every man should have one."

She winced at that. "I thoroughly understand where that sentiment is coming from," she stated, with a nod. "And I hate to have to tell you this, but they know that you're here."

"Of course they do." He stared at her. "Did you tell them?"

She nodded, with a cringe. "I'm sorry. I didn't realize it would be something you didn't want them to know about."

He sighed, as he stared over her head, and caught his brother looking at him, with a narrowed gaze. Clearly a reminder not to say or to do anything to upset his wife. Kyron swallowed back his irritation and nodded. "I suppose they were bound to find out sometime."

Her shoulders sagged with relief.

He added, "Don't expect me to sit here and welcome them though. You want to have them over, fine. It's your house. I'll leave, so you all can visit."

Immediately her face scrunched up.

He shook his head. "I get it. You want to heal the world," he stated. "You've always been that way. But some things in life just don't heal."

"And some things in life can't heal," she argued immediately, "because people won't let them."

He smiled and nodded. "You know, Sand, you could be right. But don't start using your wiles on me," he warned. "My brother is very susceptible, but I don't know that I am."

She just smiled. "What if I pulled out the pregnant woman clause?"

He rolled his eyes at that. "I'll call you on it. I've already told my brother that I would leave before I let my presence cause any trouble. So, if I need to, I will."

"Don't," she said immediately. "I'm sorry."

He shrugged. "I get your mothering instincts have kicked in, but I'm not willing to get into that kind of an issue here. I'm here to do a specific job, and I was hoping to spend time with my brother and with you, but we'll see how things go."

She nodded slowly. "It breaks my heart to know that you are on the outs with your parents."

"We're not on the outs, like this is some small thing that is temporary," he said. "I'll never be what they want me to be, and that's just a fact of life that won't change. Ever."

"I've never seen them act like that before," she noted.

"Listen. I won't discuss this with anyone," he replied quietly. "You can talk about it with my brother, when I'm out of earshot, if you want, but I don't need any more stress in my world either."

Her gaze immediately went to his missing leg, and she nodded quietly. "We all have things to deal with, don't we?"

"We sure do," he said cheerfully. "And, right now, we have to deal with the fact that we haven't eaten yet, and I'm starving."

She burst out laughing. "I'd forgotten you were such an enthusiastic eater."

"How could you forget?" he asked, with a bright smile. "You know perfectly well that my brother is the same in that regard."

She winced. "Well, that's true enough. And I have breakfast warming in the oven, just waiting for all of us to sit down together. One more question, then I'll leave you be. I still don't understand why you're here. Allen said it was something about a dog. Can you fill me in on that?"

"I can," he replied, "but it might be a little confusing." He quickly told her what little he knew.

"But, after two months, it seems like a long shot," she noted, staring at him.

"I know. I know, but I'll still do my best and give it a shot because, well, … it's an animal in need."

"And you've always been animal crazy," Sandra added.

"Maybe I should have become a vet," he teased.

"Then you wouldn't have all these problems with your family," she joked brightly.

He just glared at her.

She winced. "Okay, no more digs."

"That'll be good if you actually mean it," he replied, with a gentle note of warning.

Immediately her smile fell away, and she nodded. "I'm sorry. That wasn't fair."

He shrugged and returned to discussing the animal. "So, I have to start with animal control, the old owner, or anybody in the neighborhood, to see if I can track where it might have gone or find out if anybody has seen it." He raised his voice a bit to get his brother's attention. "Hey, Allen, you guys haven't had any police calls about a big dog loose anywhere, or a missing Malinois?" he asked.

"A missing what?" his brother asked.

Kyron pulled out his phone and brought up a picture of it.

"Oh, a German shepherd. Why didn't you just say so?" He chuckled.

"Because it's not one, and there's a fair bit of difference between them, but I get, for you, that probably won't make much difference." Kyron sighed. "Her name is Bethesda Lui II or some godforsaken thing like that, but she's commonly known as Beth."

"Interesting, I would have called her Lilly," Sandra said softly, as she looked at the picture. "Poor girl."

"Yeah, even more of a poor girl, she's also missing a leg," he added, "so we're already kindred spirits."

"And what will you do with her, if you find her?" his brother asked.

"Depends entirely on what I find, where I find her, and what kind of condition she's in."

"And is this like …" he hesitated, then continued. "Is this like a *job*, job?"

"Oh, you mean versus charity work or volunteer work?" Kyron asked in a mocking tone.

His brother glared at him. "It's not exactly an easy question to ask."

"You mean, because, in your mind, I'm not really employable?"

Immediately Sandra jumped up. "Okay, we're not going there. That will never be a topic that will go well here."

"No, it sure won't." Kyron looked over at his brother. "For the record, it's a job but not for money. They're covering all the expenses, which is why I'm totally okay going to a hotel," he said, with a warning glance. His brother backed off immediately, as he looked over at his wife, who was staring at the two brothers with worry in her eyes.

"We're fine," Allen told her. "We're still brothers. Brothers fight, you know."

"You are still brothers," she agreed, "and, if you guys would actually give yourselves half a chance, you would remember the good things about it."

At that, Allen's lips twitched. "It's really not that bad between us."

"And it's really not that good," she snapped in return.

Kyron didn't say anything because there wasn't a whole lot either of them could say. Between the brothers was a lot of time, distance, and maybe some jealousy and hard feelings, but maybe she was right, and it was time to get past it. At least with Allen, Kyron saw some hope for reconciliation. His parents? No way. At that, Kyron sighed. "We are fine," he told her. "Time has a way of dulling some of that old stuff."

"Some of that old stuff maybe," she agreed, "but there has also been a lot of pain and jealousy, and that's something that I hold your parents responsible for."

"Doesn't matter if you do or not because they never will," Kyron stated quietly. "That part of my life won't ever get any easier."

She frowned but managed to stay quiet, which he appreciated. She looked back at his phone, but he didn't have the picture up anymore. "You can check with the rescues and the SPCA."

He nodded. "Yeah, that's the plan. I need to get a vehicle. I had planned to pick one up at the airport, but Allen got there first."

"Good," she said, with a note of satisfaction. "I did send him early, just in case."

Kyron looked over at her and smiled. Then Sandra and Allen retrieved breakfast from the oven and placed it on the dining room table. "I guess I can catch an Uber up to the rental place after we eat."

"If you call them," she mentioned, "they'd probably deliver it to you."

"Right," he agreed, "that would make life easier." It would probably increase his expenses though. "It's not very far from here, is it?"

"No," his brother said. "I can drop you off on the way, if you like."

"Perfect." He dug into pancakes. He smiled as he looked over at his sister-in-law. "Excellent, as always."

She flushed with pleasure and smiled. "Make sure you get home for dinner, Kyron. Besides the home-cooked meal, we'll want to hear about any progress you've made."

"If there is any," Allen remarked.

Kyron looked over at him and smirked. "Always the pessimist, *huh*?"

Allen shrugged. "In this case, *realist* would be more accurate. Two months is a long time."

"It is, but it's not impossible. I have to try at least."

"You always did have a soft spot for the animals," his brother noted.

"And I hope I always will," he replied quietly. "There's not a whole lot in life that I care about as much as animals." At that came an odd silence. He looked over at the two of them and asked, "What?"

Sandra looked at her husband, who just shrugged and looked back at him again.

"Now what?" Kyron asked, his heart sinking.

Sandra added, "I just wondered how you felt about Millicent."

"Who?" he asked in a mocking tone. "Look. I haven't seen or heard from her since I left town, so I don't have any feelings either way." He looked at her closer. "Why are you bringing that up?"

"She's divorced and single again."

"That's nice," he replied. "Now hear this. I am not interested, so do not in any way attempt to hook me up, with her or anybody else, got it?" A note of warning was in his tone. "I'll find someone when I'm ready, and it won't be her. I don't go backward in life. I go forward."

Sandra nodded immediately. "Got it. I was just wondering."

"Don't bother, and stop trying to find a way to make me stay."

"Hey," she said, "we love you, and we want you here."

"That's nice," he murmured, "but that won't be the way to make it happen." She frowned at him, and he frowned right back.

She chuckled. "*Gawd*, Kyron, I'd forgotten how determined you always are to go your own way."

"How could you possibly have forgotten that?" he teased. "It's part of my charm."

At that, his brother got up from the table. "I'm leaving in five or so."

"Got it," Kyron noted, looking over at Sandra. "I'll see you after a while."

"Are you coming right back?"

"No. I'll drive around a bit and familiarize myself with some of the details about town these days," he explained. "Who knows? I might still have a few friends here."

"I'm sure you do," she agreed. "You didn't lose everybody just because you left."

"You'd be surprised. Millicent cost me a lot, and, because of everything that happened with my brother and my parents, it felt like I lost everybody. So I have no idea if anybody is here for me or not," he added, yet in a cheerful voice.

"You don't really care, do you?"

"Well, let's just say that I can't let stuff like that get in my way," he muttered. "I've got bigger fish to fry in my life right now, and I can't let myself be dragged down by old drama. I'm not overly concerned about reconnecting with anybody."

She stared at him, frowning. "I don't know what it's like to have been as alone as you sound," she murmured.

He looked at her affectionately. "Nope, and that's because you are a wonderful caring person, and nobody would do anything to hurt you, so you'll never be alone." With that, he got up and headed out the front door with his brother. Once they were in the vehicle, Allen shrugged. "Thank you. For being nice to her and all."

"She's easy to be nice to," he replied. "She'll be a great mom because she's a real sweetheart, always has been."

"Yeah, she is. But she is also the kind of person who always wants to heal the world."

"And I get that." Kyron groaned quietly. "But I won't be a party to any of her attempts to broker a deal to try and get me to stay."

"Are you really that against living here?"

"I'm not sure I'm against it at all," he clarified, staring at his brother. "I just don't want to be railroaded by some underhanded attempts to make me stay that are not in the best interests of me and my happiness and my healing." He shrugged. "If it happens, it happens, and that's a whole different story. But don't force it on me. If it doesn't happen *naturally, honestly, truthfully*, then I don't want any part of it."

"Right, but if it would have happened naturally, then it wouldn't be anything odd, would it?"

Kyron shrugged. "I'm not even sure what to say to that, so I'll just stay out of it."

His brother laughed. "Just keep treating her as if she's made out of bone china, and we'll be fine."

"I can do that," Kyron stated, "as long as she also remembers and respects my space."

At that, his brother sighed. "And that, as you know, is much harder."

"I do know," he confirmed, "which is why I suggested that I stay at a hotel."

"And that won't work for her," Allen replied quietly, "because she really cares, and it has broken her heart all this time you've been away from us."

Kyron shrugged. "That was sweet of her and sorry if that caused *you* a problem, but believe me. Nobody else still living gave a shit."

And, with that, came complete silence, until they reached the rental office, where Kyron hopped out and waved. "Thanks for the lift." Then he closed the door firmly in his brother's face.

CHAPTER 3

"I CALLED THE city again."

Miranda stiffened in outrage, as she looked over at her smirking neighbor, his head sticking over the old worn fence. Crazy Old Man Macintyre was another main reason for getting out of here. But anyone in her situation knew, when money was tight, selling real estate wasn't a whole lot of help if you had to buy again. And, in her case, buy larger. Not a larger house but a larger property.

"They will ignore you like the last dozen times." She knew she shouldn't even respond to him, but it was hard not to. He seemed to be on a personal mission to make her life miserable. In many ways he was succeeding.

The snort of disgust was his only answer.

She shooed the dogs inside. Even as she stood inside the small entranceway, she peered through the window, relieved when her neighbor disappeared back into his house.

"Not sure what we'll do about him," she murmured to the dogs, "but, wow, we need to do something." Selling was a last resort. It was hard to consider the logistics, the packing, just the sheer number of animals to move. … All of it was a daunting prospect. Yet her bizarre neighbor … was a compelling argument on the plus column to getting out of here. Sometimes he seemed normal and ignored her; then he went through bouts of being an asshole. Since the lost dog scenario, he'd stayed in the asshole department.

She wiped her face, then seeing it was safe, knew she should head out now to check on the barn cats. She left several bales of hay in the shed for them to stay warm but would need more with the coming winter. She grabbed a bag of cat food and an older jug of milk, slipped on her boots, and, with the dogs once again swarming around her feet, headed outside again. After that, she checked on the larger animals in the field next to hers. She leased the land from the homeowner, but, with the property prices shooting up, he'd been rumbling about selling as well.

A rumble that struck fear in her heart. Without his acreage, she'd be in trouble. Horses, a llama, a goat, ... they all needed room. And that was something she didn't have enough of.

When her phone rang, she pulled it out, checked her screen ID. Not recognizing the number, she hesitated. Giving Brownie one last brush, she stepped away from the big chestnut gelding and answered, "Hello?"

"This is Riteway Trucking. I have a delivery for a Miranda Galloway."

"*Uhm*, okay. I'm Miranda. What is the delivery?"

"I'm actually outside your house, if your address is ..." And he shuffled some papers, then read off her address.

"Well, that's my address," she noted. "I'm in the backyard. I'll be there in a second."

She quickly raced to the house, then leaving the dogs inside, she stepped out on the front veranda and stopped. Yes, a delivery truck was right there, but it was huge and had a pet company logo on the side. Surely that couldn't be bad news?

Hopeful, she walked toward the driver, who was opening

up the large door at the back of the semi.

"You Miranda?"

"I am. What do you have for me?"

"A pallet of dog food."

She stared at him in shock. "A pallet? A whole pallet?"

He nodded. "Yes." He brought out a large ramp and proceeded to move the pallet to the end of her driveway. When he was done, he held out his clipboard. "Sign anywhere."

Ecstatic, she quickly signed the paperwork and stared at the gift of an entire winter's worth of food for the dogs—likely way more. Her phone buzzed a few moments later with a text.

Did you get the delivery?

She smiled, as she finally connected the dots. The text was from Tom, the rep who had been at the vet clinic last week. They'd had a long conversation about what she was doing, and Tom had even been there, when Doug, the vet and her boss, had handed over yet another stray puppy for her to take home.

I got it! Thank you so much, she texted back. She got a thumbs-up in return. To think nice people were out there and, with a phone call, could make something like this happen filled her with joy. And made up for the guys like her crotchety neighbor, who even now glared at her from his living room window.

This delivery would piss him right off. Almost as much as it was a gold mine to her. And she didn't trust him not to do something to destroy all this. She tilted her head back and studied the weather, realizing she had bigger and more pressing things to worry about. These bags couldn't get wet. Even a tarp thrown across them wouldn't be enough. First, she had to find a place to store them; then she had to move them. If worse came to worst, she'd stack it all in her living room, if she had to. But better she only move these once.

Groaning, and knowing she had to move fast, she headed out to the back of her house, looking for storage options.

WITH THE FREEDOM of a rental truck, Kyron drove around town, reacquainting himself with some of his favorite old haunts. He'd grown up here and had learned to both ski and snowboard here. Most people chose one or the other, never both. But his father had been a snowboarder and his mother a skier, and, unlike his brother, Kyron had chosen to learn both skills. And now, as he looked down at his legs, while he sat at the coffee shop, he wondered about the common sense of trying to do either. He knew it was possible because others had done it. He just didn't know how feasible it was for him. When he looked up again, he saw a familiar face standing in front of him. He just stared. "Seriously, Miles?"

At that, his friend's face broke into a well-recognized grin, and Kyron stood and was immediately engulfed in a hug.

Miles shook his head. "I saw you sitting here, and I did a double take, thinking, no, there's no way, but, damn, just look at you. You look good." He laughed.

"That's because you're only seeing the surface," Kyron replied. "As a matter of fact, I'm a bit of a wreck."

At that, Miles turned somber, and he nodded. "I heard about the leg, man."

"Yeah, it kind of sucks."

"You know that …" he began, then stopped and

shrugged. "I'm sure you've got all kinds of adaptations and whatnot happening in your world," he noted, "so I certainly won't interfere. I just want to say that I'm really glad that you survived."

"Me too." Kyron smiled. "I'm still adjusting to the leg though."

"I'm sure you are," he agreed. "It can't be easy at all."

"Maybe, I don't know. I'm not sure it's all that hard though either. Like I said, I'm still working on it."

At that, his friend nodded. "I don't know if you're interested, but anytime you want to try to get up the mountain—"

Kyron smiled. "See? Things like that automatically come up. *Let's go up the mountain*, and then you stop and think, *Oh, shit, can he even go up the mountain?* I mean, I can obviously go up the mountain, but can I board or ski?"

Miles grimaced. "I'm not trying to make you uncomfortable."

"I know, and I get that it's something everybody has to get used to," he replied easily.

"Do you remember Jeff?"

Kyron stopped and thought about it and nodded. "Yeah, I do."

"He's in town," Miles replied. Then he hesitated a minute, before adding, "I'm not trying to overstep my boundaries or anything here, but Jeff is also missing a leg."

Kyron stared at his friend. "What? What happened to him?"

"Skiing accident," Miles replied.

"Jesus."

"I know, but he still snowboards," Miles confirmed. "So I don't know if you're looking for any tips on how to get back into something like that or if you even care at this point"—he shrugged—"but you may want to hit him up and see how he does it."

"Well, I'm sure he does it the same way we all did it," Kyron quipped. "You get up, and you keep falling down, until you learn not to."

At that, Miles burst out laughing. "Oh, God, now that brings back memories."

"Right? The good news," Kyron added, "is that I'm as physically fit as I can be, and I'm healthy. I survived what I went through, and now I'm back out on the other side."

"It's sure great to see you, and it's about time you came for a visit," Miles stated.

"I am here for a visit obviously, but I've got something else going on as well. Have you heard any rumors about a dog being a problem around here?" After Miles looked at him with a frown, Kyron explained a little bit about what he was doing.

"Is this still military work for you?" his friend asked curiously.

Kyron didn't quite know what to say about this K9 work through Titanium Corp, so he just left it fairly noncommittal and said he was helping out a friend.

"I haven't heard anything about a dog," Miles said, "but that doesn't mean much."

"Maybe not," Kyron agreed, "but you're a teacher. I thought maybe, with all the kids you're around, you might have heard some talk."

"I haven't," he noted thoughtfully, as he pondered the issue. "But, if you give me your cell number, I can ask around a bit and let you know."

"Sure enough." Kyron brought up his phone, as he also

showed Miles a picture of the dog.

"That's a beautiful animal."

"Very distinctive and easy to identify since she's only got three legs," Kyron noted. "So, yeah, I feel a kinship as well."

"Of course." Miles looked slightly uncomfortable.

Kyron shrugged. "She'll adapt, just like I will." As he watched his old friend walk away, Kyron considered how difficult it was for other people to accept his new reality, when something like this happened. Kyron understood that it was hard and that they didn't want to be rude or difficult. Yet, at the same time, Kyron fielded a million questions and still met that level of uncertainty about how to even talk to someone who lost a limb. Kyron thought somebody should be out there teaching people how to deal with it—some sort of political correctness training or something. It still sucked, but, at the same time, after having broken the ice with Miles, it seemed like every other conversation Kyron had with people after that would be easier.

But what he really wanted to deal with today was his search for the dog. Right now, he was looking for the people who had been approved for Beth's adoption and had had trouble with her. He had found out that they were both at work, so he was waiting for them to get off.

At the end of a day of driving around and checking with several rescues, Kyron drove up to the couple's address, hoping to find some answers. The minute he saw them, he knew better. The man was tall, with a pinched expression, angular features, and not a whole lot of welcome evident as he introduced himself. The woman was small, with the same pinched features, and definitely didn't look like an animal person. He asked them for details on what had happened with the dog. They looked at each other, but he wasn't invited into the house.

"The dog was a problem right away," the man stated. "I was led to believe these War Dogs were supposedly well trained and was assured that we wouldn't have any trouble."

"And yet you didn't have any problems when the first check-up visit happened, is that correct?"

"No, not at all," the woman confirmed. "Only after that she reacted really badly to my son, and we started to worry about it."

"And, of course, once fears starts …" he murmured. They looked at him sharply, and he shrugged. "How old is your son?"

"He's seventeen." She asked, "Why?"

"I'm just wondering why the dog might have perceived a threat coming from him."

"What do you mean by *a threat*?" the man protested, clearly bristling. "We didn't do anything to the dog."

"I didn't say you did," Kyron stated, "but she is definitely a very well-trained dog."

"She was also injured and didn't seem to adapt all that easily," the woman added stiffly.

Kyron nodded. "So, when did you notice she was missing?"

"The next morning," she replied quietly. "My son had let her go outside, but she didn't come back."

"What do you mean, *she didn't come back*?"

"Well, we have no backyard fence anymore," the man explained. "We had to take down a tree, and that left a gap in the fence.

"You didn't get it fixed?" he asked. "That's a problem because, as you were told, there are stringent requirements for anybody with one of these dogs, and having a secure space is very important to these War Dogs."

"Well, we would," she began, "but then the dog disappeared."

Kyron stared at her for a very long moment, as both of them shifted uncomfortably in front of him. He couldn't imagine what this dog had gone through here with this couple and their teenage son, but, from everything they said, it didn't sound like Beth had been a good fit for these people, and obviously they had decided she wasn't welcome. "What did you do when you found out she was missing?"

They looked at each other, and the father shrugged. "We didn't do anything. She was a problem, and, honest to God, we were glad to be rid of her."

"Okay, and did you notify the war department?" Of course he already knew the answer to that, and clearly several things here demonstrated this family was derelict in their duty to care for this animal. The fact that they had entered a contract seemed beyond their understanding at the moment.

They both shook their heads. "No, we didn't," the man replied. "Maybe someone could have found her again, but then they would have brought her back, and that wasn't something we were interested in."

"She could also have been rehomed," Kyron noted quietly, "and your contract legally terminated. Placement in another home would have been important to Beth."

"She was dangerous," the man stated.

"And my son was really struggling with the fact that she seemed to hate him so much," the woman argued.

At that, he turned to look at her. "Is your son here? I'd like to speak with him." They again looked at each other and shook their heads.

"No, you don't need to be speaking with our son," he

replied. "He's a good boy."

At that, Kyron's eyebrows raised. "I didn't say he wasn't, but speaking to him is important to help us understand the cues and what kind of behavior Beth exhibited when he was around. Talking to him would be the easiest way to determine that."

The man immediately shook his head and repeated, "No, and, as far as we're concerned, we're done with this."

"Ah, well then, I'll let the war department know how you feel about a War Dog who faithfully served this country, and they will deal with you directly. You do remember the contract you signed and yet apparently don't give a crap about? Well, that was issued by their department. Good day." He turned to leave, following the odd silence from both of them, as if they had suddenly realized that they would at the very least look bad, if not be in real trouble. Yet neither of them seemed to know what to say and remained silent.

Kyron walked away. It was all he could do to hold back the disgust he felt at the thought of anybody mistreating an animal who had served this country and had done so much for humankind. To listen to their weak excuses made Kyron sick. They certainly weren't the first supposed animal lovers who thought they cared for animals, only to find out they only wanted animals if and when the animals did what they wanted them to.

Just like some people never should become parents, many should never have animals. And, of course, animal abuse and child abuse were rampant among people who should never have gone in that direction to begin with.

The subject brought his brother and sister in-law to mind, but he knew becoming parents wouldn't be a problem for them, since they had been looking forward to this journey for a very long time and had already shown an amazing level of patience. Kyron wished them the very best of luck; he just wasn't sure that he had the same temperament. When it came to dogs, there was no doubt, but he wasn't so sure about people.

Sometimes he didn't like humans at all.

Back home again, he sat down with his brother and sister-in-law after dinner that evening. Sandra asked, "So, did you get anywhere?"

"I did, but some of the places that I got to weren't necessarily places I particularly appreciated." She frowned at that. He shrugged. "Some people should never be allowed to have animals. Unfortunately, even though the war department does stringent tests on a lot of these adoption applicants, they can't always see who a person really is on the inside."

She nodded carefully. "I'm sorry the animal went through such hardship."

"I also don't know," he murmured, looking over at his brother, "if anything happened that justified the dog's behavior. I mean, I want to say yes because dogs will always tell you the truth, whether it's something that you want to listen to or not, but maybe it was just a poor placement. I don't know."

"You're thinking that the teenager may have done something to the dog?" Sandra asked, gasping.

Kyron shrugged. "I'm not sure anybody has to do with anything," he replied quietly. "But sometimes a dog will take an instant dislike to somebody because they see a character trait in them that makes the dog uncomfortable," he explained. "So, was it the kid's fault? Not necessarily."

"Do you know what the kid's name is?" his brother

asked.

"No, I never did get that." He frowned, as he flipped through his notes. "It would have been helpful though, wouldn't it?"

"If I know the family name, I can get you the kid's name, but that won't necessarily help."

"I did see Miles today," Kyron added, "so maybe he knows him from school." Kyron handed over the man's name to his brother, who just shrugged.

"It's not a name I know."

"Well, that's good. It shouldn't be somebody a cop knows, given that these applications are supposedly screened, and successful applicants should have met some basic requirements in order to care for one of these dogs," he muttered. "I don't have any reason to suspect the boy or the family, outside of the fact that they took on something that they apparently weren't equipped to handle, then didn't follow up when there was trouble. Just abandoned a War Dog. And that, of course, has repercussions that affect the dog."

"So, about these dogs," his brother hesitated, "are they dangerous?"

"In the wrong hands, any animal is dangerous," Kyron replied quietly, "and, while these dogs have been trained with some serious skills, that doesn't make them inherently dangerous."

"Will they react to an abusive situation? I guess it depends on whether they bonded with the new family or not, right?"

"Getting attached isn't encouraged when you're in the K9 Unit," he noted. "That's one of the reasons why I couldn't handle it anymore."

"I presume," Allen said, "that no matter how stringent the requirements, there will always be people who fall through the cracks."

At that, Kyron nodded. "The department can spend only so many hours chasing down some of these applications. When a placement determination is made, it's pushed up or down the line. Sometimes they have thousands of applications and thousands of dogs, and it's just a matter of expediting the process."

"So, in some cases, something slipped through the cracks, and you're trying to fill in those cracks?" Allen asked hesitantly.

"Yes," he agreed. "In a way, that's exactly what I'm doing. I'm checking on dogs that were missed or have some issues. The routine welfare check that is done on all the retired dogs determined that this War Dog, Beth, was not there and hadn't been there for months. And, of course, the people who adopted Beth didn't bother to inform the war department."

"So, they might be held responsible, right? Don't they sign a contract or something?"

"Sure they do, but you also need somebody to enforce that contract," he murmured. "And people are really good at being shits in this world sometimes."

His brother stared at him.

"If they can get out of stuff, they do, and it doesn't matter what you or a contract says. Too often it's already a done deal, and you're left trying to figure out how to handle the mop-up."

"Which is what you're doing."

"Well, first of all, I'm hoping to find the dog," he murmured. "She could easily have been picked up by another family and is potentially doing very well there. She also could have been killed, shot by someone if she attacked them or was maybe looking for food on someone's property. Who knows? She's only got three legs. I don't know what her last few months have been like, but we're heading into the dead of winter."

"Some of us call that the Christmas season," his brother quipped.

"Exactly. Call it what you want, but, either way, it's damn cold out here in Aspen, and I don't want her suffering for any longer than she already has."

"You feel really strongly about this, don't you?"

"Of course I do." Kyron frowned at his brother. "You know how I feel about animals."

"And we're back to that question of why you didn't become a vet again," his brother mentioned, with a smile.

"Because, for some reason, I felt the need to go off and join the navy," he replied, with a smile in return, "but now I'm in the position to reconsider what it is that I want to do. But going back to school for what? Seven years to become a veterinarian? No thanks, not my style."

"I'm scared to ask, but what are your plans?"

"I don't have any at the moment," he replied cheerfully. "I'm hoping to let that remain a random mystery for a little longer."

His brother just stared at him.

Kyron shrugged. "What do you want me to say? I don't know what I'll do. I'm at what some people would call a crossroads crisis," he stated. "My life has been irrevocably changed, and I'm working through that. I don't really have an answer for you. So do us both a favor and don't hound me about it."

His brother nodded. "I can probably manage that." Looking over his shoulder to make sure Sandra was out of earshot, he stated, "You should know that our parents are coming next weekend."

Kyron sat back and glared, raising both hands. "Now why would you do that?"

"*Sandra*," he replied quietly.

Kyron pinched the bridge of his nose. "Even though I specifically asked her not to?"

His brother sighed. "You also know that, being pregnant, she wants everything hunky-dory and everyone happy."

"Life isn't like that," Kyron bit off.

"Maybe they won't come," Allen suggested. "Maybe they'll cancel."

"Maybe, but you and I both know that's a very faint hope," Kyron argued.

"I know," Allen replied, "but today is only Saturday, so lots can happen."

But, in his own mind, Kyron knew that not enough would happen to keep them away. And, with that, he got up, changed the subject. "I do have a couple leads reported in some of the local social media pages. Just miscellaneous dog sightings." Kyron groaned. "I contacted a few of them, but all I got was generic locations, no true addresses. I'll go drive around and take a look." And, with that, he walked out, leaving his brother staring after him.

Back in his rental vehicle, he sat here for a long moment, cussing his sister-in-law and her interference. He got it; she wanted the world to be happy, but the world just wasn't built that way. A lot of people out there couldn't for the life of them find a way to happiness because they were just so full of judgment, so busy building themselves up by tearing others down, resulting in themselves and everyone around them being constantly angry and upset. His own reaction to the prospect of seeing his parents was kind of a surprise because he had thought he'd dealt with it, but obviously he hadn't. The last thing he wanted was to see them, but he also knew getting out of it would upset Sandra, something he promised his brother he would not do.

Yet interacting with his parents could upset Sandra more.

As he turned on the engine and headed down the driveway, he saw Allen and Sandra standing in the window, arms around each other, watching him. He didn't bother waving; he just drove away, wanting nothing more than to leave it all behind. But having opened the door to his brother, he was starting to feel like he wouldn't have any choice but to open the door to the rest of his family too. Until he couldn't take any of them anymore.

Preoccupied with thoughts of his family and all the drama and hard feelings over the years, he punched in the first address he had and followed the GPS directions to one of the main town centers. As he looked around, he shrugged.

"Not necessarily a place I would expect to see a dog like Beth." He drove past a couple gas stations and then a small mall, pulling into the back, wondering if the dog would have chosen this place. If Kyron were a dog, it would be the last place he would choose, except for the fact that obviously a lot of humans were around. If she was staying close to people, then she was looking for support, comfort, a family, and that broke his heart. If she instead headed out to the wilds, then she had already given up on humans and didn't want anything to do with them. He'd seen more than his fair share of that happen as well.

He got out and walked to the back of the property, where a bunch of trees bordered the area, looking for any signs of the dog or anybody around who may have seen one. He noted a security guard, standing outside, smoking a cigarette, so Kyron walked over, introduced himself, and asked if the guard had seen a dog, like the one he was looking for.

The man immediately shook his head. "Not with three legs, no," he replied. "We do get dogs around here once in a while but not in that kind of condition," he murmured. "I haven't seen anything myself." He pondered for a moment. "However, I remember one of the other security guards talking about a lady, who had a neighbor who recently saw a dog." He frowned, pulled out his phone, and sent off a couple texts. "I'm just checking with her to see." Moments later, his phone pinged, and then he shook his head. "She doesn't know where it was, but it was three-legged apparently."

"Well, that's a very good indicator," Kyron said, with a smile. "No idea where it was, huh?"

The security guard was texting again. "It certainly wasn't here." He looked around. "I definitely would have seen that. A War Dog, huh?"

"Yeah." Kyron nodded. "A highly trained War Dog that was supposed to retire to a home here but apparently ended up having issues. The people didn't report the dog as missing, so it's been gone a couple months."

The man winced at that. "Two months in this weather is bound to be pretty rough."

"That's exactly why I've been sent here, to try to find her and to see if she's okay."

"Well, that'll be tough, if she's not okay, since it's been

so long—unless somebody is helping her or took her in, making her life a little bit better." The guard grimaced. "I really hate it when people pull crap like that. All they had to do was tell somebody that they couldn't handle the dog."

"Exactly," Kyron noted in full agreement. He left him his name and number and added, "Look. If anybody sees anything or if you hear any more about where this dog may have been seen, I'd appreciate it if you could let me know immediately."

Just then the security guard's phone buzzed again. He pulled it out and raised a finger. "Wait. … Linda says it was on the other side of town, heading out toward the highway."

"Okay, that helps."

"But that was a couple months ago, she says."

"Of course it was, and the dog could have done some heavy traveling in the meantime."

"Well, if she's good at traveling, then I would think so. But, if she's only on three legs and potentially not in the best physical shape, she wouldn't have gone too far, would she?" the security guard asked curiously.

"Well, that will be the question I'll end up trying to figure out," he replied, with a smile. "Thanks for your help, man, and, if you hear anything else, let me know." With that, Kyron returned to his truck. He still had three more addresses to follow up on and now a fourth area to check out. This last one sounded a little more promising, as the actual people reporting it sounded a little bit more viable. However, as the crow flies, he headed out to the next closest area, following the GPS. When he got there, all he saw were houses, streets, and snow. People were outside, walking their dogs and talking with their neighbors, but a storm brewed in the distance.

He pulled up beside an older man, who was walking two dogs, and he stopped and talked to him. The man shook his head and pointed to somebody else. That's what Kyron did, going from one person to another, each knowing somebody, who knew somebody else, and, at the end of a couple hours, he didn't have anybody who had a viable sighting.

As he walked a little bit farther along and studied the terrain, he realized this area was likely all wrong for Beth. The War Dog needed more room, more outdoor space. The vehicles would be something she would be quite comfortable with, but she wouldn't necessarily stick around this area because no food was here. This was a well-maintained neighborhood, with lots of dogs in residence, so garbage cans would be the only real source of food. And maybe that's what the dog was doing, going from garbage can to garbage can. Still, this neighborhood seemed too tidy for a dog living off the land.

Just as he headed back to his vehicle, someone called out to him. He looked up to see the first man who he'd spoken to, now walking toward him.

"I just talked to my wife, and she heard that, near one of the schools, a three-legged dog had been seen. Apparently someone had picked up this dog and was keeping it in a pen." The man gave Kyron further directions.

"Okay." Kyron reoriented himself and thanked the man for the information and drove down the street. At this rate he'd be talking to half the town before he had any usable information that panned out.

As he headed toward the newest lead, he noticed this area was completely different, where the homes were much farther apart, and the lot sizes were much bigger. The residences may be situated closer along the street, but some had very large backyard spaces behind them.

When Kyron noted a full pallet of dog food at the end of a driveway, he stopped and got out. It was very unusual to see the average homeowner getting that type of bulk delivery. Walking over, he met a woman coming out, clearly sweaty and tired, brushing strands of hair off her face. He stepped forward and said, "Hey, I can't say I've seen too many people get dog food by the pallet."

She looked up at him and then nodded. "Yeah, it was a donation, from one of the dog food companies." She pointed toward the back, behind her house. "I run a little animal rescue."

"Ah," he said and brightened considerably. "That makes sense. I'm Kyron. I don't suppose you've seen a three-legged dog anywhere, have you?"

She frowned. "Maybe," she replied cautiously. "Who's asking?" He smiled at that and quickly explained. She shook her head. "I'm Miranda. Wow, that's not what I expected you to say."

"No, I suppose not," he agreed, with a smile. "But does that mean you have or you haven't?"

"I have." She then pointed down the road, toward where the next house was. "Old Man Macintyre brought home a three-legged dog out of the blue one day and kept it locked up in the back. Apparently the dog had other ideas and took off."

"Interesting. Have you seen it around lately?" When she hesitated, he knew that was a *bingo* right there, and he smiled at her gently. "You obviously have your hands full here." He walked over to the pallet, bent down, and picked up one of the big dog food bags, and flung it over his shoulder. "And you obviously care about animals. I came to town for the sole purpose of making sure this one is okay."

"I guess I'm always a little hesitant because people like to keep dogs like that for the wrong reasons, as if they're curiosities or some sort of trophy." He stared at her. She nodded. "Right, I mean it's not exactly an animal you want to showcase. It sounds like he's already been through way more than enough."

"*She* actually."

"It's a female?" she asked softly.

"Yes, and fixed."

"Good." She nodded. "Most of these animals have already been through so much. I can't even wrap my head around the idea that, on top of it all, she was a War Dog."

"Well, the fact of the matter is, she's no longer a War Dog, and she deserves the best chance for retirement and the best chance at a home life that she can get," Kyron explained.

"Right," she murmured. She bent down, picked up another bag. "You can follow me with that, if you like." Then she led him around to the back, where she had the side doors of the garage open.

As he stepped inside, he noted that the entire garage was sectioned off into pet foods. Setting the bag on the floor, he stated, "I'm sure that amount of dog food is a godsend."

"You're not kidding," she agreed. "I've got hay coming tomorrow for the horses. Although I might push that back a few days."

"So, you have horses here too?" he asked. "Wow, that takes a lot of dedication."

"All it takes," she replied, her tone sounding borderline bitter, "is a heart."

He stopped and gave her a small smile. "Hey, remember why I'm here?"

She nodded. "I am trying to remember that, but I also don't know who you are. You can pretty much say you're anybody, but that doesn't mean a whole lot to me."

That sat him back on his heels a bit, and he wasn't sure how to improve things, but, if she'd seen the dog, he needed to do whatever he could. "Obviously you've come up against some jerks in this world, and I'm sorry about that," he replied. "But I'm really just here to help the dog." Walking back outside, he grabbed another bag, threw it over his shoulder, then bent down, smiling at how the knee replacements were functioning just fine, and scooped up a second bag under his arm.

When she watched him grab the second one, her jaw dropped. "Wow, nice trick."

"Spent a lot of years working in the service."

She stopped, studied him. "Were you a K9 handler by chance?"

"I was for a long time," he admitted, "and then I just couldn't handle it anymore."

"Handle what?"

"I couldn't handle the deaths, the accidents, the problems, and the fact that I wasn't allowed to love them because they had to be moved on to other trainers and other handlers as well." He sighed, shaking his head. "It ended up being something I just couldn't do."

"I couldn't do that at all," she shared instantly.

Although the garage door was open for them, he also noted a gate in the backyard fencing and quite a few dogs barking and roaming around freely. "How many dogs do you have here?"

"I've got nine at the moment," she told him, "and fourteen cats. Some are indoor cats. Thankfully I just placed the rabbits with a rescue. But I've still got a llama, horses, and a goat." She shook her head. "People get these ideas that having a pet is so great, until they realize they have to look after the animal on an ongoing basis, including buying food, getting veterinary care and training, and it seems like the minute there is a bump in the road, so many of them find a way to just dump the animal. I can't tell you how many times I've found animals tied up to my front door."

"Wow," he replied in shock, "that's just crazy."

"I know, and other rescue operations are here in town, larger facilities that are official organizations," she stated. "But anybody who knows me also knows that I lack the ability to say no," she admitted, "and they tend to take advantage."

"And yet you would want them to take advantage, if that meant securing the animals and keeping them safe, because whoever would do that in the first place isn't somebody who deserves to have them anyway."

CHAPTER 4

MIRANDA STUDIED THE man before her, obviously strong and fit, yet he walked with a bit of a limp, but he was saying all the things that she appreciated hearing. She just didn't have much faith in human nature anymore. Was he just saying it to get information from her? But really, what information did she have to offer?

Had she seen the dog? Possibly.

Could she help him get the dog? Possibly.

Would she want to do that? She wasn't sure, primarily because she didn't trust him. He carried bags and worked steadily at her side, until all of the dog food was stacked neatly in the garage. He looked around and murmured, "Got to be hundreds of dollars worth of pet food here."

"A thousand, actually," she corrected him. "I work at a local veterinary office part-time, usually just on Saturdays—unless he needs me otherwise—to cover the vet bills for my animals. The company sales rep was there one day, and we were talking about my problem with getting dog food in bulk, and he offered to send some over. Imagine my surprise when this showed up." She waved her hand at the empty pallet that the stranger, Kyron, had picked up, immediately asking where she wanted it.

"Well, I can undoubtedly find a use for it," she noted, "so let's put it in the backyard." She quickly went ahead of him, while he carried the pallet, then opened up the gate to the backyard. Immediately they were inundated with dogs. He put the pallet down where she wanted it, then stopped for a moment to survey the animals. With a big grin, he crouched down, albeit somewhat awkwardly, and gave the animals his attention.

That was another thing she really appreciated, somebody who knew when to take a moment. Because, with the animals, although they would ask for attention, they didn't always get what they wanted at the right time. They would keep asking, until they realized none was coming their way. And, with him, as a stranger, the animals were obviously quite interested in who he was. They also were calming down and accepting him at a rate that she found surprising.

She also trusted animals far more than people, and, if her animals thought Kyron was okay, well then, maybe he was. When he stood up again, laughing, he said warmly, "You have a great place here."

She frowned. "Not the usual response I get from people."

"Because they're not animal people." He shrugged. "There are definitely times in life where you have to pick the people or the animals that you want to hang out with and just ditch the rest."

She snorted with laughter at that. "Yeah," she agreed. "Except that a lot of people don't see the same side of that."

He nodded. "I get that. I'm an animal person, have been all my life," he noted quietly. "If I hadn't gone into the service, I probably would have done something along the medical line with them."

"A vet?" she asked.

"I don't know." He shook his head. "That always

seemed like far too much time in school. Honestly, you running a rescue like this gives me ideas."

She frowned, tilted her head. "Like your own rescue?" she asked. "Because, if you want to give it a shot and if you've got a place and if you can take a few animals, I am more than happy to help you get started," she declared.

He looked at her, a smile playing at the corner of his lips. "I don't know where I'll end up yet. I'm not sure I want to stay around here." He paused. "This town holds a lot of uneasy memories for me."

"I think it does for a lot of people," she agreed. "In many ways it's a wonderful town. Yet, in other ways, not so much. Aspen is a big city, and you'll have all the elements that go along with it," she explained, "including people who are great. And then the assholes come along and get pets for their kids for a holiday, then dump the pets when they are tired of the added responsibilities." She sighed. "Believe me. I've got several that were found that way."

His gaze hardened, and she once again felt relieved that he was such a devoted animal lover.

She nodded. "If you've got land, then a rescue would be huge. But you also need an income or lots of donations because these little darlings will bleed you dry." She cheerfully pointed at the animals milling around and then nodded toward the horses in the enclosure behind her.

"This is what I have, plus I lease out the backyard from the neighbor, but he's talking about selling because property prices have gone up so much, and he wants to get out of town," she added quietly. "If that happens, I have no idea what I'll do with the horses."

"And I suppose nobody's around to help you out."

"Well, apparently a great-uncle of mine just found out

from my grandma that I was doing this, and he cut me a check to help out." She beamed with happiness. "Honestly, that seemed like a miracle and has allowed me to order hay for the whole winter and to restock supplies."

"Hopefully your neighbor won't sell too quickly."

"He says he's still thinking about it, but, as you know, things can change pretty fast," she murmured. "And, yeah, moving the horses and all that hay would be a problem but not impossible."

"Have you got it yet?"

"No, it's coming tomorrow." She paused, staring at him. "Why?"

"Will they unload the truck for you?"

She nodded. "They have a trailer, and they'll just slide everything off on this side of the fence." She pointed out where she had a big rough-looking fence that held the last of the hay that she had right now.

He nodded, his hands on his hips as he looked around.

"It's pretty rough looking, I know."

"Hey, what you're trying to do is the rough part," he noted, with a shrug. "But, yeah, forty acres would be nice, wouldn't it?"

"Wouldn't it?" she agreed. "That would be awesome, but my first thought is, how much it would cost to put in fencing."

"One hell of a lot," he replied. "And yet so worthwhile."

"Well, anytime you feel like you're pulled to come lend a hand with the animals," she suggested cheerfully, "I won't say no to help."

He turned to face her. "Does that mean you trust me?"

"Let me just say that the animals trust you, and I can work with that."

He nodded. "They're pretty good judges of character, aren't they?"

"Usually," she murmured, "but they're not infallible though."

He smiled. "No, that's true, but, for the record, I've never done anything to hurt an animal in my life. And, if I could figure out a way to do something like this," he stated, "I would be all over it."

She stared at him, so curious. "Seriously?"

He nodded. "I've seen how rough the K9 military life can be, and how hard and yet still rewarding it is for the animals. They get a lot of love, a lot of feedback, and they're well treated and are supposed to be retired to good homes"—he shook his head—"which is why I'm so angry about this one."

When he told her what had happened, she could feel her own stomach clenching in fury. "I don't understand why they couldn't have just said, *Hey, guys, we can't handle this dog.*"

"Because it's admitting failure," he noted quietly. "I'm not sure how much you understand about human nature, but—"

She held up a hand. "I understand enough," she replied quietly. "And, for some reason, admitting failure or otherwise acknowledging that you can't handle something or that you changed your mind is something that most people are incapable of doing. It just pisses me off because then the animals suffer, when they don't need to." She saw that he agreed with that.

As he bent down to pet one of her dogs, he asked, "Do you keep all the dogs outside?"

"Because I have them all together in a pen like this, I

find it very hard to only let some of them in the house," she told him, "so all of them come in and out at the same time." She hesitated. "You were a great help with the dog food, so I should offer you a cup of coffee or something," she suggested. "Honestly, I could use one myself." Then with the dogs all streaking around them, she led the way inside to the big country kitchen.

The dogs filled the room. He looked in from the doorway and smiled. "Now this is a kitchen."

"Well, it was supposed to be much more refined. I bought it when it was partially renovated, thinking that I could fix it up myself over time." She gave him a crooked smile.

"But somehow there was never money—or time—to fix it." He looked at the floor, which was still plywood, and the ceiling, which was still raw beams, and she shrugged.

"Don't judge me on my house," she stated. "Judge me on the health of my animals."

He laughed out loud. "I wouldn't judge you in the first place. And you're somebody I agree with totally. The animals come first." With all the indoor animals bustling around beside them, he took off his boots, stepped inside, and sniffed appreciatively. "And you cook," he noted.

"Well, somewhat," she murmured. "I put some bread in the oven, so I'd have something to eat."

"So, you're spending all your money on feeding the animals?"

She nodded. "Things have been pretty tight, until I got that check."

"And then the first thing you did was buy hay and dog food."

"The hay was my plan, but the dog food was another

happy surprise. The hay I definitely ordered right away, since, as you saw, things were getting a little scary out there. I was nearly to the point of begging my grandmother for some money again." She sighed. "So thankfully that was averted. But, as for spending the rest of the money, I'm not even sure yet. There is plenty to spend it on, but I'm still sorting out priorities. I have vet bills, but I can pay for that by working there part-time, though even now the bills are higher than my wages. Still, it's an agreement that works well for us both. I'm able to help him by taking animals he ends up with that need homes, particularly the unadoptable ones that might otherwise be euthanized, and I get the care that the animals need at a greatly reduced rate."

"That sounds like a wonderful system to me," he noted. "You're lucky you managed to work that out."

"I agree. It's worked for the last couple years, and I'm hopeful that we'll maintain this barter agreement. What I need is more land and more money"—she shrugged—"but I imagine everybody in my situation would say the same thing."

"I'm sure," he agreed quietly. "Still, have you registered as a charity?"

"No." She grimaced. "There's all kinds of paperwork and legal fees required, and I just haven't had a chance to even look at it," she murmured. "I'm not so sure it would be worth it."

"Well, taxation-wise, it probably would help, but it is something you'd definitely need to get legal advice on."

"And again, legal advice does not come free," she replied.

"No, you're right there." He looked around and stepped over to the big kitchen table, essentially a picnic table she had taken a belt sander to, smoothing it down until the beautiful grain patterns in the wood showed up, and then stained and sealed it. "You know, in theory," he began, "what I can see is that you're doing very well."

"Well, I'm holding on anyway," she stated. "I can't say I'm thriving, and I certainly wouldn't say that any of us are doing very well, but, as long as I can keep food on the table and the animals fed, safe, secure, and warm for the winter, then I'll consider it an accomplishment for the year."

He stared at her intently.

"What's the matter?" she asked, flushing. "Have I got dirt on my nose or something?"

He shook his head. "You're just an unknown breed for me."

"What?" she asked, startled.

"A woman who cares more about the animals around her, than the latest makeup or going out for a good time."

"Well then, you haven't met many real women," she declared. "Most of the people in my circle of friends are an awful lot like me."

He nodded with a smile. "And I can really appreciate that. And I'm in no position to judge all women anyway. That's not fair," he noted. "Certainly a lot of women are very much like you and are happy to be at home with their family, but most of the time the family makes them that way."

"Well, I don't have a family of my own, just my grandma—and my great-uncle," she shared. "And I can't imagine taking care of babies and these animals at the same time." She frowned, shaking her head. "I won't be going in that direction any time soon."

His lips twitched.

She nodded. "That would be a deal breaker for me."

"Got it. But you are at least somewhat set up here."

Just then, two brown streaks raced through the kitchen, and, wrapping around his legs, they hopped up on the table.

"Wow." He laughed. "Who are these guys?"

"Pon and Pin," she said, with a sigh. "Two ferrets that were dropped off in a cardboard box one day."

"Seriously?" He frowned. "It's a wonder they survived."

"I know. Thankfully I got home when I did," she noted. "I probably could have handed them off to somebody who would be willing to adopt them, but I've grown pretty attached to them myself." She smiled at their antics. "They've been with me for a long time now."

"In that case, they're not available for adoption. They're yours," he stated. "Any change in their circumstances now would be a huge adjustment for them."

"Sure, but, when there's no food"—she shrugged—"I'm not sure that adjustment would be all that hard. I'm pretty sure I'd get replaced pretty quickly."

He shook his head. "I think you're wrong there. These animals have an awful lot of faith in you."

"Sure, and when that faith is broken?"

"You would deal with it, but, at this point, you're holding on."

"Yeah," she agreed quietly, "I'm holding on." She brought the coffeepot over to the table. "I honestly don't know how fresh this coffee is."

"Don't worry about it," he said. "It'll be fine."

She smiled. "You really don't have a whole lot of choice but to take it. I'm not sure where my coffee stash is either or if there even is one."

"Oh, running out of coffee is bad news," he stated.

She nodded. "I know. I try to keep my cupboards

stocked with a few essentials, and coffee is one of them. Even if it is the cheapest brand I can find, I still really enjoy it."

"That's important," he agreed, "especially for the quiet moments in the morning, when you're wondering what you're doing with your life."

At that, she stopped at the counter after she'd returned the pot. Reaching for the milk and sugar, she stared. "Is that something you deal with?"

"Sure. I'm recovering from an injury myself, so I'm no longer in the military," he shared. "I didn't figure I would adapt well to a desk job, so I took a medical discharge, and now I'm sitting here, trying to figure out what to do with my life." She brought back the sugar and milk, then offered it to him. He immediately shook his head. "No, black is good for me."

After returning them to the cupboard and the fridge, she sat across from him. "How badly were you injured?" she asked bluntly. His eyebrows shot up, and she flushed. "Yeah, sorry. I'm not really well-known for being too subtle."

"You know what? Sometimes it's much easier if you aren't," he replied quietly. "I lost a leg, some ribs, and a kidney. I've got more than a few scars on top of everything else, but I'm definitely still able-bodied, as you saw."

"I did see that," she noted, "and you have no idea how many hours you saved me. I was worried about getting the bags in before the storm hit, and I'm not sure I would have done it by myself."

Then his startled gaze went to the window to see the snow now falling. His lips twitched. "It's been at least ten years since I lived in this town. I'd forgotten how quickly the flurries can come up."

"Which is why I needed to get the feed in. Thanks for

the help."

"Any problems with that hay tomorrow?"

"I moved the delivery back a few days," she stated. "Considering the weather and all, it seemed like a good idea. I do have enough for a few more days, and they'll get here as soon as they can. So, with any luck, I'll be good to go."

"Right." Kyron smiled, as he watched a huge cat wander into the kitchen. "And of course you have the prerequisite number of cats."

"Six feral cats, I think," she replied. "And we have bunkers outside, if they don't want to come in. I make sure they have food, plus a warm area to tuck themselves into, with blankets—old horse blankets or anything like that to keep them warm. Then I have eight indoor cats," she added. "Not all of them are mine. Most are just, you know, up for adoption. I do keep a website up as much as I can, but that's hard to maintain. It's more word-of-mouth than anything."

"Do you have a sign up outside?"

"No, I don't," she noted. "I tried that, but some of my neighbors aren't that thrilled about what I do here."

"Of course not," he said in a dry tone. "And it was Old Man Macintyre who had this three-legged dog?"

"Well, he brought her home and told me about it. He actually talked to me over the fence, as if it were some sort of kudos to him," she explained, "which I really didn't get. But he seemed pretty excited about her. And then I heard him yelling at the dog a couple times, when the dog was barking. There was even some back-and-forth, which kind of made my hair go up, and I did talk to him about it the next day. He pretty much told me to mind my own business. Not long after that, he called me and asked if I'd seen it. I said no, asked what happened, and he told me that it had run away."

She shook her head. "For once I didn't say what I was thinking—that, of course, it ran away because that's what animals do if you don't take good care of them. They have to. It's self-preservation, particularly a dog like that one."

"And yet that dog," he mentioned quietly, "has only three legs and may not be in the best of shape."

"Particularly after Macintyre got ahold of it," she said. "He didn't beat it or anything that I know of. I would have intervened if I thought that were the case, but there are plenty of other ways that an animal can be abused."

"Exactly," Kyron agreed. "So, after coffee, would you mind showing me where you thought you saw her?"

She nodded. "Yeah, I can do that. I don't want to think of her out there suffering, assuming it's her. I didn't get much of a look."

"Did you try to get her to come in?"

"I did, and she wouldn't come close. But then I have a lot of dogs here, and I don't know how she handles other animals."

"Most of the War Dogs are raised with packs and are around a lot of animals for socialization," he told her, "but we don't know what she's been through since she ran away. It's possible she may have had a less-than-joyful experience with other animals. Particularly since her injury."

Miranda winced at that. "That's a good point. I get it."

"Their natural primal instincts would be to distance themselves from a dog like her, since she would be a target for predators. No matter how domesticated dogs are, deep down they are all about survival," he reminded her.

"I know. I just don't want to think of her out there suffering."

"Well, that's one of the reasons I want to see if I can get

close to her and if I can gain her trust," he explained.

"And then what?" she asked, with a challenge in her voice. "Do you have a home, a house, or someplace for her to go?"

"I'll have to call my bosses to figure that out," he replied quietly. "Don't worry. We'll do the best we can by her."

"So you say, but she shouldn't have ended up in these circumstances to begin with." There was just enough of a challenge in her voice that she saw him visibly withdrawing. "Listen. I get that you didn't make that decision," she added, "but you do have the opportunity to influence a decision now."

"I do," he agreed. "And sometimes these decisions aren't always easy ones."

"It's never easy," she murmured. "Why do you think I live here with all these animals and barely any food for myself?"

"Because you care," he stated, "and that kind of care can never be wrong."

"Says you," she replied, with a laugh. "And today was my half-day at work, so tomorrow will be a long day."

"At the vet's office?"

"Oh no, I was talking about a long day here," she corrected on a laugh. "That vet job is just a part-time gig, my second job. I have a regular weekday job."

"Doing?"

"I work at a vehicle supply store," she replied quietly. "And it's almost always very busy in the wintertime."

"Interesting."

"A lot of people here love their toys," she stated, with a smile.

"Do you ever hit up any of your patrons for money for

the animals?"

"Well, that would not necessarily be welcomed by my bosses. Plus, I haven't filed as a charitable organization," she admitted. "I'm sure I'd get a lot of well-intended support and advice from the customers, but actually handing over money is something not everybody is terribly enthralled about."

He nodded. "How long have you worked there?"

She raised one eyebrow. "A long time," she murmured. "About seven years, I think. It pays the bills."

"Sure, it pays the bills, but it probably doesn't pay a lot of bills."

"Nope, it doesn't," she agreed, "but what am I supposed to do? Changing jobs is not exactly an option right now."

"Got it," he said. "You must work nearly full-time hours here, alone, looking after the animals, don't you?"

"Yes, and again it doesn't matter because I still have to do more." She shrugged. "It really depends on how many animals I have at any given time."

"Do you ever have too many?"

"Yeah, and then I put out a drive to get them adopted," she replied. "Spring is the worst because we end up with cats and kittens, pregnant cats. Everybody wants a cat or a kitten, until it requires care and, you know, the inevitable medical fees. If we could just get them all neutered and spayed," she mentioned, "we would all have much less of a problem."

He nodded quietly. "Lots of service groups are in town that you could hit up."

"Maybe, if they are people who know me, that is," she noted, "but otherwise? I doubt it."

"Back to needing to get the paperwork in order, right?"

"Yes." She nodded. "I started to look into it a while ago,

and I just kind of gave up when I realized money would be an issue."

"*Hmm.*"

She cocked her head. "What?"

"Just wondering if I know anybody in the legal field who would do something like that for you on a pro bono basis."

Her eyebrows shot up. "Well, I haven't found anybody yet. I didn't think that actually worked with lawyers."

"Ah, back to that judgment again." He chuckled. "And I agree with you most of the time, but not everybody is of the same ilk."

"Maybe not," she agreed, "but I haven't had people lining up, offering to do things for free around here."

SOMETHING ABOUT MIRANDA was admirable. Even though she was on her legs financially because this great-uncle had saved her for the winter, Kyron could see that she was struggling badly but remained determined to find a way. "I don't know if I have a lawyer friend," he replied, "but I'll check out my acquaintances."

"But you said that you haven't been in town for ten years," she noted. "I can't imagine they would be overjoyed if you step into town and immediately start shaking them down for free labor."

He burst out laughing at that. "You could be right, but I have a pretty good excuse. I was serving in the navy." He frowned. "Unfortunately nobody in my family is a lawyer."

"No, none in mine either," she noted, with a wry look. "Who knows? Maybe it's not that hard. Maybe I can do it myself online or something."

"That's possible," he agreed. "I could look into it more when I get back to my brother's place."

She stared at him suspiciously. "You're staying with your brother?"

"Yes." He nodded. "I just flew in to find the dog, and, while I'm here, I'm trying to mend some fences between the two of us."

"Ah, always a few of those, aren't there?" she murmured.

"Yes, and, to be honest, I wasn't too sure that I even wanted to try, but his wife is pregnant, after a very long series of mishaps in that department. She's seven months along, so it's looking good, but we're trying to keep her calm, quiet, and not upset, so that's making us behave ourselves," he admitted, with half a smile.

"Well, maybe it's a good thing then," she suggested.

"Maybe, but at the same time she's also got this thing about trying to make everybody happy and to keep the peace everywhere, so she's done something that I'm really struggling with at the moment." He found it so much easier to talk to Miranda, probably because she didn't know anything about his life or his family. He shrugged. "I shouldn't even be bothering you with this. I'm sure you've got bigger problems to deal with."

"Well, right now," she noted, "I'm inside and warm, instead of out there, lugging dog food in the snow, thanks to you, and it's always nice to visit with another animal lover, so I'm good. Now what on earth is your sister-in-law up to?"

"She's trying to patch things up between me and my parents. She told them that I'm here and has them coming for a visit."

"Ah, so she wants to spread more of that family joy."

"Yeah."

"I wonder if that's some sort of a nesting thing," she murmured.

"I have no idea," he muttered, "but, in my world, that would be contrary to the natural order of things."

Surprised, she looked at him and then chuckled. "Meaning that, in the wild, animals tend to isolate and stay away from family?" He nodded. "And yet lots of animals are tribal or stay together as a group," she added, "so I'm not sure that particular theory fits. At least not all the time."

"I haven't had much chance to get my mind wrapped around what she's doing, but I fear it will end in disaster, with her very upset, and I'll get the blame."

"You'll get blamed because you'll be the one who doesn't cooperate?" she asked, with a knowing look. He glared at her, and she shrugged. "I can't imagine you buckling under, if some real hard feelings are there," she murmured.

"You don't know me at all," he replied stiffly.

"Nope, and you don't know me. But I do know that the animals adore you, all of them." She waved her arm at him. Kyron was completely surrounded by dogs, cats, and ferrets. "And they are a good judge of character," she noted, with a chuckle.

He raised an eyebrow with a smile.

"So, I'm not sure what the problem is between you and your family, and I'm sorry that there is a problem," she added, "because life really is far too short. But I get it because I've got problems of my own with family too." She gave a heavy sigh. "My parents are not happy about what I do here with the animals. They all want me to get rid of them and to get a life, which, in their minds, translates to *get married and have kids*. After all, isn't that what we're supposed to do?" she asked in a mocking tone.

"Well, in my case I left town and joined the navy, like my grandfather had done. He's the only extended family I've actually had in my life for a very long time. My parents didn't get along with him, so they're not happy that I followed in his footsteps. My brother, on the other hand, followed in my father's footsteps and went into law enforcement."

"Your brother's a cop?" she asked.

He nodded. "Yeah, he is. He's on the police department here in town."

"Interesting," she noted and then shrugged. "It's not like he'll know me. I'm not somebody who ever has run-ins with the law."

"Didn't think you were," he replied cheerfully. "But my brother is one of those kinds of people who is always very together. He married his high school sweetheart not long after graduating. Perfect job, perfect wife. The only thing they struggled with was having kids." He looked down at the floor, then shrugged. "But I suppose now that she's pregnant, and so far along, all has likely been forgiven in that department too."

"But not in your case?"

"No, I got badly injured, and that was more of a 'Hey, I told you so' moment for my parents."

Her jaw dropped. "Surely they didn't say that to you."

Wondering why he was even telling her any of his business, he went on. "Yeah, they did that and so much more," he confirmed quietly.

"It's also hard when you know that your brother is the only favorite," she added, "but that's what the word means, isn't it?"

He stared at her and then chuckled. "That's exactly what

it means, … but, when he's such an obvious favorite, it makes it very hard to grow up in his shadow. And to know that you're doing everything they don't want you to do, just adds to it."

"Which is why you tend to go rebel even more because some kind of attention is better than none, right?"

"Ah, look at that," he teased. "Aren't you quite the philosopher?"

"I don't know about that, but families are often very messed up and for all the wrong reasons."

"Is there a right reason?"

"In a way, yes," she noted. "It sounds like you didn't do what they wanted you to do, so that is power and control. And you did something they disagreed with, based on somebody they disagreed with, so again it's power and control. But more than that, it's probably also a case of love gone awry. If your grandfather was somebody they expected to love and to be loved by, and that wasn't how it was, they would see it as you crossing to the other side and becoming the enemy instead of family."

"That's exactly what happened," he said, drumming his fingers on the tabletop, as he stared at her. "And they've upheld their side of the bargain and basically not talked to me in all these years. In fact, I didn't phone them when I lost my leg, but one of the doctors called them to let them know I'd been injured. I was awake and stable at the time, so the doc gave me the phone, and my father went on this rampage about how it served me right, how they had told me not to enlist in the first place."

She sat here and stared at him, with enough compassion in her gaze to encompass another whole rescue of him. But he didn't want to be part of her rescue. She was a beautiful woman and all that, and they definitely had a connection between them. But he didn't want to be seen as a charity case, like with her animals, as somebody who needed help. That would never go over well. "Don't look at me like that."

"Why not?" she asked. "It sounds like you've had it tough for your whole life."

"Mostly since the accident," he agreed quietly. "That's when you find out who the people in your life really are. Like your friends, your family. … Also that's when things get boiled down, so you can see what really matters in your life."

"I agree." She nodded. "Not so different from what I'm doing. No, not to the same extent, of course, but you find out what people are really like. The ones who actually are there to help you achieve your goals, versus the ones who think this is some passing phase that you'll get over—and hopefully soon."

"Right," he replied, with a knowing nod. "Actually, I think that's what my parents had hoped, that it would be a passing phase and that I would come to my senses sooner or later."

"Preferably before you got injured, I assume."

"I don't know. I feel like they really think I deserved it. I think my dad meant exactly what he said back then, up to the present day. And now, thanks to Sandra, I'll have to listen to them while they're visiting her and Allen. In their minds, I'm sure they'll be thinking that I'll never get married or have a family because, of course, now I'm damaged goods."

"Wow, I don't like them already."

He shook his head. "The odd thing is that most people get along with them really well."

"But you don't get to know people, who they are at their

core, until you come across something like this, and you see into their souls."

"Maybe they'll change. Maybe they have already changed and are somebody different than what I used to know," he suggested. "Maybe I'm being unfair. I just don't know anymore." He sighed. "When it comes to these big emotional issues, you never quite know if it's you or them who's having the problem." Just then he heard an odd bark at the window. He bolted to his feet and stared outside.

"That was Benjie," she noted quietly, not getting up.

"He's staring at the back fence though. Look."

She got up, stood beside him, then nodded. "Yeah, so let's go see if we can talk to a shepherd."

"It's actually a Malinois," he stated quietly.

She turned toward him, one eyebrow raised.

"Similar," he said, "but different."

She laughed. "Got it. Still a dog to me and a dog that needs help. They're all the same, part and parcel, in the world that I come from. Any animal in need is an animal that I want to help," she murmured. And, with that, she shoved her feet back into her snow boots. "Let's go see if we can get close." And together they trooped outside.

CHAPTER 5

MIRANDA STOOD QUIETLY at the fence line, watching Kyron study the ground around the fence.

"The tracks are fresh," he stated.

She nodded. "Outside of the snow that's falling now, we didn't have any yesterday."

"Have you put out dog food here?"

"Absolutely," she confirmed. "And, yes, it's gone."

He nodded. "Well, that's good enough for me."

"Maybe, but we also have raccoons, coyotes, and who knows what else that could have eaten it," she explained. He glanced at her, and she shrugged. "Yes, I know. I should only be feeding dogs, particularly in my financial position. I get it, but, if I can't be sure who's eating it, how can I be sure who I'm feeding?" she asked, then shrugged again. "To be honest, if it kept the dog fed and nearby, I don't even care."

He smiled at her. "You have a big heart."

"A big heart that's keeping me broke," she stated, with a big smile. "But as long as there's enough to go around, I don't really care."

He climbed over the fence, and, when his pant leg rode up, she saw the prosthetic leg underneath. "I don't suppose your missing leg will endear you more to her, will it?"

"Not particularly," he replied. "The problem is the other way around. I understand the pain and suffering that I know she went through, and I would have done anything to have spared her that. Hell, I would have done anything to spare that for me," he said, with a head shake. "Sometimes life is just a bitch and has a mind of its own."

"I hear you there," she noted. "And it's not easy in any way, shape, or form to come back from something like that."

"No, but it's not overly hard either though," he added. "It's all about attitude."

She watched as he jumped nimbly down on the other side and into the field behind her place. There didn't appear to be any pain as he moved. He wandered around a bit there and then stopped when he caught sight of something. "What is it?" she asked.

"Other dog tracks are here," he noted. "She's not alone."

"Well, that's a good thing though, isn't it?" And then she thought about it and added, "Or maybe not. A pack of wild dogs roam around here too."

"Beth won't survive very long in that kind of environment, I wouldn't think," he noted.

"We also don't know for sure that it's the wild dogs with the War Dog," she amended. "It could be a dog from another place nearby or another stray."

"It's possible," he murmured, as he studied the surroundings. "I'll go for a walk to see what I can make of it. Maybe you should head back in, where you'll be warm."

"Well, I'm out here already. How far are you going?" she asked curiously.

"I don't know. As far as I need to go," he replied. "I promise I'll come back in and let you know what I find."

She watched him steadily for a moment and then nodded. "Please do." And, with that, she headed toward the house and called her dogs with her, yet kept glancing back, wondering if she should have gone with Kyron. But he seemed to know what he was doing, whereas she felt like she was out of her depth out there.

Tracking was something she would certainly have loved to learn more about, but it wasn't that easy to just pick up without some help. As it was, she still needed to go check the fences for wear and tear. So, turning her attention to that, she walked along the property line and then went over to the horses to check on how they were doing.

Because they were in the back pasture, she had to throw their hay on a wagon and drag it out to them. As she fed them, cutting the twine on the bale, she popped the loose flakes into their feeder. Then she walked up and down, checking on each of them. She gave them all a cuddle, a quick brush, and checked their hooves to make sure that everything was fine.

When she reached the goat, she laughed. "Hey, Gabby. How're you doing?" She immediately went *meeeh*, and Miranda laughed again. "You are a character," she said affectionately. And Gabby was.

Gabby was always with the horses, bonded in many ways that humans couldn't even contemplate, and was one of the most well-behaved goats Miranda had ever seen. That was saying a lot because, at least in her experience, goats could be pretty rough to handle. They had a sense of humor and a mind-set that got them into trouble twenty-four hours a day.

But Gabby was easy to keep, and that's one of the reasons Miranda was working so hard to give Gabby a decent life here, so she could stay. This was another one of the many animals that she had originally looked at finding a foster home for, then gave it up, because Gabby was getting on in years. If she didn't adjust well, rehoming could be really hard on her, and that wasn't a chance Miranda wanted to take with the older goat.

She needed to check in with the vet about the llama, when she got back to the house. Doug would need to run blood tests on the llama because it seemed like she was under the weather. She was looking slightly better today though.

Miranda had built a lean-to just before winter hit this year. She walked over and checked it, happy to see that it was still standing, though just barely. If it came down, it wouldn't hurt anything, since there was no substance to it, but it was one of the things she definitely needed to sort out. The trouble with building anything back here in a more permanent form was that she would lose the investment if her neighbor sold his property.

What Miranda really needed was acreage for herself, where she could move all the animals. But that just wasn't likely to happen. If she were wishing, she might as well wish for a lottery ticket, so she could have the life she really wanted. She didn't know about keeping her jobs, as long as she was dreaming, because so many of the animals were those that needed extra care.

Back in the house, she checked on the cats. She had two diabetics, and both needed shots. With that done, she checked on the other animals, then turned her attention to the coffeepot. Sadly it was empty, and, since she allowed herself only one pot a day, that meant she was done. With a philosophical shrug, she headed to her office and the mounds of paperwork she always had to deal with.

As she sat here, she wondered if it really was possible or beneficial to go through the process of becoming a legitimate charity. She wasn't even sure that *charity* was the right description and wondered if it even fit for a rescue like hers.

With that in mind, she thought about who she could ask. Immediately she picked up the phone and called a woman she knew, who ran a cat rescue.

"Hey, it's Miranda. I was just wondering about the legal status of you calling yourself a rescue and how I should be handling that." What followed was a lesson on taxation and how the state and the federal government defined the use of funds donated for animals. By the time the call was over, Miranda was armed with a lot of information and a clear path forward. One that could make her life a whole lot easier—or at least allow her to solicit and to accept tax-deductible contributions and to take advantage of other benefits afforded to charitable organizations with nonprofit status. She knew people would feel a lot more comfortable donating if she were properly registered.

The woman had also given her the name of the lawyer who had set it all up for her cat rescue. When Miranda phoned and got his answering service, she explained what her dilemma was and that she was wondering what the approximate cost would be to set her up properly. With the promise that the message would be forwarded and the legal aid receptionist would call her back with an estimate, Miranda felt good to have made at least a bit of progress. That done, she got up and headed to her bedroom, where she stripped her bed and put in a load of laundry.

The dogs and cats kept her bed completely covered in hair. She had an old mattress on the floor, where several of the dogs slept, but the rest of them tended to take over her bed. That also meant that she had to do laundry on a regular basis, just to keep the bed somewhat hair free. That was almost impossible, but what did she expect?

When she heard a series of whistles, she looked out the

big window in her bedroom. Kyron stood outside her fence again, his hand cupped around his mouth, but the whistles weren't something that she recognized. She watched to see if he got any response, and she thought she saw some movement in the underbrush. She wasn't sure at this distance. However, she hoped that the dog was probably out there listening, just unsure of what kind of reception she'd get. And, with that, Miranda's heart broke a little more.

"The poor thing," she whispered. "That's not what's supposed to happen to animals that have spent their lives in service for us." Miranda shook her head, hating that somebody actually did this to Beth. Miranda didn't know what the circumstances were, but it was hard not to judge others in a situation like this. Particularly after seeing the disgusting way people could just drop off their animals without a care. As soon as money or any effort was required, they just couldn't be bothered.

Even as she watched, she thought she saw something behind one of the trees. She wanted to call out and to let Kyron know, but that stillness to him told her that he was already aware. She watched in amazement as two dogs stepped forward. Both of them in sync, both of them together, yet standing just far enough behind him, as if thinking he didn't know they were there. She put a hand to her mouth as she watched, her heart slamming in her chest, as he slowly crouched down, still with his back to them, until he began to pivot in slow motion, then quietly called out.

"HEY, BETH," HE whispered. "Beth," he called out softly, "come here, girl." Her tail wagged, and he smiled gently. "I know. It's been tough, hasn't it?"

The other dog stuck very close to Beth, almost leaning into her. Kyron studied it for a moment. A shepherd, larger, and, yet in a way, maybe more dependent. He wasn't sure what the scenario was. He reached out a hand and called again, "Come here, Beth. Come over here, girl." He didn't want to use too many commands that would set her back, in case whatever had been there before had been part of her problem. He just kept talking to her in a calm, quiet voice. "It's all right, girl. It's okay."

In the distance, a series of shots were fired, and both dogs took off immediately, yet still so close together.

Kyron straightened up, his heart in his throat, as he watched Beth take off again. But they had made contact, so, as far as he was concerned, this was just about needing more time now. Yet something about the other dog shook him. He wasn't sure what was going on or in any way had an explanation or even a theory, but he continued to think about it, as he slowly trudged his way back to the house.

He didn't know how Miranda would feel if he camped out here several times over the next few days, trying to establish trust with the dog, but that immediately brought up something else.

Having now made contact with Beth, if he did get a hold of her, what was Kyron supposed to do? As he walked across the lawn, he phoned Badger.

"Well, I've found the dog," he stated. "She's definitely been on the loose for some time, but she's hooked up with what looks like a German shepherd. The other dog is quite a bit bigger than her, yet dependent somehow, and I'm not sure what the scenario is. I was just making progress when somebody fired some shots in the distance, and they both bolted." He paused, turned around to look in the direction the two dogs had gone, but he saw nothing. "Yet she was responding, and I know with a little bit of time, I can get her to trust me." He added, "But that brings up the larger question."

At that, Badger, his voice excited, replied, "Absolutely, it does. But this is huge, if you've actually found her. What kind of condition was she in?"

"Skinny," he said instantly, "but holding. I'm at the house of a woman who has been feeding her, well, putting out dog food, unsure if it was for this dog or for coyotes, but the food was disappearing. She'd gotten a glimpse of the dog a couple times but never got close enough to get a look at her," he explained quietly. "This woman is spending every penny she's got, trying to run a rescue here. She's got over forty animals, and it appears that she's the only one suffering for lack of food or at least nutrients."

"Ouch. So somebody else who's operating more on heart than head?" Badger noted.

"Well, let's just say that I'm sure she gets a lot of pushback from family and friends because she's working two jobs, and everything goes to the animals."

"Of course," he replied, "and you can understand that too."

"Absolutely," he muttered. "But I'm not too sure what we're supposed to do with this situation now. What if I get Beth back? I mean, I get that she needs to have a good set of choices and a good life from here on out, but do you have somebody here who can take her, somebody who'll properly look after her?"

Badger was quiet for a moment. "In that location, no," he stated finally. "Can you take her to your brother's place?"

"No, I don't think I can," he answered quietly. "I'll mention it to him, but his wife is not a big fan of dogs, and she's well along in a high-risk pregnancy, so I don't want to cause any trouble. In fact, I'm not sure I should even be there myself."

"Right," he agreed thoughtfully. "Let me talk to the rest of the team about it and see what we can come up with."

"Will do," Kyron said. "I just don't want to see Beth go to another scenario where she ends up struggling, you know? Plus, she's broken out of two different places here, so we'll have to keep that in mind as well. And she seems strangely bonded to this other dog."

"Right," Badger noted quietly. "We've got to find the right placement. That's why we took on this K9 project, to make sure all these animals ended up in homes that are safe and sound. We might find a rescue that can take her there or maybe adopt her somewhere within the city itself."

"And it's possible," Kyron admitted. "Certainly decent people are here, but we've seen some lately who haven't been all that easy to deal with. Like the people who got Beth originally."

"Right, and I can contact the war department and see what can be done about that."

"Haven't you come across this problem before?"

"No, not yet," he said.

"Well, what happened with all the other dogs you found?"

Badger laughed. "You may not want to hear this."

"What?" Kyron asked.

"Every one of them was adopted by the man we sent out to find them."

Kyron froze, as he thought about it. "Damn."

"Why damn?" Badger asked.

"Because, I have to admit, it already crossed my mind. She is a dog I can handle because it's work that I've done in the past," he noted, "but that doesn't mean that I'm ready to settle down."

"No, and I'm not saying you have to," Badger answered carefully. "This isn't a trick. We're not trying to get you to sign up for something like that, particularly if you're not ready to put down roots. The dog needs a home where she can stay for good, where she doesn't have to be rehomed yet again," he explained quietly.

"More than that, she needs a place where she feels safe, and it's very obvious, based on her current mannerisms, that she hasn't felt safe in a long time," he noted. "I did get a tail wag out of her eventually, but she's wary, very wary."

"Do you think she's been hurt?"

"I wouldn't be at all surprised, though I don't have any evidence or any other reason to say that," Kyron admitted. "Obviously something went on at her placement home that wasn't at all what we'd hoped for."

"Of course, and, if she's been on her own for any time it makes more sense too. It makes me damn angry with the ass who didn't let anybody know she was in trouble. They were only thinking about themselves and how much trouble they would be in," Badger snapped. "Believe me. It's not the first time we've seen something like that."

"It's still wrong, no matter how many times it happens though," Kyron muttered.

"Sure it is, and *being wrong* is just one aspect of how these poor dogs ended up slipping through the cracks," he replied, "but we're doing what we can. As is the war department."

"I know. I hear you," Kyron said. "Let me think about it. I might have some solutions here."

"Do you know people who are solid and serious in their commitment to handle Beth?"

"Maybe." Kyron turned to stare at the house. "I don't know. I'll have to give it some thought. Talk to you later." And, with that, Kyron hung up the phone and walked toward Miranda's house. He knocked on the back door, and she opened it almost immediately.

"You got close to her," she exclaimed.

"I did, but then some shots were fired or a truck backfired or something. I'm not sure what I even heard," he explained. "Her reaction does make me wonder if she has PTSD though."

Miranda winced immediately. "Oh, the poor baby."

"Exactly." Hesitating a moment, he began, "Look. I don't want to impose, but I'll need to come back and forth over the next few days to see if I can gain her trust. Also a second dog is with her."

"I saw that, at least I thought I did," she added. "I could just see you from my bedroom window. I was up there stripping the bedding to get it in the laundry, to rid it of all the dog and cat hair," she said, with an eye roll. "I heard you whistle, then looked out, and later saw that you got somewhere."

"I got somewhere. I'm just not sure where yet," he admitted. "And honestly, a lot of progress is necessary in order to get her to the point where I can take her home—or to a home." He hesitated. "I'm not too sure how long that will take."

"And what about the second dog she's with?" she asked anxiously.

"That's the next problem. I wasn't expecting a second dog, and they seem to be bonded."

"What about your brother? Would he take it?"

"Nope."

"Well, you need to spend whatever time you can give her," she stated. "Come on back in again and get warmed up."

He stepped inside, happy to feel the warmth. "Thank you, and I sincerely mean that. It helps that you're an animal lover, so I can take time getting Beth's trust, without pressuring her."

"As long as you'll look after the second one as well," she stated immediately.

He winced at that. "I know. I need to. I called my boss to see what they want to do about this."

"Well, I can't have you taking them out of here to a worse situation," she stated.

"Worse?" he asked, with a wry look.

"Yes, worse," she confirmed, nodding.

"At the moment, now that we've found her, we have to move into the second stage, which is gradually gain her trust and get a leash on her, then see what we can do from there."

She nodded. "And your brother?"

He shook his head. "My brother would probably be okay with it temporarily, as he's an animal lover, or at least he used to be. But my sister-in-law is not." She frowned at him. He frowned right back.

"I really can't condone letting the dogs go into an unhealthy scenario," she stated, crossing her arms over her chest.

He hated that he immediately noticed how plump and firm her breasts appeared over her arms. He gave himself a mental shake. "I get it. Let's get all our options together, and I can come back tomorrow." He looked out the kitchen window at the darkening sky. "Would you mind putting out more dog food for Beth today?"

"I can do that." She smirked. "As you saw, I have plenty, and thankfully you helped me unload."

"Right." He nodded, still in his own thoughts. "I'll bring a harness, some leashes, and dog food for Beth and her friend tomorrow morning. And see what I can do over the course of the day to hopefully gain her trust." And, with that, he smiled at her. "Thank you for the coffee too."

"Thank you for the help moving the dog food."

"I'm just so glad you found Beth in the first place."

She gave him a big grin. "Hey, any animal in need."

"I get it, and I'll see you in the morning." And, with that, he headed back to his vehicle.

CHAPTER 6

MIRANDA CLOSED THE door, stepped inside, and warmed up some of the soup she had in her fridge. During the winter she often kept a pot of stew or soup on hand. As soon as that was done, she would have to do the evening chores. As she did, she took out more dog food for the two dogs outside the fence, calling out to Beth and the strange one with her, putting the dog food underneath a branch.

She headed back to make sure that all her animals were tucked in well for the night and then she went back inside. She thought she heard another odd sound, then turned around to the nearest window but couldn't see anything. The dogs were calm and quiet, but, in the distance, more shots were fired.

She knew that several of the neighbors did target practice at times, and the sound of gunshots was not uncommon here, but it was dark already, and surely that would rule out target practice. She couldn't help but wonder if someone was after the two dogs. That would break her heart. She studied the area outside through a now-open window, wondering if she might hear anything moving. There was just an odd feel to the night.

When another shot rang out, she immediately bolted outside, grabbing her jacket on the way. She headed out to her backyard, yelling as she ran.

"Stop shooting! Stop shooting! Damn it!" She first went over to check on the horses, but they had been spooked and were still running around in circles. She called out with a calm whistle, trying to get them to settle down.

That was another damn reason she needed to find her own property and to get out of this in-town living situation. Just too many people were around who thought it was funny to get the animals going, like the horses, but it caused their stress levels to go through the roof. It was definitely not healthy.

Then another shot rang out, followed by still another. After that, the silence was deafening. She turned slowly around, wondering at the odd sound she heard in the trees behind her. For the first time in a very long while, she was actually nervous. She slowly made her way closer to the trees, and, as she got there, she heard a heavy growl in the shadows. She frowned and then called out, "Beth, is that you?" The growl continued. "Shit." She grabbed her phone and quickly punched in the number that Kyron had given her. Thankfully he answered right away.

"You need to get back here. I think she may have been shot."

KYRON RACED BACK toward Miranda's house. His heart slammed against his chest at the thought of the poor dog having been shot. What asshole had done that? That he'd heard shots fired earlier didn't bear thinking about. He'd heard them, but it was impossible to determine where they came from or even that they were gunshots.

If Beth had been shot, it also could have been an accident, although Kyron struggled with the concept of accidents when it came to shooting animals. Maybe the neighbor had seen Beth and had decided that, since she had taken off from him, she would just be a problem he should deal with by shooting her. Kyron didn't know.

The fact that Miranda got close enough to hear the dog growling and not whining, meant that it was a dangerous situation. If Beth had been severely hurt, it was hard to say if she would survive, since she wasn't in great condition to begin with.

The roads were heavy with snow, and it was coming down even heavier. He had just enough medical gear to maybe help a dog out in an emergency, but he didn't know. He also needed a decent vet around here, who would take emergency cases, and, if it cost a lot to save Beth, they'd just figure it out. Maybe Miranda's vet would help out if they needed him. Kyron could pay; he still had his savings, which was substantial at this point in time. Enough that he had to give serious consideration as to what he would do with that kind of money.

Would he buy a place here or move somewhere else, where his money would get him a little bit more? But he also had a piece of property that his grandfather had left him. He'd been the only one to receive anything from Granddad's estate, and, of course, that had just caused even more problems within his immediate family. But Kyron didn't know what condition it was in or what the place was worth, if it was worth anything at all. It was one of those things he had walked away from a long time ago when he had walked away from Aspen and his family and hadn't really considered since. The tax bills came due on Granddad's place, and

Kyron paid it automatically, without even looking at it. It had just been another reminder of the negative part of his world.

And maybe that was wrong; maybe he should be reassessing that negative part of his world and seeing it more as a gift from his grandfather because it was. Kyron also knew he wouldn't inherit anything from his parents, and his grandfather had seemed to realize that too, so he'd given the place to him. Predictably then, his own son, Kyron's father, felt like he'd been stiffed, felt that what should have been his had gone to his son.

It seemed that these situations always ended up creating bad feelings. At the same time, Kyron didn't really feel like it was his problem, since his father and grandfather had had such a breakdown in communication between themselves that they weren't even speaking by the time his grandfather died.

It had broken his heart to lose him, but Kyron thought, for the rest of the family, the old man's death had been a relief. That had hurt Kyron terribly because he'd loved his grandfather deeply, something that nobody else seemed to even realize. Allen may have, but Kyron doubted that Allen cared enough to even remember when his grandfather had passed. It was one of those sad scenarios that there was just no coming back from, once it had happened.

Snow was coming down at a steady pace, but it was by no means a storm. It was just snow. It was just Aspen in the winter. Something Kyron both loved and hated, yet how much was that hate tied to his other memories? And what would it take for those ugly memories to fade away? He knew in his heart of hearts that he no longer held anything against his brother and wondered if it had even been fair to have held something against him in the first place. Kyron didn't know, and he had no solid cohesive thoughts about it at this point in his life. Yet Kyron had been through so much that he was a completely different person now.

The snow picked up as he got closer and closer to Miranda's place. By the time he pulled into her driveway, the snow was coming down heavily. He got out of his rental, pulled on his gloves, and stomped his way up to the front door. "Hey," he greeted her, when she opened the door and watched the relief on her face.

"Thank God you're here," she said. "I didn't know what to do."

"Can you tell me where she is?"

She nodded. "Give me a minute." She stepped into big mukluks, grabbed a pair of heavy gloves, and said, "They're around back."

"Did you get very close?"

"No, and I didn't try. She was growling pretty good."

"No, that's important too. I don't want you to come with me, but I do need you to point out where I should be going." And that's what they did. She unlocked the gate, and her dogs came running. He looked down at them.

"I figured they'd be inside in this weather."

"They would be, but they know Beth's out there and that something isn't right," she noted.

"Animals are great that way, aren't they?" he said, with a smile.

She nodded. "They are. At the same time, my dogs are also very wary. I go by that instinct of theirs as much as anything to know that this is a serious situation."

"Got it."

When they got around the side of the house, she pointed

into the back corner of her fenced-in property. Not where the dogs would have been or where Kyron had caught sight of them before but over by a group of trees.

"They're in there. Or they were," she murmured.

"Right. And you heard it from here?"

"I heard gunshots and ran outside. I was standing at the back field here, when I heard the growls."

"Right. Stay here." And, with that, he headed out to the back.

There wasn't much light, though she had turned on the outside lights. As he headed down toward the back, it got dimmer and dimmer. He was about ten feet away from where Miranda thought Beth was, when Kyron heard a growl. He took two more steps and then came to a stop, as the growl became even more fierce.

"I'm here, Beth," he said softly. "I get it. It's been a really crappy day. I'm so sorry, sweetheart." He kept talking to her as he crouched down, but he was on the wrong side of the fence in terms of getting close enough to her. It was hard to see as it was. As he leaned forward, she growled again. "I get it, girl," he murmured. "You don't trust anybody, and I'm so sorry because that's not how life was supposed to be."

He started to whistle, a whistle that he would use with the dogs when he was in training all the time, just a light happy sound that said everything was fine and that they were having a great time.

Her ears perked up, but she didn't respond.

He took two more steps, and she immediately went from a growl to a howl. "I got it," he murmured. "I'm just here. I'll stop." Of course he was about four feet away, but, in the dark, it was hard to see anything.

He stepped one more foot closer, and she seemed to

growl and to whimper at the same time. He wasn't sure what the change was, but he pulled out his phone, turned on the flashlight, and took a look. Sure enough, blood was all around her. The second dog was tucked up behind her. "Damn," he whispered. "You're hurt, aren't you?"

She whimpered again and glared at him.

He snuck another step closer, and she immediately crouched and growled at him again. He gave her a command to stand down, to calm down, and to rest. She looked at him, her ears twitching, as if cataloging the commands. Then her head slowly lowered, and the other dog followed suit.

Kyron smiled. "Good girl. You came to people because you knew you needed help. But I have to get over there to help you." The other dog just stared in his direction. "Is it you or her that's hurt?" he asked in the darkness, trying to keep his voice calm and patient, as he analyzed the fence all around him, wondering how he was supposed to get over to Beth. He saw a gate, although it was ten feet off to the side. He walked cautiously toward the gate, staying in her line of vision, and unlatched the gate.

He took a quick look around, but all the other dogs were inside the house now, which was a good thing. If Miranda had managed to get all the dogs inside, Kyron wouldn't have to worry about them surging in and fighting these two. He opened the gate up wide and said, "Come on, girl." She just stared at him and growled. He walked through the gate and stepped forward. Now nothing was between them, if she decided to attack.

Keeping his hands calm and steady, he walked forward until he was about six feet away, then he stopped and said, "I need to check you over, and I need to check your friend too," he murmured. Then he bent down on his knee and gave her the order to come. She growled and howled but slowly got to her feet. He wasn't certain that she was the one that was hurt, though enough blood was on the ground to cause problems. It could have been either or, indeed, both of them. She took a few steps toward him, but they were wary.

He held out a hand. "Good girl," he murmured, "good girl. You can do this." She took another step and then froze and looked back at her friend. Kyron shifted the light so he could look at the other dog, who looked at him warily. Then the other dog laid down, whined, and dropped her head onto the ground. With the flashlight, Kyron saw that she was the one bleeding badly.

"Damn." He got up and walked closer. He was sure it was Beth, at least according to the markings on her back, plus her response to her name and to the commands. No way for him to confirm it until he saw the tattoo, could scan for a chip, and could look for an ID tag. She growled at him again. "Come on, Beth. You know I have to help her," he said quietly. He took two more steps, keeping an eye on Beth, and, when he got close enough, he held out his hand. Her tail gave the tiniest bit of a twitch, and she sniffed his hand and growled again.

"I know," he said. "I didn't bring food. I didn't bring anything, did I? You and I have to get to a level of trust that has nothing to do with rewards right now. Because one or both of you needs medical attention."

He crouched in front of Beth, and, as soon as she sniffed forward again, he reached out a hand and very gently laid it on her neck. As he stroked her neck, she trembled under his touch, as if afraid that hand would cause her pain.

In Kyron's world, the only people who ever hit a dog were cowards and were people who didn't care enough to actually learn how to live with these beautiful animals. As soon as he had her somewhat calm, he ran a hand across her back, down her belly and flanks. He found nothing wrong on the one side facing him, and she had made a few steps toward him. From what he saw at the moment, the other dog was badly injured, and Beth was standing guard.

"Good girl," he said gently, "good girl." She looked over at him and then started to whine. Her tail wagged against him several times, and he nodded.

"You have to let me in a little closer now," he murmured. "I need to see the other side of you too." She shifted a little bit, as if understanding what he said. She moved enough that he could come up on the unchecked side and run his hands down along her flank. It came back with blood, but she didn't hiss or howl in any way.

"So it's her, is it?" he asked. He hated that there was relief in his voice, but, at the same time, Beth was the dog that he had been tasked to get, and now he needed to see what was wrong with the other one. He bent down in front of the other dog, who barely lifted her head when she saw him. He took one look and swore because, indeed, he found what looked like a bullet hole amid all the blood.

He pulled out his phone and called Miranda. "Hey, that vet of yours, does he do emergency surgery?"

"Yes," she replied. "I already gave him a heads-up that I had an injured dog out here."

"It's the second dog," he noted quietly. "And you're right. I think she's been shot."

"Damn it. I hate people," she cried out.

"I know. But, at the moment, we have to get her to the vet, and that'll be a bit of a problem."

"You think?" she asked. "Can you get close to the one

that's hurt?"

"Well, I got close enough to the wounded one so that I could check around her, and the War Dog stood beside me as I did that. However, when we try to move her hurt friend, Beth's likely to get defensive."

"Well, we can take her in my pickup," she offered. "I do have a cover on it that flips up, where I put animals inside a lot."

"If you want to get it ready," he said, "I'll see if I can get the two of them to come."

"And you really think both of them will come along?"

"I don't think we have much choice," he noted. "Beth seems determined to stay at the other one's side."

"And I don't blame her. When you make a friend, you do everything you can to keep them," she said, with a smile in her voice.

"Well, particularly when one's been hurt," he replied, his voice gentle. "See you in a bit." And, with that, he hung up, then looked over at Beth and said, "Hey, girl. You know I have to take her in. I'm just not sure how to do it." Using the light, he studied the wound closer, a bullet up in the flank. He didn't know if it had gone through and through or had just ripped through a large chunk of skin. A lot of blood was everywhere, but he also knew that sometimes these bleeder-type shots didn't necessarily mean major damage; it could have just nicked something and left a big mess.

As he studied her, he got a little closer and bent down and talked to her. She didn't raise her head, but she jerked when he laid a hand on her. He held his hand against the ruff of her neck, gently scratching and petting her.

"Hey, little one. You got yourself in a spot, huh?" He didn't have a clue who she was or why she had no collar. No way to know if this was just another dog that had been dumped or if it was something else entirely. But right now she needed care, and whether she survived that care was an entirely different story. He looked over at Beth, standing beside him, whining deep in her throat.

"No, you're right, and I'm glad you warned us," he said quietly. "That was a good girl. Now I'll have to pick up your friend and carry her to the house." He knew that would be the dangerous part. As he reached over and checked the dog again, he noted that her breathing was slow and steady, but she didn't even appear conscious now. And that was a good thing, as long as he could pick her up and get her moved fast. Getting ready, he put his phone in his pocket and positioned his hands underneath the dog and scooped her up in one fell swoop. Immediately Beth fell into step beside him.

"Right," he said. "You knew people here would help you right now and would help her too, so let's get going, and we'll see what we can do." He carefully carried the dog around to the gate where he'd come through, thankful it was still open. He kicked it closed and as he stepped forward, Beth kept to his side. He walked toward the driveway and noted Miranda had already pulled out the other truck and had it running and had opened up the back. He nodded and gently laid the dog inside.

"Oh my goodness," Miranda murmured, "she looks pretty rough."

"Yeah." Kyron nodded. "But that doesn't mean she can't pull through."

"No, it just means that she's had a rough go of it and that people should be shot themselves," she snapped, her voice hard.

He smiled at her. "Which really won't solve anything."

"Well, it would make me feel better," she said, with a smile.

He agreed with her, but the time for that discussion wasn't right now. As he laid the injured dog in the back half of the truck box, into this big almost built-in cage, Beth hopped up beside her friend and laid down beside her, whining.

"Oh, look at that," Miranda whispered.

"Now, the question is, how will she feel being locked up in this?" Kyron asked, looking at Beth.

"Well, it's not very far to Doug," she noted, "so I suggest we go now, and we'll see if we can get her treated. I told my boss that I'd meet him there."

Closing up the back of the truck, Kyron grabbed his bag from his rental vehicle, then hopped into the passenger side of her truck.

"Of course the weather is crappy too," she stated, with a sigh, as she slowly drove through the snow.

"Is it ever not crappy when you've got an emergency going on?" he asked curiously.

"I don't know," she replied. "I've never been so lucky yet."

He nodded. "You know what? Me either. It seems like, whenever there's an emergency or disaster or something that you've got to deal with, the weather just decides to make life miserable."

She laughed. "It's kind of funny in a way, but you're right. Almost like Mother Nature is testing our resolve. Like asking us, *Do you really want to do this?*"

"Well, the answer tonight is a flat-out absolutely." Kyron watched as she drove into a parking lot.

"And the nice thing," she said, "is that we won't have to

wait in line." Indeed, another vehicle was in the parking lot, and the lights inside were already on. As the vet opened up the back door, he stepped out to look at them. "I'm grabbing a gurney," he stated, then disappeared, only to return moments later. The trouble was, even empty, the gurney was hard to move because of the snow. Kyron immediately grabbed the other end, brought it closer to the back of Miranda's truck.

"Hey, I'm Kyron," he greeted Doug. "I'm the one who's been looking for the War Dog. Thanks for coming out."

"Well, looks like you may have found her," he noted. "I'm Doug. Let's see what we've got here." When Miranda opened up the back end to her truck, Doug saw both dogs huddled close together in the pen. "*Uh-oh*, are both injured?"

"No, just the one. The other one is the War Dog, who's been keeping her warm."

"Interesting," he muttered. "Will it be safe to get her out?"

"I hope so," Kyron stated, "but honestly, I don't know."

"Of course not," Doug replied. "Well, I haven't been bitten in a few months, so let's hope today doesn't break my streak. We've got to see what's up with the other one, and, from the looks of it, we better get moving."

"Yeah, she's lost a lot of blood," Kyron noted, as he opened the cage and placed a hand on Beth. "Hey, girl, we have to take her out now."

Beth stared at him, and then realized Kyron was trying to move the other dog, so Beth shifted enough so that the dog could be slid gently forward and onto the gurney.

With that, Kyron told Miranda, "I'll lift the other end of the gurney to take the dog inside. Don't move. Don't do anything with Beth, okay?" Miranda nodded, and he grabbed the other end of the gurney, and he and Doug carried the injured dog inside. Once they saw the dog better under the bright lights, Kyron noted, "It looks like she took a bullet to the flank. Not sure if it went through or not. She's not looking too great."

"Maybe not," Doug replied, "but I've seen a lot of dogs survive some pretty rough shit, so we won't count her out yet."

"Never, I wouldn't do that either," Kyron stated, "because, like you, I've seen them come back from some pretty amazing scenarios. Dogs are really tough and resilient."

"Well, let's hope we have a happy ending this time," Doug murmured. "Because you know that Miranda out there will be pretty upset if it's not."

"Yeah, not to mention the War Dog won't be happy. No pressure, Doc. You're right about Miranda. She really comes from the heart."

"She does, but that neighbor of hers, he's a bit of an ass. He's threatened to shoot her animals before. He used the excuse that they get loose and kill his chickens."

"Did they?" he asked.

"She didn't think so at the time because she didn't have anybody go loose, but, for all I know, it could have been these guys killing the chickens, just trying to survive."

"That is definitely possible, and maybe he's the one who shot them."

"Maybe, but listen. I wouldn't put it past this guy to shoot Miranda either. He's just pissed off enough half the time. Honestly, from the stories she's told me, he's three-quarters' crazy."

"That's not good."

"Leave me with her for a few minutes, while I get an IV

going and some anesthesia into her. Go check and ensure Miranda is okay with that War Dog of yours. She looks like she can take off somebody's face pretty fast."

"Yeah, Beth could," he replied, and he quickly moved across the room.

At the edge of the door, the vet looked up at him and added, "I know this will be one of those questions that I don't like the answer to, but I guess the war department won't pay for these injuries because it's not the War Dog, *huh*?"

"I'm not sure they would pay even if it was the War Dog that I am here for," he noted, "but I'll pay for the surgery."

The vet looked at him in surprise and then nodded. "Well, we'll see what ends up happening," Doug stated. "We could be premature even talking surgery at this point."

And, with that, he returned his attention to the dog.

CHAPTER 7

MIRANDA WAITED BESIDE the truck, talking gently to Beth. "Hey, sweetie. Kyron's coming back, and we'll make sure that your friend gets all the care she needs," she explained. When she heard the back door to the vet clinic open and close, she continued. "See? Here comes Kyron right now. I told you that he'd be back." But, at that, the dog immediately shifted and turned to stare at the door. "She looks like she's waiting for her friend," Miranda told Kyron.

"Honestly, if we were alone right now, and she had just managed to get here with her friend inside, I suspect she would stay here on guard, until her friend came back out," he explained quietly. "I've seen that before, and, if Beth's been isolated all this time and has now bonded with that dog in particular, it's not surprising."

"But she can't stay here," Miranda stated. "Not only could she be dangerous in her own right, but she could get picked up or shot by somebody who reports her here."

He nodded. "Dogs loose in the city is never a good thing." He walked closer and then bent down. Beth wagged her tail ever-so-slightly. "I know. Trust is hard, isn't it, sweetie?" he asked quietly. "I did manage to get some dog food on my way home today, and I've got leads and stuff in my bag up in your front seat," he told Miranda. "If I can get a lead on Beth, she should be a lot more amicable."

"Will she?" Miranda asked, with a wry tone. "She looks like she's ready to bolt to me."

"Of course she is. She's spent a little too long away from the good side of humankind, and now her friend is hurt, at the hand of a human," he stated, looking over at her.

"Right," she agreed. "So, like you just said, trust takes time."

"More than time in this case," he noted sadly.

"Well, you've done well with her so far. Let's hope that we can get her somewhere. Get your leash."

He walked to the front of the truck and pulled out the bag he'd thankfully grabbed before they left. He quickly took out the leash, and, holding it in a big loop over his hand, he bent down in front of Beth, petted her gently, and, as she half closed her eyes, Kyron slipped the lead over her head and tightened it ever-so-slightly. Almost immediately she snapped to attention. "Good girl," Kyron said.

"I've never seen a dog react to a lead like that before," Miranda noted curiously.

"It's part of the training," he replied quietly. "She's likely forgotten some of her training, but she's not forgotten all of it. And, as much as she wants to remember that people had been good to her in the past, she's currently dealing with the fact that people haven't been good to her in the present."

"Right," Miranda agreed. "I still feel like just an awful lot of shit is out there in this life, and it's got to be so hard for a dog to actually learn to trust again."

"And yet they have hearts as good as gold," he murmured. "So we'll give her every chance to have a good life again." He slowly straightened up and walked several steps. Immediately the dog fell in line and walked with him in the heel position.

"Look at that," she noted, marveling.

"Generally," he added, "she should be even better behaved on a leash, but there shouldn't be any noticeable difference between her behavior on or off a lead. But in this case—"

"Of course." Miranda's heart went out to the dog. "I mean, he's beautiful—she's beautiful, I mean," she corrected.

"She is, indeed, and she's all heart because she's looking after her friend."

"Speaking of which," Miranda stated, "I'll go in and check on Beth's friend and see if Dr. Doug needs any help. That is, if you're okay to stay out here with Beth."

"Will do. I sure hope that dog makes it."

"I do too, more for Beth's sake than anything," Miranda admitted.

"You know that that just means they'll have to stay together," he said, staring at Miranda. "Had you thought of that?"

"I know." She nodded. "Bonded pairs come up in my work with some regularity. Had you thought of it?" And, with that question, she headed inside. As soon as she saw Doug, he looked up and nodded.

"She's alive, but she's been shot in the flank," he told her. "She's lost a lot of blood and has a fair amount of tissue damage. I'm just running through the x-rays now," he explained. "She'll be here a little while, and I'll need to keep her overnight."

"So how bad is the damage? That's the real question," she noted.

"I know," he agreed. "Give me a few minutes to complete the x-rays." She waited inside, where it was toasty and warm, and wondered what would happen now that Kyron had rescued two dogs.

If she had the room, she would take them. Honestly, it came down to that she would *find* the room. But this dog was injured, and that would require some separate space to heal. What Miranda really needed was her dream rescue facility, back to that hope for forty acres and a ten-bedroom house.

She shook her head, as she thought about it, trying to figure out some way to make this work. She wasn't alone this time because Kyron was helping.

When the vet stepped back in with Miranda again, he stated, "We'll just give it a minute to develop." He looked over at Miranda. "Kyron seems like an interesting person."

She nodded. "I just met him today, when he came looking for the War Dog."

"Well, considering that this dog looks like it's been living pretty rough for a long time, it was good timing that he actually found both of them."

"And I had just heard about the three-legged dog from that crazy neighbor of mine about a month ago, and then was hopefully feeding her in the back of my place, while I waited to see if it was her or not. But you know? Sometimes good things happen."

"I hope so in this case," Doug replied. "He did offer to pay for any surgery."

Miranda looked up at him, her eyebrows raised.

Doug shrugged. "You know that I'm not against it. I do an awful lot of helping out for free," he stated. "But I have bills to pay too."

"I hear you," she said. "Sorry that I'm always putting a strain on that."

He laughed. "No, you do way more work than I have to

anyway," he noted. "So I have no problem with that, but you know, if it was the War Dog that needed medical help, I was hoping the War Dog Department would take care of it, but Kyron said there was no guarantee on that either."

She frowned. "Oh well, I was hoping he would at least pitch in and help with the food cost at my place, if I took them on."

"Considering he offered to pay for whatever this costs," he noted, "I suspect that won't be a problem."

"But then again," she added, "I don't really need dog food. I just got a huge pallet delivered." He turned to look at her, his eyebrows raised, and she smiled. "Remember Tom, the sales rep that was in on Saturday?" He nodded. "We were talking, and he offered to send some food over. I figured he'd send some samples or something. Never did I expect a whole pallet."

"Well, that's huge," Doug replied.

"It was sitting in my driveway when Kyron drove by, while he was looking for the War Dog. He stopped to ask me if I had seen or heard anything about the dog and ended up helping me move and stack all that dog food. And it is huge," she admitted. "I'm finally looking into becoming an actual registered charitable organization, so donations can officially be tax-deductible. I'm hoping that will help with contributions."

"That's not a bad idea," Doug agreed. "Particularly if you can find a lawyer to set it up without killing you with the costs."

"And that's the trouble." She nodded. "You know there are just so many costs that you don't even think about."

"Absolutely," he said, with a smile. Then as he started to walk out, he added, "The x-rays should be done by now." A few minutes later, he returned, a smile on his face.

"So there's no damage to the bone, and there are no bullet fragments, but it's done some pretty good muscle damage, and she's lost a fair bit of blood. I've had her on IV fluids, trying to get her more stable. But her needs won't be as invasive as I'd thought they might be."

"Another *she* for sure?"

He nodded. "Yes, it's a female and fixed. I'll clean the wound, stitch her up, and keep her overnight, and then we'll take another look at her in the morning," he noted.

"Okay then, shall I scrub in and give you a hand?" When he hesitated, she added, "Look. I brought her to you, after working hours and on an emergency basis and everything, so it's the least I can do."

He laughed. "Now that's a good point," he agreed, "and it will save some time, although I still owe you big-time for taking that diabetic cat, so I didn't have to euthanize it. What about your buddy?"

"Yeah, I better give him an update," she noted, "if we have time for that."

"Just tell him to come on in and sit in the waiting room. He and the dog don't need to be out in this weather."

She nodded. "I don't know if he'll agree, but, hey, we'll see." She walked back outside to the parking lot and looked around. "Kyron?"

"Over here," he called, and she turned to see him by the woods, walking with the dog.

"Hey," she said, walking over to meet him. "So Doug got the x-rays done and there's no bone damage or bullet fragments to remove, which is great. However, she sustained a lot of muscle tissue damage, and she'll need several layers of stitches. He's got her on IV fluids. He said she is pretty emaciated, as if the last few months have been pretty rough on her," Miranda noted. "So, all of that is adding to how badly she looked tonight."

"Of course," Kyron agreed. "So will he do the surgery now, the stitches and all?"

"Yes, and I'll suit up and give him a hand. I feel like it's the right thing to do, since I got him into this and all. Plus, it will get her finished quicker."

"Absolutely," Kyron noted. "We're fine out here."

"He also said you could come inside and wait where it's warm, if you like."

"I'll see." Kyron pointed at Beth. "Right now we're just getting acquainted."

Miranda smiled, as she looked down at the War Dog. "And I don't know what your friend's name is," she noted, talking to Beth, "but she's a very good girl." At that, Beth wagged her tail enthusiastically. "Wow, she's come a long way already, hasn't she?"

"I find most often with dogs like this, if they've spent a lot of time with humans, it's almost a relief to them to get back with one, as long as it's a decent one, of course," he murmured.

"I agree." She nodded. "But how do they weed out the bad from the good? Even then, Beth ran away the first time, only to get caught by my crazy neighbor. It must be hard for them to get away from these people, until they do something like Beth had to do—escaping a second time."

"Do you think your neighbor had Beth?"

"I assume so." Miranda frowned, as she looked down at Beth. "I can't be sure of course as I never saw her up close, but to the best that I could identify her, yes."

"Well, her back leg is missing. She's pretty strong regardless, but I can see a bit of a pull on the one side."

"Maybe have Doug look at her too?"

Kyron nodded. "After he helps her friend, yes."

"Okay, I've got to go help Doug, if you're okay out here. Otherwise just come on in, when you need to get warm." She waved as she ran off. Miranda hadn't mentioned bringing the War Dog inside, but she figured it was a given that Kyron would bring Beth inside if it got too cold out there.

As soon as she headed back inside, the doc looked at her and smiled.

"Good, suit on up, and let's get this show on the road." And that's what she did.

"WELL, I DON'T know how long we'll wait out here," Kyron said in a conversational tone to Beth. "And of course I didn't bring any treats for you, not that you're necessarily looking for any." However, he did note how she definitely kept eyeing the building ahead of her.

"Do you want to go in and wait?"

She barked at him.

"I'll take that as a yes. So, just how close are you to this friend of yours?" he muttered. That definitely complicated things, or at least it did if he was hoping to keep the two of them together. It was hard enough to get anybody to take one dog, but to take two, especially two midsize dogs and one already potentially dangerous. "But you're not very dangerous, are you, girl?"

The trouble was, in the wrong hands, these War Dogs were still quite a weapon, and no animal would tolerate being abused for very long, though in her case it seemed maybe more about neglect. At least he hoped so, but it was hard to know, especially since she'd run away from two different places. There was always a chance the asshole of a neighbor had done something more severe, but there was no way to know for sure yet.

When Kyron got up tomorrow morning, he would go talk to the neighbor and see. He would find out where he'd gotten the dog from and verify if it was the one in question. The neighbor had no claim to Beth as far as Kyron was concerned, but that didn't mean the old man wouldn't have something to say about it. The fact is, the dog had taken off, and chances are the asshole neighbor had no proof it was his dog anyway.

But it was a conversation Kyron would have to be prepared for.

He quickly sent Badger a text with an update, then sent photos of the dog on her leash. He wasn't at all surprised when he got a response with a thumbs-up. He sent back a quick explanation about the other dog and added that he would talk to Badger in the morning.

Then realizing that it was already eleven in the evening, Kyron slowly headed toward the vet's door. Beth followed along right behind him. "Do you want to go in?" The dog barked at the door. Kyron took that as a yes and opened it. The dog came in without a qualm.

"That's a good sign," he noted quietly. "Now, if only we can figure out what else you seem to think you need to do here, then we'll be fine."

As they sat down on the bench under the lights of the waiting room, he had a chance to take a closer look at Beth and her coat. She obviously had endured some difficult months, as her hair was thick and rough. There was some flesh on her bones but not nearly enough. She'd obviously suffered recently. He frowned at that because he hated to see any animal suffer ever.

When he finally had a chance to calm her down enough that she could relax, she rolled over and showed him her belly. He immediately took several photos of the tattoo. In order to see if she had an ID chip under her skin, he would have to wait until the vet had a moment to check her over and to scan for it. And it was quite possible that she did, providing it had survived whatever rough living she'd endured over the last few months. With Beth calmer now, he finally relaxed himself.

"I don't know how long we'll be, Beth, but it wouldn't be a bad idea if we got a nap." Of course that wouldn't happen for him, but, as long as his voice helped calm down the dog, as she continued to stare at the surgery room door, the better. He spied the jar on the counter, filled with puppy treats. He dropped the leash first, so Beth just watched him. He got up and walked over. Seeing where he was headed, Beth seemed to know exactly what was coming, and she hopped up and joined him.

When he gave the dog the treat, Beth took it delicately between her teeth, then walked over to the surgery door and laid down about six feet in front of it, just waiting. She didn't eat the treat, apparently wanting to give it to the dog on the other side of the door. Shaking his head, with his heart melting, Kyron walked over with several more and put them down in front of her. "Go ahead, Beth. You get to have some too." The dog looked at him with yearning and then ate the one in her mouth and sat here, with the others in front of her.

"Not quite what I had in mind," Kyron stated, "but I guess that's the closest I'll get right now." And, with that, he took a picture and sent it to Miranda inside.

By the time she came out, she was clearly tired, but she had a smile on her face. "Hey." She stopped and looked down at Beth. "Your friend is doing much better, honest."

The dog just wagged her tail but kept looking at the other room.

"You do realize you can't separate them, right?" she asked Kyron.

"I know. I've been sitting here trying to figure out what to do," he replied. "I'm not sure she'll let us out of here without that dog."

Miranda winced at that. "I know. I was wondering about that myself. Her friend does need to stay overnight though."

"And that'll be fun." Kyron looked around the waiting room. "I don't suppose Doug would let us sleep on the bench here, would he?"

She stared at him, then looked down at Beth and asked, "Do you think it's that bad?"

"Well, as far as a way to gain her trust, that would be a huge one," he admitted. "Beth doesn't want to be separated from her friend, and she knows her friend is here. If I drag her away, even if I bring her back tomorrow, she's not likely to rest, and she'll worry all night."

"Wow." Miranda scrubbed her face with both hands. "The things we do for animals."

"I know," he said, with a twitch of his lips. "But it is Sunday tomorrow, and I presume the clinic isn't open, right?"

"No, it isn't," she confirmed. "So, in theory, you wouldn't be disturbing anybody, but I can't say that Doug will be happy about it."

At that, the surgical door opened, and Doug walked through. "Happy about what?" Kyron explained what the problem was. Doug looked down at Beth, still waiting at the surgery door, staring, guarding.

"Wow, she really is intent on making sure that dog's okay. She knows she's in there. Although the dog is sleeping and will probably smell odd to Beth, if we took her in there, at least she would know that her friend's okay," Doug suggested. "So why don't we do that and see what happens?"

Immediately Kyron picked up the leash, as Doug opened the door, and Kyron walked Beth into the back room. There he walked toward a large cage at the far corner, Beth pulling the way forward, as she sniffed out her friend, and Kyron bent down beside her. "See? This is where she is," he explained, as she barked and whined gently. But of course the other dog wasn't moving. "She's hurt, and she needs a bit of time," he added. Then he looked over at Doug. "Would you have any objections to me sleeping on the outside bench with this one?"

Doug stared at him. "Do you really think it's necessary? That is not a comfortable bench," he noted.

"No, it's not," Kyron agreed, with half a smile, "but you can bet I've slept on a lot worse."

"Well, if you were doing anything with dogs like these before, then you sure have," he agreed thoughtfully. He shrugged. "I guess I don't mind. We don't have the clinic open tomorrow. Obviously I'll be back in to take a look at this girl, but it's not like you'll disturb anybody."

"I promise I won't break into the back and steal anything," Kyron teased.

"The place is full of cameras, so if you do," Doug noted,

"we'll know who was behind it. Just try not to break anything in the process," he said, with a grin. He looked over at Miranda. "What do you think?"

"I think he's nuts," she stated, "but then I need my sleep."

"I do too," Kyron agreed, "but I also need this dog to trust me. Right now her entire focus is on that other dog. If I try to drag her away from here, it's quite possible she'll put up a fight in a big way. To me, it's just not worth the risk of that kind of setback."

With that, Doug nodded. "Be my guest. Make yourself as comfortable as you can, and I'll see you in the morning. I'll call it a night." And he headed out.

Miranda looked over at Kyron, frowning. "You won't get any sleep."

He nodded. "I know," he admitted, "but we'd all be safe, and, considering the events of the evening, that's not a bad outcome and maybe the best we can hope for right now."

She nodded. "Fine. Let me grab you a couple blankets. We use them to warm up the dogs when they need it, but they are washed in between." Pulling out several, she handed them over. "Go grab your backpack from my truck, and here, you might need these."

"Thank you," he said, with a smile, appreciating the gesture. He walked out to snag his pack and returned to see her standing there looking at him, shaking her head. "You know that, if I didn't like you before, I definitely do now. Anybody who would make a sacrifice like this just to make the dog more secure is okay in my book."

He laughed. "You liked me just fine before," he stated, with a smile.

"Well, that's true. I did, but it's much easier now. At

least you can spend your sleepless night thinking about what you'll do with both of these dogs in the morning."

"I know. Believe me. I've been thinking about it already."

"Well then, I'll leave you to it. I have a lot of other animals to go home to." And, with that, she walked to the door and gave them both a long look. "Text me if you need anything," she offered, as she walked out.

CHAPTER 8

MIRANDA DROVE HOME, hoping she could sleep through the night, but, of course, knowing Kyron was staying at the clinic, while she slept in a warm bed, didn't make her feel any better. Sure, he was safe in there, and so was Beth, and it was warm enough, so it's not as if they would go through any undue hardship, but it wouldn't be comfortable in any way. But it was also his call, and he'd made it, so she had to respect that.

She didn't know what to do about a place for the dogs because she knew perfectly well the one would need time to recover, and Beth would still need time to assimilate. They needed a home together, which was something she didn't think Kyron had really considered at all.

When she got home, she crashed, but woke up very early in the morning, then rolled over, slept for a bit, and by six o'clock gave it up. She got up and headed outside, but almost immediately her neighbor yelled at her from his side of the fence. She turned and stared. "What?"

"Did you see my dog?" her neighbor growled and shifted the rifle in his hand. She stared at the gun, looked at him, and took a step back. He nodded. "Yeah, you damn well better step back, you bitch," he yelled. "Where the hell is my dog?"

"Well, I don't know what dog you're talking about," she

replied, "and what are you doing with a gun?"

"I'll pop it for good this time," he yelled, like she was hard of hearing or something. "You think I give a shit that you're some do-gooder? If you don't get me my goddamn dog, I'll kill all of yours, one by one until you produce it."

"If you kill any dog in my care," she snapped, "I'll have you up on charges so fast your head will spin. Then I'll slap a lien against your property, and I'll take your home and anything else you've got."

He stared at her, his jaw dropping. "You've got no call to do that," he finally said, raising the gun.

She pointed at him and his gun. "If you raise that one more time in my direction, I'll call 9-1-1 as soon as I get in the house."

And, with that proclamation, damned if he didn't raise the gun and point it in her direction. "Now what will you do?" he asked, with a sneer. She looked at him and realized there really wouldn't be any way to defuse it now that she'd set it off, and she bolted for the house. And, sure enough, he fired, and the minute she got inside, she called 9-1-1 and explained the situation. The dispatcher said they'll send somebody out immediately, but Miranda knew it wouldn't be enough. Crazy Old Man Macintyre had now become a major danger in her world, and it was something that she definitely didn't want to deal with.

Keeping the dogs in the house, she wasn't sure how to get down to where the other animals were, but this asshole had pinned her down into her own home, and that was a whole different story.

She waited anxiously for the cops to come, and, sure enough, two cruisers came by. As soon as she saw them, she raced outside and told them what happened. He looked at her and asked, "Did you take his dog?"

She stared at him and asked, "That's the question you have? Whether I stole his dog? No, I didn't steal his dog. He abused the animal, and it took off, weeks ago." He stared at her in surprise. She shrugged. "Last night a bunch of shooting was going on, and he shot one dog, which I took to the vet for emergency treatment. So you can talk to the vet about that if you want," she snapped. "And the other dog, you'll need to talk to Kyron about."

"Who's Kyron?"

"Somebody who is here on behalf of the War Dog Department," she snapped. "It's a long story, but apparently there's a good chance the dog this guy has been abusing and may have shot last night belonged to the War Dog Department." Of course, that wasn't precisely true because the one he'd shot wasn't Beth, but Miranda was too flustered to even worry about minute details like that.

"Whoa, whoa, whoa," the cop said. "How is the War Dog Department involved in this?"

She glared at him. "The man just fired at me," she roared. "Can't you get that in your head? I can't even leave my back door to go check on the other animals because of that lunatic."

He raised both palms. "Look. We'll go have a talk with him."

"Yeah, you do that," she said, glaring at him. "Then you can call Kyron when you get back here, and he'll explain the rest of it." At that, the two cops shook their heads, and one headed to talk to the neighbor. The other cop came up to her and asked, "Do you happen to have any cameras?"

"Yeah, I do," she replied. "Why?"

"Because it will help back up your story."

She stared at him, nonplussed. "You know what? It never even occurred to me that you guys wouldn't believe me."

He held up a hand in a conciliatory motion. "Hey, it's not that I don't believe you, but we do get complaints and neighborhood disputes all the times. You should hear some of the accusations that people can level against each other," he shared. "It would just clarify things if you had something to back it up."

She reached up, rubbed the bridge of her nose. "Yeah, but with the lighting out here, it won't show anything."

"Can I take a look?"

She nodded and led him into the house. Immediately the dogs surrounded them both.

"You have a lot of dogs here."

"I'm in the process of becoming a legal charity. The dogs were outside, but, with that lunatic shooting at us and threatening to kill us all," she snapped, "I had to bring them in."

"Wow," he replied, "that's a really nice guy over there."

"No, not at all," she stated, her tone turning desperate. "And now that he's made threats against the animals, how am I supposed to let these poor things outside at all?"

"Well, let's do one thing at a time," he replied.

She led the way to the computer and brought up the camera software. She quickly flipped back through the images to the incident with her neighbor. Sure enough, there was the argument with the neighbor, and then a very clear image of him picking up the rifle and firing it in her direction.

"Wow, he really is an asshole, isn't he?" he muttered. "He shot right at you."

"He did, though I'm sure he'll say it was nothing and

that I just pissed him off or something."

"Still, he's not allowed to shoot firearms at people," he stated.

"Yeah, and you'll cite him for some misdemeanor. And he'll be back home in no time, and the next thing I know, my dogs will be dead." She shook her head, trying to calm herself down. "He needs to be stopped."

At that, the cop looked at her sharply. "Don't you get involved any more than you already are."

"Sure, give me the reprimand," she snapped, glaring at him. "The guy shoots at me, threatens to kill all my dogs, and you're telling me to not get involved. Jesus," she snorted. "You know what? Sometimes life just really sucks."

"I'm not saying that we won't do anything about this," the cop added. "I'm just trying to tell you that obviously this guy is a loose cannon, and anything you do that will trigger his behavior will get you in trouble. I'm just trying to keep you safe."

"Yeah, well, if you want to keep me safe," she stated, "you also need to keep my animals safe."

Long after the cops left, Miranda was still restless and unsettled. She had to go out and deal with the horses and other animals, but she could feel her crazy neighbor's eyes boring into her back. She was pretty sure that he'd been pissed off over the visit from the cops, but, after they spoke with him, the cops told her that he'd been reprimanded and warned what would happen if he did it again. So he would likely just be biding his time.

She didn't know how she felt about that, but it was pretty hard to relax with this asshole free to just watch her and to make his plans in the background. She always knew he was dangerous; she just hadn't figured it would ever be directed at her. She always thought just her having the animals were the issue. That was bad enough, but realizing that this guy was determined to hurt them and her as well was a whole different story. What if he killed her? She lived out here by herself. Her animals would die without her. That was one way to kill them all and with just one bullet.

By the time she finished with the animals, she was tired, mostly just from having to keep up her guard. There was no way to protect herself; that was the part that really got her. Being out here right now like this was just bad news.

She made it back inside, leaned against the wall inside, and could feel the tears against her eyes. The stress would kill her. She knew she would have to move, but wow. What was she supposed to do?

When her grandmother called at seven, Miranda was barely back in control.

"What happened?" her grandmother asked, hearing the trouble in her voice.

"You don't want to hear about it." Miranda rubbed her head, then poured herself a cup of coffee. "And I can't talk long anyway," she replied. "I'm heading into the clinic."

"Why on earth would you go to the clinic on a Sunday?" she asked, astounded.

"Last night we took in a dog that was shot," she explained, "and we think it was shot by my crazy neighbor. On top of that, he threatened me this morning too."

There was silence at the other end for a bit. "You know you need to get out of there," her grandmother stated immediately.

"And where would you like me to go?" she asked, barely keeping her tears at bay.

"I don't know," she said, with worry in her voice. "But

that man's been getting worse and worse over the years."

"I know, and it's heading for a really ugly confrontation," she admitted, "but I still can't just walk away from all these animals, and I can't just find a place that'll keep them and not have any problems."

"No, you're right," she agreed quietly. "Let me give it some thought." With that, she hung up.

Think about it all you want, Gran, but it doesn't help or solve anything. At least it hasn't yet. Miranda got up, dumped the rest of the coffee because it tasted like crap, then bundled up, and she headed out to her vehicle.

She had actually driven Kyron to the clinic last night and left him there, which made her feel even worse. Even if he had wanted to leave, he couldn't have. When she pulled in, Doug had already showed up. To think that Miranda was the last one to this party shook her. She walked in with a bright smile, to find the two of them talking intently. She watched as the doctor looked up at her and smiled.

"She did fine overnight," Doug stated. "We're just about to let Beth here into the back to take a look."

At the mention of her name, Beth stepped up to the side to watch as Kyron, after flashing her a bright smile, led the former War Dog through to the back, where she headed straight for the cage where the other dog was recuperating.

The second dog wagged her tail ever-so-slightly. Beth whined, her nose tight against the cage.

"Well, that's a good sign," Kyron noted, with a gentle smile.

"It's a good sign, but it also means that they would both do much better together," Doug stated, looking from Miranda to Kyron and back again.

At that, Kyron nodded. "No argument here," he agreed.

"Clearly they are bonded, and both benefit from the other."

She asked, "Did you think about that scenario overnight at all? I can't imagine you got much in the way of sleep."

"I tried to sleep," he replied, "and I got a couple hours."

Miranda studied him, and it was obvious that he hadn't gotten any more than that. "I told you it wouldn't be very comfortable."

"I didn't need comfortable," he stated. "We just needed to know that this one was safe." He backed out of the room toward Miranda, drawing the vet with him.

"How did Beth handle the night?" she asked Kyron. "She appears to be obeying pretty decently."

"She's doing fine right now," he agreed, "but she's been pretty anxious about her buddy."

"Well, that one needs a name," she suggested. "We can't keep calling it *her buddy* or *the other one*."

"No, that's true enough." Yet Kyron frowned, as he walked closer to Miranda. "What happened to you?"

Miranda stared at him. "Wow, I must look really terrible if you can take one look at me and see a problem."

"No you don't," he said, shaking his head. "I'm not that easily diverted. What happened?"

She groaned. "My neighbor's a dick," she snapped, "and he showed up this morning demanding *his* dog back and actually threatened to kill all my animals until I turn over Beth. Then he took a potshot at me for good measure."

At that, Doug raced over. "What?" he asked.

Kyron's reaction was more interesting because he reached out, grabbed her by her shoulders, and asked, "Are you okay?"

She nodded but felt the tears in the back of her eyes. She brushed them away impatiently. "It just added to what's become a very trying situation."

"Did he hurt you?"

She shook her head. "No, he didn't hit me. I think it was like a warning shot. I called the cops, and they came, warned me not to set him off, went and talked to him, gave him a warning that you know will do absolutely no good at all."

"Well, for someone who actually went so far as to fire a gun at you," Doug stated, "a warning won't do anything at all."

"I know," she said, sniffling. "Damn it! I hate it when I get teary-eyed."

"Did you get any sleep?"

"I did, but you wouldn't know it now," she snapped.

"What you're feeling is shock," Kyron stated. "Let's head back to your place and leave this one here. I'm thinking about naming her something like Betty, but it doesn't seem quite right. I don't know. There's got to be some better name. Any ideas?"

"How about Grace?" Doug suggested. They both looked at him in surprise. He shrugged. "This whole situation between these two dogs has a distinct note of grace, don't you think?" he asked, shrugging and looking embarrassed. "Besides that's a perfect accompaniment to the war dog – and yes her scan confirms that."

"I like it," Kyron stated immediately. "Grace, that's perfect. Thanks, Doc. Come on, Miranda. We'll come back and pick up Grace later today," he said, "assuming Doug says it's okay."

"I would think so. However," he added, "you must have a place to put her. I can't release her into your care if you don't."

"Right." Kyron looked over at Miranda. "How do you feel about a few house guests for a few days?" She stared at him, frowning. "Obviously I need a place for Grace and Beth for the moment, and you need somebody to keep an eye on that neighbor of yours."

"He'll still be there when you leave though," she noted, "so, while I appreciate the sentiment, I don't know that it will help resolve my problem."

"Well, it might be a help to you and your animals," he stated, his voice turning hard. "Believe me. I fully intend to go over and have a talk with him."

"That would just make things worse," she replied quietly. "He'll just wait and choose the one time that you drive away. Then he'll come over and do something to terrorize me."

At that, both men stopped to look at her.

She shrugged. "He's never liked me, and he's been getting a lot worse over the last few years," she stated. "I don't know that he's all there mentally, but he's been getting even crankier and more miserable with every day that passes. So, yeah, he's dangerous as hell, and apparently the cops can't do anything about it."

"You know what? I'll talk to my brother about that," Kyron added. "That is just unacceptable."

She laughed. "And that is also life. What I really need, for a variety of reasons, is a new place, and I've got to find out what my options are with that," she stated. "But the prices are pretty tough, so I know it's not practical to even consider it."

"Do you want what you have?"

She nodded. "I do, but, even without the crazy neighbor, it still really isn't big enough."

"So, do you think you could find something that would work if you moved outside of town?"

"I don't know," she murmured. "Potentially. I just hadn't gone down that road because the cost of a move seems like an unrealistic goal at this point. But given the state of the neighbors—one crazy with a gun and the other one who rents me his horse pasture who may sell—I have to seriously look into it."

"Right." Doug winced. "I remember the last time I moved. Just paying the Realtor's fees was pretty rough."

"Exactly. How is that even possible to sell when the fees alone cost so much? I mean—" Then she stopped and shook her head. "It doesn't matter." She looked over at Kyron. "Are you ready to go?"

He nodded. "Absolutely." He reached over and shook Doug's hand. "Thanks, Doc. I'll see you back here to pick up Grace at about what, three?" Kyron patted Beth, talking to her specifically. "See? We'll come back soon for Grace. Okay?" Beth barked and seemed to understand the process.

Doug nodded. "Three works," he agreed, "but give me a phone number in case I have to push that one way or the other, depending on what the day looks like for my kids."

"Right." Kyron smiled.

"The kids' days always end up a whole lot busier than we think. They have a more active social life than I do," Doug quipped. "And I guess that's good, but, at the same time, trying to get them where they need to be at specific times can be a problem."

"Got it." Kyron nodded and gave the doc his cell number, then walked out to the vehicle with Miranda and Beth. He asked Miranda, "Why don't you let me drive?"

"I got to sleep though. You didn't."

"And I'm not the one who's stressed out and dealing with the shock of being shot at this morning." She stopped and stared at him. "You don't have to be a tough girl all the time, you know," he said. "Let somebody else help for a change."

She frowned and handed over the keys to the truck. "I really am okay to drive."

"I'm sure you are," he agreed quietly. He opened up the back door and helped Beth up into the back seat.

"Do you think she'll be okay there?" Miranda asked.

"Well, this will give us a chance to see." Kyron hopped into the driver's seat and turned on the engine. When Miranda was in and buckled up, he started it up and put it in Reverse.

"Do you remember how to get back to where I live?"

"Yep, I do." And, without any assistance from her, he drove back to her place.

"I guess you're pretty good at navigating," she muttered.

"I'm good at a lot of things," he stated. "The accident didn't change any of that. It just made life a whole lot more memorable in the sense that I need to enjoy every day a little more."

"Can you do that though?" she asked. "It seems like we're always told to do that, but it's not so easy."

"You're right, and I don't think it is easy. I think it's one of those things you have to intentionally work at and have to keep reminding yourself on a regular basis that other things in life are important too."

"I guess so," she replied quietly. "It just seems like, … I don't know. I guess I'm more shocked than I thought I would be."

"Getting shot at is no joke. Regardless of his intentions,

you could have stopped suddenly or changed directions, and he might have actually hit you. You could have been killed," he murmured.

She nodded and stayed quiet.

ONCE THEY DROVE up to her house and parked, Kyron hopped out and asked, "How about the chores?"

"They're done for the moment," she stated. "I figured I'd be damned if the animals would go hungry because of that asshole."

"A stubborn one, huh? And what about coffee and breakfast?"

"No, I tried for coffee but it didn't taste right so I skipped both of those," she replied. "I felt bad leaving you at the vet's office without a means to get home again."

He shrugged. "I could have called a cab if I wanted to leave."

"Didn't even think of that," she noted, with a wry look in his direction.

"And that goes along with being stressed," he added. "So let's get going. I've got dog food for Beth and Grace, but I don't think it would work to separate Beth from the other dogs."

"No, it won't," Miranda agreed, "and she's certainly welcome to be with the other dogs, but we'll have to see how she handles being in a society with a lot of other animals. It might stress her out."

"I'll bring her in on a leash," Kyron offered. "We'll introduce them as slowly as possible," he said, with an eye roll.

"Yeah, good luck with that," she teased. "Most of them

are okay, but a couple could get a little possessive."

"And they would sort it out," he noted quietly.

"Without bloodshed?" she asked, an eyebrow raised.

"Without bloodshed," he confirmed, "but, hey, let's see how it goes." He waited until she had the door opened and the dogs called back, before he stepped up with Beth. Her tail was wagging as she saw all the other dogs.

"She really is social, isn't she?" Miranda stared at Beth.

"A lot of the War Dogs are, and they're used to being surrounded by a lot of people as well," he noted quietly. "It makes sense that being isolated, like she was, abandoned really, was the hardest thing for her."

"Not to mention going from an environment, where every need was met, to one of trouble and chaos, and then finally she had to survive on her own."

"Exactly," he murmured. Going one by one, as Miranda calmly held them back and released them one at a time, Kyron slowly introduced Beth to them. Finally, with all of them having had a good sniff at each other, they gradually disappeared to various corners, except for a dachshund that seemed to be stuck at Beth's side.

"Who is this guy?" Kyron asked.

"Rocky," she replied, with a smile. "I'm actually hoping that maybe he's more adoptable than most. A lot of people like the smaller dogs, and some people don't always do so well with bigger dogs."

"That makes sense," Kyron agreed. "The bigger ones just need a little more work, but they also get a bad rap because people don't always know how to handle them."

She nodded.

"So do you mind if I put on some coffee?" he asked. "I promise I'll go pick up some later."

She shook her head. "You don't have to do that."

"Oh, absolutely I do," he stated. "I know that things are tight here because you've given everything to the animals. I won't run you short on coffee."

"You've done already a ton," she said, with a wave of her hand. "The least I can do is get you breakfast."

"I won't say no to breakfast," he replied, with a smile, "because honestly, I am on the hungry side."

"Good. Did you let your brother know what was going on?"

"Yeah, I sent him a text last night, so they didn't worry, and another one this morning. If you don't mind, I was going to call him and ask about your rights and try to find out more about this guy who is your neighbor. For all we know he already has a couple misdemeanors on his record."

"That would be too much to hope for," she replied.

"And then," Kyron added, "I'll take a walk with this dog in full view, where he can come out and attack me if he wants." She stared at him in shock. He smiled. "I know. That sounds like I'm being aggressive, but, if it's this dog that he seems to think is his, we need to nip that in the bud right off the bat," he snapped. "And, if he thinks that you're alone and unprotected, he also needs to know that's not the case."

With that, he motioned at the coffeepot. "I'll put a pot on when I return. Let me go out and have a look around. I want to check on the horses and introduce Beth to the outside animals as well." And, with that, he pushed his way out the back door.

CHAPTER 9

KYRON WAS DEFINITELY confident in his ability to handle the dog, and, so far, it had been proved out, but Miranda wasn't at all sure about his ability to handle her crazy gun-toting neighbor. She'd seen Kyron's prosthetic leg, and he'd mentioned a bunch of other injuries. Though Kyron seemed strong enough and very fit, her neighbor was obviously not quite all there, and that made him unpredictable. She also worried about Kyron being a little more aggressive than she thought would be necessary, but, if he thought it was important, she didn't know what to do anymore. She really had no choice but to let him take the lead on this one.

The fact that his brother was a cop couldn't hurt either. Maybe it would give her an inside line, but she wasn't sure. Just so much crap was going on in her world right now that she was a bit overwhelmed. The trouble was, she needed to solve her property problem, and that was really the big issue. But how could she do that when she didn't have nearly enough money? She'd spent quite a few hours in the last couple weeks looking at real estate online, and sure, moving out of town would definitely help the situation—but not enough, definitely not enough.

She watched from the window as she put on the coffee, but Kyron and Beth walked outside, completely undisturbed.

Her neighbor didn't call out to Kyron or point a gun at him or threaten him. Kyron walked all the way down to the horses and out of her view. She stepped out to watch him, as Beth made acquaintances with the llama and the horses—everybody apparently quite content with each other, which Miranda put down to being a well-trained War Dog versus an animal already afraid of horses, something that they all would pick up on.

As he slowly walked back to her, Kyron smiled and waved. She stepped out a little farther, cautiously looking over at her neighbor's place, but saw no sign of him. As Kyron reached her, he noted, "Doesn't look like he's home."

"Not home or else he's just waiting," she muttered darkly.

"Is that a possibility?"

"With him, yes," she replied. "He seemed pretty convinced that I had stolen his dog, and Beth's presence here just confirms it."

"Well, you didn't steal Beth, and neither did I," he stated. "If he wants to go to court over this, that's fine. This is a War Dog, and he has absolutely no legal claim to it."

She brightened at that. "Right, although I don't know that the government will back you on that."

"I don't know for sure either," he replied, "but a lot of people won't go down that pathway regardless."

She nodded. "The coffee is ready. Come on in." With that, they slowly made their way back inside. As he stepped forward to close the door behind him, she thought she heard something. She frowned. "What was that?"

He shook his head. "I didn't hear anything."

She motioned at the door. "Can you push that open again?"

Kyron pushed it open, and he stepped back out again, this time without the dog. He looked around, listening. "I'm not sure what you heard, but I don't see anything."

She stepped out beside him and frowned. "I don't know either. I guess I'm hearing things."

"Or you're just being naturally cautious," he added, "and that's a good thing."

"Doesn't feel like a good thing right now," she argued. "It feels like a bad case of nerves."

"And, if that's what it is, that's just what it is." He shrugged. "Don't go blaming yourself for being cautious."

"I don't know what to say anymore," she noted. "He's got me twisted up inside."

"Got it," he agreed, "but still, this is not your problem."

"Maybe not," she replied, "but he'll think it is. And you don't know what he's like."

"No, so I may go over there and talk to him myself," he stated. "I wonder if he's still as aggressive when he doesn't have a gun in his hand and when he's confronting another man."

"I don't know," she admitted, "but I'm telling you that he is the kind to take it out on me later." He stopped, looked at her, and frowned. "So yeah," she stated, "it would be very helpful if you consider that part of this before you go piss him off even more than he is already."

"Got it," he replied thoughtfully. "First, let's get some coffee and food. I'll be in much more amiable mood to talk to him if my stomach is full."

"Coming right up," she said, with a smile. "Anything to avoid a huge collision of testosterone, with the two of you duking it out."

"Duking it out would be fine with me," he agreed, "but

I don't want to bring a knife to a gun fight."

She stopped and stared, then winced. "Right, now that's not exactly a thought to sleep on," she muttered.

"Don't worry about it," he told her. "We have enough things to deal with right now."

"Yeah, which one of the many worries were you thinking about?" she asked, with a laugh. "I mean, I'm trying to pay bills that I can't afford, buy a larger property in the country that I can't afford, and deal with a gun-happy neighbor who hates me and has gone off his rocker," she spelled out. "Have you got anything else in mind?"

"Lots," he said cheerfully. "But I'm not necessarily sure where or what."

She stared, yet nodded. "I guess you still have to figure out your family stuff, don't you?"

"Even that seems really small compared to everything you're going through," he noted, with a shake of his head.

"I don't think it is," she muttered. "It's just a matter of each of us sorting out the things that we have to deal with, and, while mine seems impossible to me, I'm sure that yours seems impossible to you."

"Maybe, … but it does bring up an issue about whether I'm staying close or what I'll do," he muttered.

"I guess you weren't thinking about staying local, were you?"

"I wasn't at first," he admitted, then looked down at the dog lying at his feet. "And then I see a dog like this, and I realize that I really do have some skills to offer. I can do rehab K9 training or all kinds of related stuff for that matter," he noted quietly. "I did get a pension, and I was medically discharged, so it's not like I'm destitute. However, I would still need something meaningful to do with my life."

"Well, you're right in the sense that you would certainly be a welcome addition around here," she agreed. "There are definitely K9 units in Aspen, but I don't know whether any local trainers are here or there's a need for someone here. I assume they bring them all in from out of town."

"I could be a local one, if and when there is a need, which would be something I could consider," he stated. "Animals have always been a huge part of my life, and to see how people treat them? Well, that has always upset me. And now I may have just inherited two dogs," he said, with a smile.

"Can you keep them both?" she asked.

"I can if I want to, yes." Kyron reached a hand toward Beth. Almost on instinct, she lifted her head, looked up at him, and nudged his hand with her nose.

"There is a bond between the two of you," she noted. "I'm quite surprised that it's already there."

"I'm not because it was a long night at the vet clinic, and we did lots of talking together. Lots of reminiscing, discussing our rough childhoods and all the other stuff that we have had to deal with," he admitted on a humorous note.

"Ah." She nodded. "All the lovely bonding that goes into any good relationship."

"Apparently," he replied. "Though I can't say I've had too many of those either."

She asked, "Relationships?"

He nodded. "At least the good bonding kind."

"But you were always leaving town, weren't you? Not everybody is happy to have a man who's not around."

"Exactly, which is also why, once I realized that would be a stumbling block, I decided it wasn't a big enough deal that I wanted to go in that direction," he explained, "so I didn't really worry about it. You know that short-term relationships work just fine, if everybody knows and agrees on it from the start."

She nodded. "I can see that, though I think it's kind of sad in a way because you military guys probably needed that security to come home to, a reason to come home for every time you left. Yet, if it wasn't the type of relationship you wanted or that you could count on, that's probably worse than not having a relationship at all."

He stared at her and nodded. "That actually was part of my thought process for a lot of friends of mine. More than a few came home to find that their wives weren't faithful while they were away."

She nodded. "I've heard certain things like that myself over the years, and that's always sad, so maybe, in your case, it was probably better that you didn't go in that direction."

"Yep, and now I don't have a job—or a visible means of support—or a lot of other things going for me at the moment. Just a broken-down body. So most people, most women," he corrected, "won't be interested."

She stared at him. "Wow, I guess you've been meeting all the wrong women."

He burst out laughing at that. "You know what? I probably have. But are you really telling me that a guy who's already got a prosthetic leg and a whole series of injuries to deal with is somebody you'd be interested in for a relationship?"

He had asked her in such a way that it was not geared personally to her, but Miranda still wondered if some level of that question was directed at her regardless. She answered him as honestly as she could.

"Given the fact that I've seen what you can do with the

animals, and how you care about the animals," she replied, "I couldn't give a crap about how broken your body is. Because your soul and your heart, those are both intact. At least I can *see* the physical damage, versus these guys who have broken and cracked hearts and blackened souls that are hidden from view. Their bodies may look pretty, but the rest of it is festering and corrupt." She visibly shuddered at the words. "Those are the guys I don't want anything to do with. Yet it's hard to find out which ones are the good guys, unless you spend some serious time with them."

With a reassuring smile, she continued. "So, Kyron, don't worry about that broken body. You're doing just fine with what you've got. Obviously you're doing the best you can, as you learn to adapt to this new life. Even if no further improvement is coming, you're still doing just fine right where you are at now. It's a miracle you're even alive." He stared at her, while she shrugged. "But then, that's just my take on life."

"Hey, I kind of like the world according to Miranda," he replied.

"Good," she murmured. "Because anything less than that is short-changing yourself. You're a good man, Kyron. Don't ever let the bad people in the world get you down."

KYRON SPENT SUNDAY morning having a belated breakfast with Miranda, enjoying the coffee and the company, getting to know her better. He had learned about her family hating the choices she had made for her life, the fact that potential boyfriends refused to have anything to do with her, and that her sister thought she was something to be ashamed of. At one point in time, Miranda even shook her head.

"They're all so stuck on, you know, being part of the Aspen social scene," she explained, "but they forget that we came from a dirt-poor background."

"Which is another reason why they're trying so hard," he added. "They prefer this *We didn't do it ourselves* mode. *We just came from rich families who ended up finally dying off and giving it to us* mode."

"Maybe," she noted, "but nobody gave me anything. Otherwise it would have gone to the animals."

"Maybe it hasn't come down to this generation yet."

She shook her head. "No, it hasn't. Though I do have a great-uncle in town, as I was telling you earlier, and he's been a big help with that check. But I know that these are stop-gap measures and that I need something that's a whole lot more stable."

He nodded.

"Would you really consider staying here?" she asked suddenly.

"I'm thinking about it, yeah. And yet you know, up until meeting Beth, I wasn't thinking about anything but getting the hell out of town as soon as possible, hopefully before I had to see my parents."

She stared at him. "Yeah, I know how that family stuff can be really poisonous." She nodded quietly. "I'm the one to talk. There's already been a lot of hardship on my side."

"I'm sorry for that," he shared. "It sounds like we have a lot in common."

"We do," she agreed, with a smile. "Oddly enough, instead of scaring me, that actually makes me feel better."

"Why would you be scared?" he asked curiously.

"Because my family always tells me that there's no way I

will ever have a real relationship and that nobody would ever want anything to do with me because they'd have to live with smelly animals." She looked over at him. "I presume that's not your attitude."

"Not at all," he stated. "Although I might have a problem with sharing the bed, if there isn't room for me to sleep."

She burst out laughing at that. "Honestly, I do have problems with that too. I've put a secondhand mattress on the bedroom floor, trying to encourage at least some of them to sleep there, and it has been moderately successful."

"That sounds like a great solution," he noted, chuckling.

"Because it's still important to get a good night's sleep. Especially for you, I suppose, after the injuries?"

"Not so much," he noted. "I just really do better with sleep. I can get cranky and groggy if I don't sleep, unless I'm on a mission of course. I hate it when it's the perfect time to be sleeping, then I toss and turn and can't sleep for some reason." He shrugged. "That is guaranteed to make me crabby."

"Duly noted," she teased.

He looked at her and started to chuckle. "You know what? It does sound like we're getting all the details out of the way before we start a relationship," he said gently.

"You're right. It does," she agreed. "And we've actually already been through a night and a morning and shared breakfast and multiple coffees. A lot of people could say we've spent the night together."

"Oh, and, if you'd stayed at the vet clinic with me," he added, "that would be justifiable wording."

She nodded. "Believe me. When I got home, I felt terribly guilty about leaving you there. I didn't even sleep very much myself."

"Now that was a waste," he noted. "Why on earth would you ruin your chance for sleep? It's not like you could do anything to help me."

"No, but, once I realized that I had left you there, without even a way to leave"—she shrugged—"it just felt like I'd done the wrong thing."

"Well, you didn't," he argued quietly. "It was a good time for me and Beth, and we got a lot closer during the night," he added. "I spent a lot of time handling her, talking to her. We talked to her friend, to Grace, through the door a lot, and we got up and walked around several times. It actually was a good thing for us."

"Good," she said, her relief obvious. "It's just such a strange thing to even think about."

"After a while we'll need to see about getting Grace home again," he noted, checking the time. "And you didn't answer me earlier by the way."

"About what?" she asked curiously.

"About a house guest."

She nodded. "You are perfectly welcome here," she replied, "including both dogs." She looked over at him and smiled. "Honestly, I wouldn't mind having you here just because of the neighbor."

"That's part of my thought process too," he agreed, "along with the dogs of course." Smiling, he continued. "And while we're at it, I wouldn't mind spending more time with you."

She looked at him with a pleased smile. "Ditto."

His phone buzzed, and he checked it to find a message from the vet, confirming that Grace was ready to be picked up.

Just over an hour later, inside Miranda's guest bedroom,

Kyron stepped back and looked down at Beth beside Grace, who seemed like she was in more pain than he would have liked. "She'll probably need a few days to recover a bit," he murmured. Reaching down, he placed a gentle hand on her head, but Grace just laid there, not moving. "I hate that she doesn't even react to being touched."

"I noticed that too. It's like... I don't know... it makes you wonder whether something more serious is going on or it's just the effects of all the months of abuse and neglect. We really have no idea where she even came from or what she's been through. Either way," she added, "it's too much and will make it harder for her to recover."

He agreed, but it was obvious that they could do only so much right now. "Well, I guess we should just leave the two of them alone now. Grace may well relax and get more rest if we aren't here." And, with that, they headed out of Miranda's spare room, downstairs in the back of the house. "You know what? If it weren't for the animals, this would make a great office for you."

"It would if I was staying," she noted quietly. "But now that I have to consider the safety of the animals, threatened by my crazy neighbor, I have to look at other options."

"Yet you know crazy neighbors can happen anywhere."

"God, I don't even want to think about that," she admitted quietly. "I have to keep a positive attitude and believe there will be an end to this."

"I am totally in agreement with that," he replied, with a smile. "And, by the way, thank you very much for allowing us to stay here. I know this is the best situation for Grace. And Beth."

Miranda nodded. "I wouldn't turn away anybody in need, and in this case, there are three of you." She smiled.

"Besides, with a crazy neighbor out there ..." She stopped, then just left her words hanging.

But Kyron understood. "It is a difficult situation, and I'm really sorry you're going through this."

"I have to make decisions about my future anyway," she muttered. "It's just been kind of rough."

"It is rough, and things go on in this world that we wish we didn't have to experience. Yet these are the cards you've been dealt," he stated. "So, we'll deal with it the best we can, and we'll try to find you a safe way forward."

She shook her head. "You won't be here long enough for me to fix all that." She stopped, asking, "Will you?"

He stared at her and shrugged. "I know I asked for a couple days here, and I certainly won't take more of your time than necessary. However, I do want to make sure that the dog is more than happy and healthy before I move her."

"Do you have a place to move to?"

"I'll go take a look at that later today," he noted. "I have property locally that I inherited from my grandfather." She stared at him. He shrugged. "Remember that part about my grandfather loved me, and I loved him, but nobody else could stand him?" She nodded quietly. "He left me the property years ago, and, of course, that made for a big drama, since it didn't go to my father. They told me how Granddad had let it go to waste, and it's useless anyway. It was such a sore subject that I'd basically put it out of my mind. I pay the property taxes every year and hadn't given it much thought, but I guess, in the back of my mind, I was always wondering about making it home. More out of love for my grandfather I think than anything. But, with so many ongoing problems with my family, I just never came home."

"Got it. I understand critical families," she noted. "Still, that would be huge if you could find a place close by."

"Well, it would be in some ways," he admitted, "like we were saying, how maybe I could work on training K9 units or something to do with dogs."

"Or maybe you don't even need to do that right away," she suggested. "Get yourself resettled, find a place, and make it a home for you and the two dogs, if that's all you've decided on so far. Then, as you work your way through whatever it is you want to do, you'll eventually find a way to make peace with it all."

He looked at her and smiled. "Wouldn't that be nice? I feel like a lot of my problem is family."

"It sure sounds like it, and that is just sad and such a waste," she murmured. "I doubt that your grandfather would be very happy about that."

"No, he wouldn't be. Not at all. Plus, some personal stuff of his is probably up there," he said thoughtfully, staring out the window. "I really should have done something about the property a long time ago."

"Well, as usual, real estate is crazy expensive here."

"Yeah, I know. Aspen's a big tourist trap. It's been that way for a long time."

"I was actually wondering how your brother managed to buy a place, being a cop. Did he get help when he bought his house?"

Kyron nodded. "Yeah, my parents kicked in a large chunk toward the down payment. My brother was obviously grateful but, at the same time, afraid it would cause some stress between us."

"But, if you got an inheritance from your grandfather, it works out, right? You each got a home."

He smiled. "And that's the thing. I'm okay with it. I also

know that the greatest value of my grandfather's place is the land, while, in Allen's case, it's the house."

"Sure, but you would rather have land anyway," she stated, with a shrug.

He laughed. "You think you know me that well, huh?"

"Absolutely," she confirmed. "You are the last person to care a crap about a big fancy house, if you couldn't fill your property with dogs."

"And maybe that's what I'll do." He thought back to the two they had just left for a rest.

"It sounds like you need to go take a look at the land first."

He nodded. "I do, and honestly? It's something I've been avoiding."

"Sounds like it's painful."

"Sounds like I should be an adult about it and go deal with the situation." He frowned.

"Well, if you need any company or support, I could come along."

He looked at her for a moment. "And how does that work?" he teased.

"Well, I need to look at properties myself. In person. Not just online. Even if I sell this place, I still have to find something big enough, and everything I've looked at online tells me that I can't afford anything." She sighed loudly. "That's more than depressing."

"But you have this property in town, so, if you go farther out, maybe the prices will be lower."

"I know we've discussed that before," she agreed, "but farther out doesn't seem to mean all that much."

"Well, we can go take a look."

"Do you think Grace will be okay?"

"She'll be fine."

"It will be time for her pain meds soon, before we go," she noted, "and it's better that she doesn't try do too much moving anyway. Maybe if we leave her, she'll just sleep."

"Well, we'll shut the door to her room. That should keep her contained somewhat, right?"

She nodded. "She's already had a bathroom break, and that was painful enough for her. However, she is moving, and I think right now she just needs to rest. How far away is your grandfather's property?"

"It's out of town." He stopped to think. "Maybe fifteen minutes or so. So that's not bad, half an hour round-trip drive time, and a few minutes spent there," he estimated.

"That kind of fits in with the schedule," she replied.

"Is there a schedule now?" he asked in a teasing voice.

"I don't know." She laughed. "You kind of threw things into a bit of a tailspin, so whatever schedule we have will partially be dictated by these two gals."

"Right, well, it would be a good chance to walk Beth again," Kyron suggested. "Would you want to bring some dogs along?"

"Sure, but probably just Travis." She pointed to the big shepherd.

He looked at that one and nodded. "And he does seem to get along well with Beth."

"Looks like it so far at least," she agreed. "It would be good if we had a little more one-on-one time with them."

At that, he nodded. "I've got a rental truck, so why don't I drive this time?"

"If you want to," she stated, with a shrug. "It's your gas."

At that, he burst out laughing. "Always aware of every penny, aren't you?" He chuckled.

"Always," she murmured. "If it means putting that penny back into the animals."

"Well, I certainly won't argue with you on that. I have a vet bill to pay for too."

She nodded. "I would imagine that Doug will probably give you a discount, but I can't be sure," she warned. "I know he has obligations to meet, like everyone else."

"Of course he does. It's not a problem either way." And, with that, he led Beth out of the sickroom and closed the door on Grace, so she could sleep in peace. He'd be back with her medication in a bit. Then, with Travis at her side, they all headed out to his rental.

As they drove toward the property he hadn't seen in a decade, she asked, "Has it never occurred to you to sell it?"

"No," he replied immediately. "Remember that part about loving my grandfather? He was the rock in my world, when the immediate family seemed to be something I couldn't count on."

"It sounds like your family cared more about fighting with your grandfather than loving you."

He thought about that for a moment. "That's not a bad way to look at it, as sad as it sounds."

"Well, it does sound sad," she agreed. "Life is way too short for that kind of stuff."

"Yet we see it happening all the time."

"That doesn't mean it's right," she murmured.

"No, it sure doesn't." He chuckled. "But, hey, let's go take a look. I should warn you. I don't even know if it's habitable. I did have somebody I know come and check on it last year. He told me that everything was fine and that I should get my ass home and live in it."

"Well, you know what they say about vacant houses and

how quickly they can degrade," she murmured.

"Good point, and I haven't seen it myself for quite a while. It sounds like my parents have driven past it a few times, but I've never given anybody in the family a key." He paused. "I did let a couple friends stay there a few years back, and this other buddy of mine stayed a couple times, more just to keep an eye on the place."

"Sounds like a really good friend," she noted.

"Yeah, he's one of the better ones," he replied quietly. "And we're still friends, even after the accident."

At that, she looked at him sharply. "Are you telling me that you lost friends because of your accident?"

"Sure, lots of people aren't terribly comfortable when you come out of hospital with major injuries," he noted quietly. "You really do learn who your friends are."

"That's just horrid," she said instantly.

He burst out laughing. "Until you actually see what people are like, they will continuously surprise you."

"It's sad though," she noted quietly. "There's absolutely no need for people to treat others that way."

"Well, I do have good friends now," he replied, "and some of them are actually in the trades, so maybe, if we needed to do some work on the property, I could have them come out to show me a thing or two. Guess I should get a look at it before I make any plans."

"You know what? From what you've told me about your family, you don't have a true home," she noted. "You're kind of lost in a way, so maybe coming back and living in your grandfather's house would help you find yourself again."

"Do I sound that lost to you?" he asked.

She frowned. "Not lost, but—" Then she stopped. "Yeah, lost," she confirmed. "You don't know what you're doing in your life now. You don't know where you're going after this gig. You have this incredible property that's yours and available, and yet, because of conflict within your family, you haven't been able to enjoy it."

He pondered that for a long moment. "*Huh.* I guess I did allow stuff with my family to keep me from enjoying it."

"And yet you know nothing would make your grandfather happier than you moving into his house and living as he wanted you to live all these years ago."

He smiled. "Well, you're right about some of that. Granddad would be tickled pink if I moved in again."

"Again?"

"Oh, yeah, there were times when I was just not welcome at home, especially during my teenage years. I didn't think I was a difficult teen, but, because I couldn't see eye to eye with them, it seemed like everything I did was wrong and that everything my brother did was right. There were times when I just couldn't handle it, and I would go to my granddad's and spend a weekend or longer," he explained quietly.

"Then it's high time for you to really take possession of your grandfather's house." She spoke with such a positive tone that he wasn't sure how to take it.

"In what way would that help?"

"It will help to reorient yourself. When your grandfather was there, that's exactly what you did. You went to him for that stable base, for that time to get your bearings and to remember what was important to you, before you had to head back into the maelstrom of the life you lived with your family."

"I had to go home each time," he stated. "Every time I went to my grandfather's place, it caused him and my father stress. I wasn't trying to do that. I was just desperate to find a way to survive what wasn't a very happy home life."

"And I'm sure your grandfather understood that."

"I think so," he agreed. "He kept telling me not to ever let them stop me from coming to see him and that I always had a home there, if I wanted it."

"Sounds like he was already planning on leaving it for you then," she murmured.

"I don't know. I hadn't really thought about it—but maybe." He was a million miles away for a moment, as he considered the years gone by. "I was lost when he died," he stated simply. "And it definitely pushed me into enlisting in the navy faster than I might have if I'd had a chance to adjust to the grief first."

She didn't say anything, but what was there to say? It was his young adulthood, his whole childhood, really, that Kyron had to deal with. Maybe she was right about the whole *coming home* thing and all. "I think you may be on to something there," he noted quietly. "If nothing else, it does feel like I'm coming home right now, in a way."

"Good," she agreed. "It's long overdue. Maybe if you can find peace with coming home, you can find peace with your family. And if you can't, that's not your problem."

"Meaning?"

"Your family will always be there, but that doesn't mean you need them in your life. If they don't want to have a life with you, and you can find a way to come to terms with whatever it is that you have or don't have as far as a relationship with them right now, then you don't have to see them," she stated simply.

"I wonder how they would handle my moving into Granddad's place."

"After all this time I would suspect they won't care, and your brother might even find some joy in it—you know, what with him having his house already."

Kyron doubted that, but who knew?

As he made a series of turns, she looked around. "I don't even know this area."

"It was just a place that my granddad made his home."

"Exactly," she said, with a bright smile. "And it definitely feels like a place that you can make into your own now. You've avoided it, but yet there's a home for you already. Right here." She paused for a moment. "Honestly, this gift is something to be cherished. To hell with anybody in your family who tries to make it anything less. The years with and memories of your grandfather are something to be cherished as well. We don't always get the time that we want to have with people before they're gone, and we're suddenly just left with nothing," she explained. "So any time that you can spend now, here, in this place so full of memories of him, a place that always felt safe for you, can only help you." She turned in the passenger seat to face him. "Honestly, I don't know why you haven't come here before."

"Most recently because I was recovering," he replied quietly. "I wasn't in any shape to make the trip."

She looked at him sharply. "And here I thought you were doing really well."

"I am now," he confirmed, "and I have been for the last few months. I'm just getting to that place where I'm beginning to feel like I'm back to normal now, whatever that new normal is. But it feels good, and I feel strong," he stated. "But, even six months ago, I was still recovering from the surgeries."

"Ouch." She went quiet for a long moment, until he

turned down a driveway, and then her thoughts burst out of her with such force that he knew she'd been mulling it over, stewing on it for quite a while. "I just can't believe that, after such major injuries, your parents haven't been there for you."

"They haven't been there for me all my life," he noted. "So that's not likely to change now."

"Got it. They suck," she snapped. "That's it. I officially don't like them."

At her pronouncement, he burst out laughing. "You don't even know them," he teased.

"No, but anybody who doesn't show unconditional love to both of their children and who blatantly favors one over the other just aren't very nice people. The issues with your grandfather were theirs, not yours. They should have set aside the trouble enough to at least recognize that your grandfather was giving you something they were unable to provide, something that you desperately needed," she stated emphatically. "Just like with animals. They need things that we can't always supply. You do your best, but sometimes animals want or need something different. And, with kids, it's far more pronounced," she murmured.

"And as a troubled teen, or whenever they seemed to think you were troubled, your grandfather gave you something that was precious. That your parents chose not to see that and didn't act accordingly is on them." She shook her head. "You've come into yourself over these last few years—or maybe even the last decade," she guessed. "I don't really know, but that they haven't had a chance to even see who you are is just sad for everyone," she murmured. "And that might be something that you see going forward. The fact that they don't recognize who you are anymore because maybe they're looking back at times gone by, realizing how much they've missed."

At that, he pulled down a long driveway, and she gasped. "Is this yours? This is the property?"

He nodded. "Yes. This is it, starting here at the road. The driveway is pretty long," he murmured. "Although I didn't remember it that way."

"How did you get from your house to here?"

"Sometimes I came right after school, or sometimes I called him for a ride, or sometimes I'd hitchhike," he explained quietly. "Anything to get away."

At that, she fell silent, her gaze intense as they headed down the long driveway. When they got to the end of it, she shook her head. "Dear God." She turned to stare at him. "You have this, and you haven't even been here? I've been desperate to find anything that would suit all the animals and couldn't even have imagined getting something like this."

He didn't know what to say to that because she was right, and yet, as he sat there, he hated that his throat thickened as he was flooded with memories of his granddad. He shook his head and whispered under his breath, "I'm so sorry, Granddad. I should have come long before." And, with that, he looked over at her. "Let's go take a look around."

CHAPTER 10

MIRANDA HOPPED OUT, the dogs jumping down too, as she stared in rapture at the huge old farmhouse in front of her. "You didn't tell me that it was a farmhouse."

"And I probably wouldn't have described it that way either." He smiled, enjoying her reaction. Just seeing how overjoyed she was at all this reminded him of how much he had allowed his family to change and to affect everything in his life, when he really should be right here. He should be recovering here; he should have been recovering here the whole time. Even his friends had mentioned that a couple times, and he'd been almost instinctively resistant to anything that had to do with coming home.

And yet he wasn't coming home to his family; he was coming home to his granddad. *That* mattered, but somehow he had lost sight of that. Miranda was right. He had lost his way. He was lost. And now, maybe because of her, he was found. He looked over at her, then watched in amusement as she raced around, looking at the huge old sprawling residence.

"How old is this place?" she asked.

He shrugged. "No clue. At least fifty years plus, I would think."

She nodded. "If not twice that," she muttered. "You are so blessed," she said, for the twentieth time.

By seeing this through her eyes, he realized he was blessed, more so because, for the first time, somebody else was here to help him see something he had walked away from. He hadn't recognized the value of what he needed, even though it stared him right in the face. "Come on. Let's go in."

She followed him up the wide front steps to the huge full-length veranda with a happy sigh. Looking around the property, she added, "You know that you could put all kinds of animals out there. Horses, even lots of dogs, like, if you wanted to train dogs. You could have kennels, boarding kennels, all kinds of stuff."

"*Huh*. I never even thought of boarding kennels, but that is something I could do to supplement my income."

She frowned. "I hate to ask, and it's definitely none of my business, but is this place paid for?"

He nodded. "Yeah, my grandfather owned it outright."

She nodded. "So, it's really just your living expenses that you would need to cover."

He agreed with that and reminded her that he did get a pension, but what was lacking was that sense of purpose, that sense of needing to do something. He knew he had to honor that aspect of his life too, or he could never be happy.

As they entered the massive old house, she gave a happy sigh. "Wow, what a perfect place. I know it's worth a lot of money, but, if I could ever buy this type of property, with a wonderful house and all this acreage, something like this would be ideal." Then she explored the massive living room with a huge fireplace and headed into the big country kitchen, complete with island. She shook her head. "You know what? Updated a bit and this place would look amazing, but, even just like this, it's incredible."

"It is, isn't it?" he noted, with a smile. "Thank you for opening my eyes up to it again."

"The whole situation is really a shame. Your grandfather obviously cared about you very much, and I'm sure would have been hurt to know that, even when your situation changed and when you suddenly needed a home, you couldn't let yourself make use of the perfect one you already had waiting for you right here." She shrugged. "I'm sorry if I'm overstepping. The good news is that it doesn't have to stay that way. Everything here is something you can deal with now."

There wasn't a whole lot to say to that, but he knew she was right. He knew it and was already looking at the idea of maybe setting up a few things and moving in here.

"It's also odd to me," she added, "that you're asking me for a place to stay with your two dogs, when you already have this."

He stared. "Because I wasn't even thinking in those terms," he replied quietly. "I wasn't thinking that I would move back here in Granddad's house or even stay in Aspen very long. My plan was to be here for a couple days to find the dog and then maybe travel for a while. I just didn't know where that might be."

She nodded. "I don't mind either way," she stated. "Obviously Grace still needs a lot of medical attention, and, since I work for a veterinarian, I understand a lot of the signs and symptoms of the problems, so it makes sense. Yet she seems to be doing very well. One thing I will say," she said, pointing at Beth, who was even now racing around the main floor, "is that these dogs have a unique relationship, and both could decline in health if they were separated. So, if you are planning on keeping either one of them, please consider keeping them both. And this would certainly be a wonderful place to do it."

"I hadn't even considered staying in town," he stated, "and now my mind is going one thousand miles an hour, asking myself, *Why? Why would I have walked away from all this when obviously so much about it is absolutely perfect?*"

She nodded. "That, in itself, is huge, the fact that you can even see that now, I mean." She was beaming. "I, for one, will be overjoyed to see this place come alive. I can practically hear your grandfather telling you to do it!"

He laughed at that. "And you wouldn't be too far wrong." Kyron smiled. "My grandfather was a real character."

"I'm sure I would have liked him," she said, with a definitive nod.

"I don't know about that," he teased. "He wasn't necessarily a huge animal lover."

"Oh, I would have won him over to my way," she stated instantly. "I've gotten an awful lot of people on my side when it comes to looking after animals."

"And maybe," he admitted, "I shouldn't be second-guessing anymore. I know without a doubt that he loved me." And, once again, his emotions built up and choked his voice.

She reached over and gave him a gentle hug. "He was instrumental in you becoming the man you are today, so just honor that and move back in. This place is what allows you to really come home, despite how things go with your family. My God, what an amazing gift." And with that, she was off and running. At the staircase, she stopped, looked at him, and asked, "May I go upstairs?"

"Sure." He chuckled and gave her a wave of his hand.

"Check it all out. Besides, you'll have to help me move the dogs in here."

She stopped several steps up and turned to look at him, grinning broadly. "So, you're moving in?" she asked in delight.

He shrugged. "Maybe," he replied, with a wry look in her direction. "I mean, it seems odd that I wouldn't be, when I have this available to me."

"Do you think your brother wondered about that too?" she asked quietly.

"I don't know. I think he probably just thought like I did. He may not even know that I still own it. Maybe he thought I sold it years ago."

"You would never sell it. I'm not sure very many people in this world could understand or honor the value of what you have here," she noted. "It's not just your future. It's your past and your future rolled into the present. That's a massive gift." And, with that, she dashed up the stairs, looking at everything she could possibly see.

THE VERY STRANGE and unsettling visit to his grandfather's place brought out a whole lot more memories than Kyron expected or was prepared for. And yet, at the same time, something was so very right about it all. He walked upstairs and looked around.

"It's still got your grandfather's furniture, I presume," Miranda guessed. "All the stuff downstairs and up here?"

He nodded. "Yeah, he went into hospice from here," he replied quietly. "And I left it just as it was. I was pretty wrecked over the whole thing. It's kind of like a mausoleum."

"No, not at all," she argued. "While you may want to honor the rich history and memories of the time you spent here with your grandfather, you don't want it to be a shrine. You want to make it your own, which honors him by default. That gives us lots of options."

At her use of *us*, he smiled. "What now? You'll help me move in too?" he asked.

"Well, somebody needs to," she stated. "Otherwise you probably wouldn't."

He winced at that. "Wow, is it that obvious?"

"I don't know about *obvious*," she admitted, "but you definitely have some heartfelt issues to sort through. And, as you know, we do have two dogs that need a home, I certainly want to see them settled."

He nodded. "And I'll take any help I can get, but I feel like I shouldn't even be at your place right now."

She waved her hand. "Honestly, it's the best place for Grace right now, and, this one, she won't want to be away from Grace for long. So it's fine," she replied. "But I do suggest we make a list of everything that needs to be done to get you moved in here." She paused, frowning. "Though honestly, it's really not very much. You've got power on already. I don't know if you need to get the gas heat turned on or not, and you'll need firewood," she noted. "You'll want a fire at this time of year. That will be good for the house as well. So maybe you should turn on the thermostat and get things warming up around here, so it will be more comfortable next time for you and Beth and Grace."

And, with that, they returned to the first floor and sat down in the kitchen to make a list.

She added, "Of course you'll need food, for you and the

dogs, and we should check out the kitchen pantry and see what else you need, not that any of it is worth keeping after all this time."

"True, and the list just gets longer and longer." He stared down and shook his head. "Somehow I just became domesticated."

She burst out laughing. "Oh, you're a long way from domesticated yet, but adding a couple dogs to the place will help." At that, she hopped up. "Hey, why don't we go out and take a walk around the outbuildings and have a look?"

"I agree with that totally." Then, as Kyron called Beth, and Miranda called Travis, they headed outside with the dogs on leashes, just because. As they walked the property, she stopped and asked, "How big is this place?"

He shrugged.

She turned and stared at him. "Seriously, like do you have acreage here?"

He nodded. "Yeah, I think it's like twenty acres maybe. … No, there's more attached to this place." He turned, looking. "I think it's a total of forty acres."

"Good God," she muttered.

And he realized what it must be like for somebody like her, who wanted something like this so badly. "Hey, it's all good."

"Yeah, it's more than good, I would say." She continued her survey of the property, turning, getting a full 360-degree view. "What do you think properties like this out here are worth?"

"I have no idea," he admitted. "Would you sell and come out this way?"

"In a heartbeat," she stated. "If I could get something like this—or hell, even something one-quarter this size—this would make my life a whole lot easier."

He nodded, unsure what to say to that because he had already seen what she could do with just a few acres. "You do realize that, as soon as you get more room, you'll fill it to capacity."

She nodded cheerfully. "That just means there would be more animals getting help."

He smiled. "It's all about the animals for you, isn't it?"

"Well, it needs to be about the animals, not about me," she declared honestly. "And I do know that I need to bring some kind of balance into my world. I just haven't managed that yet," she muttered, shoving her hands into her pockets, as she continued to stare around in amazement.

"I bought my place quite a while ago. As it happens, I bought it off my grandfather," she added—something else they shared in common. "He didn't like the property and didn't want anything to do with it, and my grandmother was more than happy to let me have it. Although I still paid pretty close to market value," she muttered.

Miranda continued. "My parents didn't have the money then, but apparently my grandfather had stashed away quite a horde of cash for my grandmother, for when she was left all alone, if that were the case. When he passed away, she found it and was in a pretty sweet situation."

Kyron turned toward Miranda. "Now I'm going to ask a personal question. Do you have a mortgage on your place?"

"A small one," she replied, with a nod. "I would love to get rid of that, but, if I go bigger, then chances are I can't avoid a mortgage."

He shrugged. "Maybe you should contact a Realtor."

"That wouldn't make me terribly happy because they are like bloodsuckers," she noted, with a laugh. "They'll take a chunk of whatever money I make off my place, and I just don't know that I can afford that."

"But maybe they can save you money on the other end," he argued.

"I don't know. Maybe. I'll have to see."

He nodded at that.

"Your fences look decent though," she stated, as she looked around. "Just a couple of those back ones need work."

"I can fix those myself," he noted, as he studied several panels that were down.

"It'll take longer to walk all of this," she admitted, "but you could cross fence it."

"I know," he murmured. "We can close up a couple fences near the house and let the dogs have room to play and roam outside. Then, as I get these external fences fixed up, it will expand everybody's outdoor living space tremendously."

She nodded enthusiastically. "Well, you wanted a project."

"Did I say I wanted a project?" he asked, sending her a sideways look.

"Yes." She nodded, looking at him. "Just not quite so clearly as you probably expected."

He snorted. "Are you always this enthusiastic?"

"Always. Except for when I'm not," she quipped, her mood plummeting. "Like when I think about my home situation." She shrugged. "But I will solve it, just like I've solved everything else."

When their initial inspection was finally done, he said, "Come on. Let's take Beth and Travis back. We have a long list of things to work on. Plus, I don't want to leave Grace too long." As they headed back, he suggested, "If we want to hit a grocery store, I'll pick up steaks for dinner and get the other groceries that we need."

She nodded. "Well, I won't say no to that."

"Good. I'm a guest, but I won't take advantage of your hospitality."

"Hey, groceries are always welcome," she stated, with a laugh.

With that, they made a quick stop on the way back to Aspen at a grocery store.

As he parked, Miranda stated, "I don't want to leave the dogs alone in the truck."

"Got it. Are you okay to be left with Beth?"

She nodded. "Beth's a sweetheart."

"Maybe so, but you also know what would happen if somebody approaches you?"

"I'll keep the windows closed then," she promised, "and you won't be that long."

With that thought, he raced inside, picked up coffee, fresh vegetables, milk, cheese, a lot of staples that he hadn't seen at her place, what he needed for their steak dinner tonight, plus hamburgers with all the fixings for tomorrow. At the last minute he tossed in dog treats and dog food. If he was using her dog food, he needed to replace it.

By the time he got near the exit, he heard the dogs frantically barking outside. Quickly pushing the cartful of groceries outside, he checked out his vehicle, and she was inside, but somebody was slamming on the door beside her. Beth fiercely barked, and Travis was excited as well.

Racing over, Kyron quickly gave Beth a command, and somewhat reluctantly she laid down, silent and confused, and Travis followed her lead. Then Kyron turned his attention to the man. Must be her crazy neighbor, Old Man

Macintyre. "What are you doing?"

At that, the grumpy older man turned and looked at him. "None of your fucking business! Now get the hell away."

"Well, that won't happen," he said, as he went to the back of the truck and unloaded the groceries, "but you better stop tormenting Miranda," he snapped. "I don't know what your deal is, but this will never be okay."

Macintyre stopped and asked, "Who in the hell are you?"

"What's it to you?" Kyron asked.

"If you're her latest boyfriend, then you're just another guy who'll get sucked in by a piece of tail, then ends up having to pay for dog food for her whole bloody nightmare of an illegal rescue," he snapped, snorting.

At that, with the groceries completely loaded up, Kyron turned, faced Macintyre. "Are you the asshole who shot at her this morning?" he asked, his tone low and hard.

The other man backed up. "What do you know about that?"

"Oh, don't you worry," Kyron stated. "I know plenty, and so do the cops. If you think you're getting away scot-free on this one, you're wrong."

"You can't do anything about it," Macintyre stated. "My gun accidentally discharged. And, hey, accidents happen."

"No accident happened," Kyron argued. "And it will not happen again."

"And if it does?" Macintyre asked, giving Kyron a sneer.

"I'll make sure that it's more than your rifle that I'll break over a block of wood," he stated.

Macintyre's eyes widened. Then he started to bluster, "Are you threatening me?"

"No, what I'm doing is letting you know that I will protect this woman and the animals on that property, and, if you think anything else is going on here that you feel like insulting her over, I suggest you run it by me first," Kyron snapped, "because I can tell you right now, I won't tolerate any of it." Then he looked from Macintyre to Miranda, who sat staring at the two of them, and he saw the fear in her eyes.

"The fact that you actually attacked an unarmed woman and are running around shooting dogs," Kyron added, "is absolutely despicable. But I get it. Slime is found all over this world. Just some of it landed beside her place."

Macintyre glared at him. "You don't know anything about me. All you're concerned about is this bitch here," he muttered at the vehicle. "Don't worry. You'll learn what she's really like soon enough."

"Yeah, and why don't you tell me right now," he demanded. "You seem to have a lot of hate for her. What's it all about?"

"Those animals are everywhere. They bark all the time, I don't even know what the deal is with the horses on the other side. If the owner knew that she was feeding these horses there all the time, I'm sure he'd have a shit fit too," he replied. "I have a good mind to go over there and tell him what she's up to."

"Well, you could, but she leases that land from him. So seems he's totally okay with the agreement they have," he explained. "But, if you feel like that's something you want to do, fly at it. Still, you haven't told me anything that's changed my mind about who she is and where she is coming from."

"Of course not," he sneered again. "Women like her always convince guys like you to belly up for them. You'll learn soon enough, just like everybody has."

"I don't think anybody learned anything bad about Miranda. Her standing in the community is just fine," he retorted. "You're just a sour old man who hates life, who hates everyone, and somehow thinks that reality should be how you want it to be, instead of the way it actually is."

Macintyre continued to glare at Kyron, but the old man backed away.

"Keep on backing," Kyron yelled, "and, if you ever bring that rifle into my view again, anywhere near her property, making threats or taking potshots at her or me or any of those animals, you'll be dealing with a hell of a lot more than you bargained for."

"And there go the threats again," the other man replied cheerfully. "I'll just go have a chat with those cops she called on me and let them know she's got you harassing me too now."

"Are you sure you really want to go there?"

"Why not?" he asked, with a smirk.

"Be sure and introduce yourself to my brother while you're there."

That wiped away the man's smile.

"Not only is he a cop but we don't take well to bullies," he muttered. "And that's what you are. You threatened a woman. You shot at her, and nobody on the planet believes it was an accidental discharge. So if you are stupid enough for there to be a next time, believe me. There'll be a hell of a lot more pain in your world than you're ready to deal with."

"Who the hell are you anyway?" asked Macintyre. "You're just nothing but her latest winter ski buddy," he sneered.

"Oh, I'm hell of a lot more than that," he replied. "I haven't been home in a long time because I've been off in the navy, but you can bet I'm home now, and I'm here on behalf of the War Dog Department. So this shit of yours won't fly. So lay off or face the consequences."

And, with that, the older man shot him a hard look, then turned and stumped off.

Turning back to the truck, Kyron quickly opened the door. "Are you okay?"

She nodded immediately. "He'll never stop though, will he?"

Kyron studied her for a long moment, looked back at the old man, and then shook his head.

"Instinct tells me the answer to that question is no. For some reason, he's got a hate on for you, and it'll take a lot more than just me warning him to keep you safe."

"Great." She blew the loose strands of hair off her face. "Maybe I will call that Realtor."

"I suggest you do," he added, "and maybe you can negotiate a smaller fee."

She gave him a wry look. "Yeah, right. This is Aspen."

He nodded. "Good point." And, with that, he quickly checked on the dogs, then hopped in and drove home.

CHAPTER 11

WHILE MIRANDA WAS broiling the steaks in the oven, foregoing cooking outside on the barbecue, with her lunatic neighbor running free, Kyron sat nearby at her kitchen table, working on his list and periodically making calls. She was still absolutely stunned that somebody could have a place so beautiful and not even have been there for the last ten years. She understood, due to his circumstances, but still, she found it heartbreaking. Today had been a hell of a day and would have been worse if she hadn't postponed the hay order even then she had to call and give the new address. Not that she wanted to fob that job off on Kyron while she was at work but she couldn't even begin to deal with a truckload of hay right now.

When she realized Kyron was currently on the phone with his brother, she tuned in a little bit closer. Some fascinating family dynamics were going on there that she'd never seen before. Her parents didn't appreciate anything that she was doing in her world either, but she hadn't had to deal with the same level of animosity. Mostly now all she got was the cold shoulder.

But the fact that she and Kyron had so much in common made her smile. The fact that he was also a hell of a good man and had gone to bat protecting her several times already had helped as well. He was one sexy male, and, though she'd been too busy to even really notice men for what had seemed like a very long time, it was slightly troublesome that her perspective had changed so drastically.

When he finally got off the phone, he looked over at her. "I told my brother that I would be staying here for a few nights with the dogs and that I'd be over to collect my personal belongings."

"And was that okay with him?"

"As long as I promised to show up for dinner with the parents," he winced.

"Well, maybe you should go, just to see if they are as bad as they were before," she murmured.

"I told Allen I would, as long as I could bring somebody."

She looked at him, startled. "Who?"

"You, who else?" he replied quietly.

She slowly turned to face him, her hands at her hips. "Are you trying to hide behind me?" He burst out laughing, then got up, walked over, and pulled her into his arms. Stepping back, she said, "Oh no, you don't. I'm not such a pushover as all that."

"Is accepting or giving a hug being a pushover?" he asked. "I just wanted a hug."

And that made her feel terrible. "Do you say things like that on purpose just to make me feel bad?" she asked, as she stepped back into his arms.

"Nope, not to make you feel bad at all," he replied. "But I actually meant it. Seems like a long time since I've had a hug. My grandfather was really good with them. My parents, on the other hand, didn't give me the time of day."

Her face pinched at that. "You know what? It might be better if I don't come with you."

"Why is that?" he asked curiously.

"Because I already don't like them."

"And maybe it'll be good then," he added, "because you'll get a better opinion of them and can understand me a little more."

"Is that important?"

"Absolutely it's important," he replied. "If you're convincing me to stay here, I think it's only fair that we stay as friends."

"Agreed," she murmured, looking at the floor. "I'm not sure exactly what we are right now as it is."

He laughed.

"I would say more than friends, but we haven't known each other very long, and we bonded over an animal," she added, with an eye roll.

"Is there anything better than that?" he asked.

"No, maybe not," she agreed, "but I know, for a fact, my family won't appreciate it."

"No, probably not," he stated, grinning. "Is that a problem?"

She stared at him and then slowly shook her head. "No, I guess not."

"And what about your grandmother?"

"Oh, you'll like her," she said, instantly brightening.

"But will she like me? That is the question," he added.

"I think so."

All without any idea that Miranda would find out the next day.

MONDAY MORNING, AS she finished cleaning up the

kitchen from breakfast, she watched from the window as Kyron finished the chores outside. She heard the doorbell, frowning, as she walked over to see her grandmother standing there, with an older gentleman. She reached out and gave her a hug. "What? No warning phone call?" she asked, in a joking voice.

"No, definitely not," her grandmother stated. "The last couple phone calls I've made to you have seemed kind of … cryptic. Your side of the conversation has been a bit of a mystery. So I decided to come and to see for myself what was going on."

Miranda stared at her grandmother, nonplussed, and then looked over at the older man beside her. "Are you Uncle John?"

He nodded slowly, a smile lighting up his face. "I am." He held out a hand, but, when she stepped forward, her arms opened to hug him. He immediately accepted that too.

"It is lovely to meet you after all this time. Come in, come in." And then, as he passed by, she added, "And thank you so much for the generous check, by the way."

"You're more than welcome," he replied. "I understand you need more."

"Don't we always," she quipped, with a sad smile. "There are always more animals in need." As he stepped farther inside her house, he was completely overwhelmed by the dogs. With a few sharp commands, she managed to move them back and away, so that everybody could come easily inside.

"Grandma, how did you know I would be home today?"

"Oh, I heard about the pipe bursting and flooding the store."

Miranda frowned. Wow. Her grandmother may be better connected to the community than Miranda was.

"Are they always in the house?" her grandmother asked anxiously.

"Not always, but, with the weather, plus I've got fences down," she added, "not to mention the fact that I have a neighbor running around with a gun, threatening to shoot everybody. So I'm generally keeping everybody in for now."

"Oh, gosh," her grandmother replied. "Didn't the police talk to him?"

"Yes, they did, and then he harassed me at the grocery store too. What he didn't know, however, was that Kyron was nearby and quickly set him straight, but I don't know that he'll listen to him either."

"Kyron?" her grandmother asked delicately.

Miranda stared at her and flushed. "The man who came to Aspen, looking to find a missing dog from the K9 War Dog program," she explained, "which we did find, by the way." She ushered them into the kitchen, and her grandmother immediately sat down at the big table.

"This is a beautiful house, but it does need a lot of work," her uncle noted.

"Definitely, but it isn't worth putting the time and effort into doing the work here, when I need a bigger property anyway, not to mention getting away from my crazy neighbor," she muttered.

Her grandmother nodded. "You definitely need to make some decisions."

"I know. I know." She raised both palms. "That's been brought home to me more than a few times lately, particularly now that my neighbor has gone round the bend," she muttered.

"It sounds serious that he's actually threatening to shoot

you," her great-granduncle noted, staring at her with concern.

"Well, unfortunately he already took a shot at Miranda," Kyron stated from the doorway. At that, both of the older people turned to look at him. He stepped forward and reached out a hand to her grandmother. "Hello," he said to them both. "Miranda has been very generous in allowing me to bring an injured dog here, along with the War Dog that I came here looking for."

At that, the elderly man looked at him. "Army, air force or navy?" he barked.

"Navy," he replied, seeing someone of the same ilk. Kyron reached out to her great-uncle and shook hands, adding, "Former Navy SEAL actually."

Her great-uncle's face lit up. "Well, I was Army. A pilot in World War II, Third Battalion."

Miranda watched as the two men exchanged measured glances and accepted each other, just like that. *Now why did that never happen with people who needed healing, like her relationship with her parents, like with Kyron's relationship with his immediate family?* Miranda put on more coffee and then sat down with her grandmother.

"At the grocery store yesterday, it was actually very helpful to have Kyron there because, besides buying a ton of groceries for the place, even though he didn't have to"—she sent him a hard look—"my crazy neighbor found me and started pounding on the truck door and yelling at me to move out of town and to get the hell away or my animals were toast again."

"But that's not allowed," her grandmother cried out softly, clearly distressed.

"No, it's not, but you also know what happens when

you get somebody hell-bent on causing trouble," she added. "I contacted a Realtor this morning just to see what the property's worth. They'll come out in the next few days and do an assessment."

"It should be worth a lot," her grandmother noted.

"Is it? I don't think so."

"Well, I think it is, but you do have a mortgage on it, don't you?"

"I do, so therefore, trying to find another place that's got more land, well …" She just shrugged and didn't say anything more. Everybody knew what the problem was, but nobody really had a solution. She looked over at her great-uncle. "So, are you staying in town now?"

He nodded. "I'm liquidating everything and taking care of my financial affairs. I'm not getting any younger." She didn't have a clue how old he was. When he noticed her assessing gaze, he smiled. "I'm eighty-eight, my dear."

Her eyebrows shot up. "Oh, for somebody who's eighty-eight, you're looking mighty fine," she added.

He gave her a beaming grin. "That's a nice way to treat your elders." He chuckled.

"Do you have a family nearby?" she asked.

"No, I never did," he replied. "I took a lot of turns in life, but that wasn't one of them."

She nodded. "Well, that's their loss," she murmured. "I think you would have made a great father and grandfather," she murmured.

"Well, aren't you just too kind," he said. "Keep it up. Keep it up."

She chuckled, then got up and poured the coffee. As she did that, she heard the other two questioning Kyron.

"How dangerous is this neighbor?" her grandmother

asked Kyron.

"Dangerous," he replied immediately. "I don't know why he is so angry over her animals or how much trouble he's caused anybody else. I did ask my brother about his background." Kyron explained, "My brother is a local cop here. He checked the record on him, which shows some complaints and disturbances but nothing so serious as this."

"So, a *slipper*, huh?" said her great-uncle. "And call me John, by the way." At that, Kyron nodded. "What will you do now?" Uncle John asked Kyron.

"We went out yesterday, looking at a property that I inherited from my grandfather quite a few years ago," he shared, trying to keep the story simple.

Miranda listened, as Kyron perhaps intentionally changed the subject and drew their attention away from her and her problems.

"Because I've been away for so long, I never did anything with the property. We went to see what kind of shape it's in. As it turned out, it's a bit like a time capsule, just sitting there. I've had friends stay a couple times over the years, but that's it."

"But there obviously were problems, if you didn't go there until you arrived in town," her grandmother stated, as she studied him carefully. "I feel like I know you."

Miranda looked over at him in surprise.

"No, but maybe you knew my grandfather. He was certainly well-known in town." Kyron pulled up a picture and held it out for her.

She immediately looked at the picture and smiled. "Wow, this is Robby. We called him Robby Burns because he used to make up lyrics all the time like the Scottish lyricist."

Kyron nodded at that memory. "And he used to play guitar, until his hands got too bad," he stated, with a smile.

"Do you play?" Miranda asked him, as she turned to face him.

"I used to at one time," he noted, "but do I still? I don't think so. But again, maybe it's something to go back to." While the others were obviously confused, he added, "I was badly injured in the navy, so I'm out on a medical discharge. I've just come back and am helping out the war department to track down a War Dog, while looking at what the rest of my life will be. After yesterday's visit to Granddad's place," Kyron stated, "I think the next step will be to reopen that house and to see if I can find something in my life to do now that makes sense," he murmured.

At that, Miranda's grandmother smiled. "You know what? I think your grandfather would love that."

Smiling, Kyron replied, "I think he would too. He was quite a character and always very full of love for everyone."

At that, her grandmother frowned, staring down at the picture still. "And yet wasn't there a problem? With his son, wasn't it?"

"Yes, they never got along, and most of my childhood was spent with my grandfather rather than with my parents, and I think that caused Granddad a lot of trouble too."

Miranda interrupted with coffee refills, and, when everybody had a cup, she looked over at her great-uncle and repeated, "I really do appreciate the assistance. You can't imagine what a help that is."

He nodded. "I was talking to your grandmother about it, about selling off most of my assets, as I simplify my life. So I'm happy to help you a little bit more," he stated cautiously. "But I think you're in one of these situations where it's a problem that has no end."

She chuckled. "You are quite right about that," she stated, with a smile. "If people would only stop abusing and dumping animals, that would make my life easier, but it doesn't seem likely to happen."

He nodded, turned toward Kyron. "And what is your role in all this?"

He shrugged. "I came looking for the War Dog, and, with Miranda's help, found her, but in a bad state," he replied. "We also found a second dog that Beth, she's the War Dog, was protecting, and now, at the moment, we're all here, while the second dog recovers from a gunshot wound.… Most likely, thanks to the crazy neighbor. So your granddaughter's generosity and assistance brought us to this point," he stated, "and now that I've had a chance to take a look at my property, I'll be working on getting it back up and running."

"Will that take long?" Miranda's grandmother asked, her gaze bouncing from her granddaughter to Kyron.

He understood the grandmother's innate fears of Kyron hurting Miranda. "No, I don't think so. Definitely a few things need to be done, but we should be able to get the house opened up in just a couple days," he noted quietly. "Obviously I have fences to fix and cleaning to do, plus stocking up on groceries and things like that, not to mention firewood."

At that, the grandmother nodded. "But still, that's a huge boon for you, isn't it?"

"It is, indeed," he agreed, with a smile. "And I'll be getting out of your granddaughter's hair as soon as I can."

"But you don't have to rush." Miranda reached out a hand, placing it over his. She looked back at her grandmother. "When you're thinking about him leaving, please remember my crazy neighbor."

At that, her grandmother winced. "No, she's right. You should stay here until this is solved."

He let out a bark of laughter. "Well, that could take weeks to months."

Her grandmother nodded. "It's a big house, so it should sell easily."

"Which is why it would fetch a decent price right now." Kyron looked over at Miranda.

"Maybe, but maybe not enough to do what I need to do."

Kyron nodded and didn't say anything more.

After the visit, he stood in the doorway and watched as the older pair left. "They seemed quite nice," he noted, looking at her.

She nodded. "Honestly, I've had nothing to do with my great-uncle in all these years because he was living abroad, I believe. So I only had my grandmother nearby."

"And your parents?"

She shrugged. "They both live in Boston and both teach at the university. They've largely washed their hands of their renegade daughter."

He wrapped his arms around her shoulders. "Looks like we're in the same boat there too."

"It appears like we're in the same boat in many ways," she agreed, with a smile.

He grinned. "Well, what's next on the list? What do we need to get done?"

"Tending to the horses," she said quietly. "Beth probably needs a walk, and Grace needs to be checked." At that, they heard a bark, and they looked over at the doorway they had left open, so Beth could come and go, to see Grace standing there.

"Oh my," Miranda gasped. As she stepped forward, Kyron held out a hand and said, "Hang on a minute."

"Why?" And just then, Beth walked over to Grace, wrapped her head against her buddy, and then still touching, the two dogs moved out into the living room. The other dogs raced in, and Beth stopped them. but let them sniff Grace.

"Interesting," Miranda noted. "Beth really is a caretaker for her, isn't she?"

"I meant to ask the vet, but I didn't get a chance and then forgot," Kyron stated. "With the way Beth is acting, I'm wondering if Grace isn't blind."

At that Miranda stared at him, startled. "That would explain why Beth is taking over her care so much, wouldn't it?"

"Beth would know that Grace wouldn't survive out here on her own," he stated. "I don't know how they found each other, but the fact that they have really confirms that we can't separate them."

"You weren't planning on separating them anyway," she stated, with a chuckle.

"I was hoping not to," he agreed, with a nod. "And honestly, after seeing Granddad's place yesterday, there's no reason to."

"I'm quite jealous, if you haven't noticed," she admitted quietly.

"Well, you're more than welcome to come visit anytime," he offered, looking over at her.

"And I now know somebody with lots of land, in case I run into trouble with way-too-many animals," she teased, with a big fat grin.

He rolled his eyes at her. "I have to figure out all that too," he noted. "Some fencing and cross fencing would be good right away though."

"Not only would it be good but remember that my other neighbor is looking to sell his land where my horses are," she stated. "So, for me, that's another huge headache waiting to strike."

He winced. "When your Realtor comes, at least you'll have an idea of what you can get for this place."

Almost on cue, Miranda's phone beeped with a text message. She glanced down at her screen. "The Realtor wants to come over and take a look. Like *now*."

"Good, let's do it," he stated.

"The house is a mess," she added quietly.

"And that's not the problem right now. The Realtor doesn't care about that. As long as it's cleaned up for showings, it won't be an issue."

"Maybe," she murmured. "I guess it just seems like a big step."

"A big step you need to take," he reminded her quietly.

She nodded and picked up her phone. When she got off the call, she looked at him and said, "They'll come over in an hour." She glanced around and winced.

"Let's do what we can do in an hour," he suggested. "That's all you can do. Then I'll go deal with the horses, while they're here, so you can talk with them alone."

She looked at him gratefully. "Thank you for the help, but you certainly don't need to run away."

"I'm not running away as much as trying to give you some space and some privacy," he explained. "Since I moved in on you, you haven't had too much time of your own."

She smiled and shook her head. "I hadn't really noticed that it was an issue either." She laughed. "As a matter of fact, it's been kind of nice to have somebody who is also animal oriented and generally on the same wavelength to talk to."

"I get it," he agreed. "And your grandmother seems to be one of the good guys."

"Definitely one of the good guys," Miranda agreed. "And honestly, my parents are fine—especially when compared to yours. Mine just think that I'm wasting my life."

"Ah," he noted. "I've heard that a time or two."

"Right? But it's time for people to understand that we want different things than they want and that difference should be okay."

"In some cases, I don't think they'll ever understand," he stated, with a smile. "Although my brother, since he's having a family now, might want to reconsider having a pet. Don't all kids want pets eventually? Maybe Allen will come around."

"Not likely if his partner isn't animal oriented."

"I guess it's pretty important that you find somebody in life who thinks like you do, isn't it?"

"Absolutely," she stated. "Look at us. We do fine, but, if you married somebody who didn't like animals, then that would take the dogs out of your world. She'd demand that you choose her over them."

He winced. "I can't imagine the animals even tolerating somebody like that."

She burst out laughing. "The idea would be, from people like my parents, that you'd need to get rid of the animals."

"Well, that won't happen," he replied, then looked over

at her. His gaze twinkled. "You still didn't answer about coming to dinner with me that night."

"Am I coming as a date, coming as support, or coming to run interference?" she asked. "If it's running interference, I'll probably fail."

"Well, giving them the benefit of the doubt after all these years, I think we should just consider respecting who they are first," he explained. "That's all I ask of you."

"If you can do that, then I can do that," she admitted. Then she stopped to stare at him. "You still didn't answer *my* question."

"No, I didn't," he agreed. "I guess I'm looking to see what answer you would like."

"The truth," she said.

"Good. How about a date, running interference, and support?"

She stared at him, then her laughter rang free. "Oh my. That dinner reunion sounds like it'll be a heck of a time."

"It will be," he admitted, "hence the *support* part."

"Got it, and, in that case, I'm absolutely looking forward to it."

He grimaced. "You might change your mind about that part when we get there, you know."

She shrugged. "Well, I'll forewarn you now. I won't tolerate them badmouthing you, after everything you've done for me. So, whatever." She looked at the time. "Oh, crap, now we have about forty minutes until the Realtor gets here." And with that, they got to work.

As soon as Kyron saw a vehicle drive up, he told her, "I'll head over to the horses now."

She nodded, grateful that he was somebody who just helped and that he was quite capable of handling whatever needed to be done. She let in the two Realtors, surprised to see more than one, but the woman explained that they worked as a team and asked Miranda to give them a tour of the home. That took a good hour, as they walked through, talking about her reasons for wanting to move, which did not include a mention of her crazy neighbor.

Miranda explained about the animals' need for a larger place, so that launched a series of questions about what she was looking at buying, which she assumed was them looking to see if they could score another commission out of Miranda.

She just shrugged and explained it would depend on what she could get for this property and that she was prepared to move out of town in order to get more acreage.

With that, encouraged to know that possibly two deals were on the table, the Realtors did a quick assessment and said, "Look. We'll have to post some stats, other sales in this area and such to find the going market rate for similar properties," she explained, "but I would think that, given the market right now, you can expect quite a bit." She then specified a range that was way higher than Miranda had expected.

She stared at them. "Really?"

They nodded. "We think so, although the house needs a lot of work."

"I know," she admitted. "At its core, it's a good old farmstead. But, of course, I've been living here with many animals for a long time."

"Exactly, so, without repairs, the selling price could wind up substantially lower than that first estimate."

"Right," she stated, "but still, I need to know a ballpark figure to work with."

"But also, once we head down this pathway, if you get offers, you have to decide if you'll accept or not." They discussed the business terms further.

Miranda nodded. "Let me think about it." And, with that, Miranda escorted the Realtors to their vehicle. When the Realtors left, Miranda ran inside, put on her winter work jacket, grabbed a couple dogs, and headed toward the horses, wondering why Kyron still hadn't returned.

She called out, "Kyron, are you out here?" When no answer came, she looked around anxiously because she saw no sign of him. She pulled out her phone and quickly texted him, but still there was no response.

"Damn it, where are you?" she muttered, immediately turning to look at her crazy neighbor's place to see if he'd done anything. She glared in his direction and, not seeing Macintyre worried her more right now, as she raced down to the far side, hoping against hope that nothing bad was going on. When she got a little bit closer, she was tackled almost immediately and dropped to the ground.

"Stay here," he whispered. "Your neighbor has been outside, moving around with his rifle," he murmured. "He's already shot at me once." Her jaw dropped, and he nodded. "It's gonna get ugly."

"It already is ugly," she stated. "I can't even imagine trying to sell the place with that asshole around here making life difficult."

"Did they give you a price?"

She mentioned the range they'd given. "But they weren't prepared to commit to that without checking comparable sales and such, partly because of the condition of the house. They wanted to do some other assessments first."

"And that's also a typical real estate ploy to sign you up

at a higher amount, and then force you to commit to a lower price later," he stated, with a shrug. "Although, given the market right now, that actually doesn't seem like it would be a bad price."

"I would be thrilled if I could get that, but what if my crazy neighbor shoots at someone interested in the property? All my chances at selling this place will be doomed," she moaned. "But, even if he doesn't do that, even with money in the bank from selling this place, I still don't know that I can buy anything else because, if that's where the market is at on my acreage, then chances are I can't buy those additional acres that I need because it will be out of my reach."

"Which is also why you have to move out of town."

"Any property close to you for sale?" she asked. "Something like that would suit me to a tee."

"It's possible," he noted. "We'll have to take a look."

She nodded. "Well, obviously that's not happening while I'm flat on my back hiding from my neighbor," she stated, getting angry all over again.

He lifted his head and pointed. "It looks like he's heading back inside."

"So he missed you?"

"He may have missed hitting my body, but he did puncture my jacket."

She stared at him. "That's just unbelievable. How is that even slightly okay?"

"It's not," Kyron agreed. "And believe me. I'm heading off to my brother's right now. The chores out here are all done, so I want you to go inside and stay there, until I get back."

"Okay," she said, with a warning. "But you know that this just makes me want to sell all that much faster."

"So call the real estate people back and tell them to hurry up on the report because you've made the decision that you want to move forward."

"Will that make any difference?"

"It sure will. In this market, they need to make sure that they get it on the market fast and before another Realtor snags the listing."

"And what about the fact that there's not a whole lot to be done about the condition of the house?"

"You let the new buyers worry about that," he explained. "There's a buyer for every house. Don't ever doubt it."

She pondered that, as he hustled her back into the house. "What will you do?"

"I'm taking my truck, and I'm heading to my brother's," he told her. "But you can't go outside and don't open the door to anybody."

She nodded. "I won't. As long as you're not gone for too long."

"I won't be," he said, "but I do want to have a personal talk with my brother about this and show him my jacket at least. It's beyond stupid." And, with that, he walked outside to his truck and tore off on his own.

As she turned to look around, Beth stood up on the back of the couch, staring as he left.

"You've already bonded with him, haven't you, sweetheart?" Her tail wagged ever-so-slightly, but Beth looked over at Miranda, more warily than Beth looked at Kyron. "And I get it. He knows how to handle you. He knows what you're comfortable with, while I'm still in the dark," she admitted. "You're an animal in need, and I'm here for you, but obviously he can give you a whole lot more than I can." That explained a lot because Miranda had a ton of heart, but sometimes animals needed more than that. This was a prime example.

She headed into the kitchen, then phoned the real estate agent and asked them about a time frame. When they told her three to four days, she mentioned she might phone a couple other Realtors, since she was looking to get it to market as soon as possible. Sounding alarmed, they said they could get her an answer quickly.

"Well, that's good," she replied, "because I want to move things along." And, with that, she hung up. She figured she would get numbers back fairly fast. Then she wondered if she should contact somebody else anyway and get a second quote. With that idea in mind, she quickly phoned another company and asked for a fast assessment.

"Is there a rush?"

"Only if you're interested," Miranda replied, "because I may sign with another Realtor." And, with that, she hung up. They phoned back almost immediately, saying they could be here in an hour.

"Good," she noted, "and then how long before you get me the information I need in order to set an asking price?"

"We can do that right on the spot. We're already pulling comp reports for your area, so we'll have what we need."

"Good," she replied. "I'll expect to see somebody soon then." She continued to clean while she waited, knowing that it was one of the reasons that the other company had said an awful lot of work needed to be done on the house. She didn't know how good they were at seeing past everything or whether they even cared.

As long as they saw that they could sell it, that's probably all that was on their minds. In what seemed like no time at all, she watched the vehicle pull up. She led them in, walked them around the house, and discussed what her plans were. "Okay, so what is it worth?"

They immediately named a figure within the range the other Realtors had suggested. "What about the current condition of the house? Will that drop it much?"

"I don't think so," the one Realtor replied. "Right now the market is hot, and we've taken that into consideration. People are trying to get in at this price point all the time."

She nodded. "Interesting," she murmured. "How long before I can close on it?"

"It happens right at the same time, unless you want a special contingency. Is it because of the animals?"

"Yes," she stated. "I'll need to know ahead of time, as we'll need some time to move."

"Right, and do you have another place to go?"

"Not right now," she stated. "But I do have a place in mind where I could move the animals in the interim, while I find another place to buy." She smiled at that because the one thing she felt confident about right now was that Kyron would be okay with it.

"Good," one of the Realtors said. "In that case, we have a contract waiting. What do you want to do?"

"Let's sign and get this moving," she said on impulse. She quickly signed the documents.

The Realtor added, "We'll have a photographer in and get the photos posted online, hopefully within forty-eight hours."

"Well, I would like it sooner than that, if you can," she explained.

They nodded. "Are you prepared to drop the price to make a faster sale?"

"No," she stated bluntly. "I need every penny I can get

for the sake of the animals."

"Got it. We will see what we can do about arranging a photographer." And, with that, they left, and she stood here, wondering if she'd made a huge mistake. When her grandmother called not long afterward, Miranda admitted in a heavy tone, "I may have done a stupid thing." When she explained it, her grandmother's reply was gentle.

"You did what you needed to do," she stated. "That's all anybody can expect of you. Your neighbor is making life very difficult, and I don't understand why he's not in jail," she added.

"He took a shot at Kyron today."

"Oh, good Lord. I don't even want you there right now."

"Well, particularly right now, as I'm alone, because Kyron left to go talk to his brother about this latest shooting," she explained. "But, yeah, I want out. I want out now. The property's already too small. I just don't know what to do or where to go."

"Have a little faith," she murmured. "You said that Kyron has a really nice place."

"Yes, it's a great old place, and the best part is that it's at least forty acres," she stated enviously.

"Which is what you need."

"Exactly," she agreed.

"So tell me," and then her grandma hesitated.

"What?" Miranda asked.

"I just wondered what the relationship was like between the two of you."

"I really like him, but honestly, I hardly know him. I'm definitely not looking at his property as the answer to my problems."

"Of course not, but—"

"*No,* no buts. Now, temporarily could I board the animals with him? Yes, I suspect I could. However, beyond that? No, that's not happening."

"Right, but at least that gives you an option," her grandmother noted, with relief.

"Well, I'm hoping so, but he's not here right now for me to talk to about it, but I'm hoping that, since I helped him out with these two dogs, he will help me out as well."

"Sweetheart, he really likes you," her grandmother told her, "and the vibes between you two are positively humming."

"Sure, but that doesn't mean we're the kind of people who just pick up and move in together," she argued. "He's at a big transition point in his life, deciding what he wants to do next. Plus, he's still dealing with a lot of his family issues."

"As you are," she stated quietly. "And nobody is sadder about that than me."

"Maybe, but I can't help my parents to see anything in my life in a positive way right now. They're very determined to be completely absent."

"And maybe absent is better than negative at this point," her grandmother offered.

"Maybe," Miranda said, thinking about Kyron's family. "You could be right there, but, at the moment, it's much more important for me and the animals to stay safe."

"Absolutely."

"And I am terrified about having the animals outside now." She walked to the window, shuffling the curtains back.

"Well, Brant Macintyre is dangerous," her grandmother stated. "I wish Kyron hadn't left you there alone."

"He needed to," she replied, "and I've still got injured dogs and other animals to care for."

"Is he at least helping out?"

"Yeah, are you kidding? He filled the cupboards with food," she stated. "Which made me feel terrible because I haven't had much time to shop lately."

"Time or money from the looks of it," her grandmother replied severely. "Why didn't you tell me that it was that bad?"

"Because you've already helped so much," she replied. "At what point in time do I have to *not* rely on you for groceries?"

"When you're on your feet," she stated simply. "Do you think I want to see you suffer like this?"

"Well, hopefully if I can sell the house—"

"You still have to find another place," she responded.

"I know. I'm just not sure what to do about that yet. I just can't be this close to town with this many animals and feel comfortable about it. You know it'll just become more of a space problem here."

"Absolutely, and you've already had warnings from the city, haven't you?"

"Yes. I'm also in the process of trying to get the legal paperwork submitted to become a registered charity, but you know how that documentation is not all that easy."

"None of it is," her grandmother agreed. "But nothing worth doing is ever easy. It seems like you may have found a kindred spirit."

"If you mean Kyron, then, yes, absolutely," she said, with a smile in her voice. "Believe me. It makes me smile and sleep a whole lot better at night knowing that he's here, but I can't be dependent on him either."

Her grandmother sighed heavily.

"I can't, Grandma. He could get up and walk out at any time. In a matter of days, he'll be heading out to his place," she said, with a laugh.

"No, that's true. I forgot about that," she noted thoughtfully. "I don't know what he has there, but maybe you could move in and rent for a while."

"I have no idea about that either, but, if the money I get from the sale of the house isn't immediately tied up in real estate, it'll be way too easy to spend it, and then I won't have enough money to buy again."

"No, that's a good point," she murmured. "I have been talking to your great-uncle, but he hasn't made any decisions yet."

"I understand," she replied quietly. "And he needs to consider himself first. Plus, for someone like him, I'm probably just a crazy cat lady."

"Maybe," she agreed, "but he seemed pretty impressed with the work you're doing, and he was very unimpressed with your neighbor."

"Of course, but he seemed to hit it off with Kyron."

"That's because the two of them are servicemen," she said, with a laugh.

"Yeah, I suppose if a man would impress him, it would be another one just like him."

"Well, that's good. I'm glad something worked out."

And, with that, Miranda hung up, then walked around, cleaning up, doing dishes, and making spaghetti sauce instead of burgers with the ground beef Kyron had bought. It was a cold winter day, and, if there was something that she really enjoyed, it was a good spaghetti.

With that simmering away, she heard an odd noise at

the door. She hesitated and then walked to the kitchen door and opened it, and, sure enough, the back porch was empty. She closed it tight and said, "See, Miranda? You're just going crazy." But when an odd *mew* came, she returned to the door again to see a cat, not one that she recognized, coming toward her, dragging an injured leg.

"Crap." She bent down and picked up the small animal. It looked like a four- or five-month-old kitten.

"What happened to you, little one, and how did you find me?" She didn't understand how all these animals kept finding her. It was great that they did because they needed care, but it always amazed her that animals in need seemed to show up at her door. Just then she saw the fresh blood. Frowning, she checked it out and found a wound at the side of the leg. It was remarkably similar to the wound on Grace.

"Did he shoot you?" She gasped in horror. Quickly she brought the little cat into the kitchen and examined her under the light, her heart breaking at the sound of an animal in pain. She immediately dialed the vet. "Hey, I think my neighbor now shot a cat."

"Alive or dead?" he said, all business.

"It's alive, a kitten, and hollering pretty loudly."

"Of course it is. Bring it in," he said. "Let's take a look. I wonder when the hell the cops will stop this guy."

"I'm not sure," she replied. "Kyron's gone to talk to them because he was shot at earlier."

"Good Lord, this is terrible."

"Yeah, well, it isn't allowed, but, at the same time, the cops still need to stop this guy." At that, she looked up just in time to see Kyron pulling into the driveway. "He's back now, so I'll head down with the kitten." And she raced to her driveway, pulling on her coat and holding the kitten in a small cat bag.

Kyron took one look and frowned. "What happened?"

"I don't know for sure," she admitted, "but the wounds look remarkably similar to Grace's."

His frown deepened, and he swore. "He's really a loose cannon."

"He is, indeed. I presume your brother didn't say anything helpful."

"Another warning, basically they'll take the firearm from him if he continues to be a shithead. But, so far, there's only been misdemeanor charges or fines for hurting animals."

Miranda took off with the kitten, while Kyron remained behind to look after the other animals.

HATING WHAT HE'D just heard, Kyron raced into the house and headed back outside, finding the tracks of the kitten and where it came from. The blood trail was a direct line to the neighbor. At that, Kyron swore.

The neighbor came out with a big sneer on his face. "Hey, I'm looking for a kitten," he called out. "I thought you might have seen one."

"You mean, the one you just shot?"

"I wanted to put it out of its misery," he said, with a shrug. "After all, it was injured."

"*Injured* doesn't mean it needs to be killed," Kyron snapped, "and you're the one who injured it."

"You can't prove that though, can you?" he noted, with a laugh. Then he went back inside.

This was becoming an all-out war; yet, at the same time, his brother hadn't been very optimistic. As Kyron went back inside, he called Allen and replayed the conversation with his brother.

"A case like this is notoriously hard to deal with," Allen had said quietly. "You know that."

"I do know that," he stated. "I just don't understand why, when he's shooting at me, not just animals."

"That was a misfire," Allen replied.

"And he misfired at Miranda too? You know that's BS."

"I know it, and you know it, but, short of any kind of proof either way," Allen continued, "he's been given a warning. "If he does it again, that's a different story."

"And yet he had already shot at me and punctured my jacket," he reminded him, "as I showed you earlier." His brother went silent on the other end of the call. "But I guess you'll say that's just coincidence too, right, Allen?"

"No, I didn't say it was a coincidence in the first place," he said in exasperation.

"I get it. This is a really frustrating scenario for all involved, but mostly for Miranda and her animals."

"I guess he's just more or less completely fed up with so many animals. And, by law, she is not allowed as many as she has."

"So that gives him the right to shoot me?" he asked in astonishment.

"No, absolutely not," he replied. "Believe me. We'll take that very seriously." He hesitated and added, "Look. I'm not on duty today."

"Whatever," Kyron said, beyond irritated.

"I get it. It's personal to you. I'll call somebody on duty and let them know what's going on."

"It should be personal to you as well, since I'm your brother, Allen, but whatever." Kyron disconnected the call.

He had left his brother's place irritated, and now, after this follow-up phone call, Kyron was even more irate. He knew that telling Allen how the neighbor had shot a kitten wouldn't do any good, especially when the asshole next door was already saying it was injured, and he was trying to put it out of its misery. But Kyron felt like he was up against something even nastier than it seemed.

He walked over to the fence behind him, and the asshole neighbor stepped out and roared, "Leave my fence alone!"

"I didn't touch it." He shrugged. "I'm just checking to see if you're the pervy Peeping Tom type too."

Macintyre stared at him. "God, why would I even want to look at the ugly bitch who lives over there? The only reason I would want to see in there is to count the animals for when the city people come around next week to look into this mess."

"So, you really have no heart then, do you?"

"God no," he replied, "not for women like that and damn sure not for all those stupid animals. You mark my words. She's nothing but trouble." And, at that, he laughed and headed back inside again.

"Unless I make you pay," Kyron replied.

The guy stepped out and asked, "What was that?"

"I said, unless I make you pay."

"More threats?" he asked. "Don't worry. I'm recording all this."

"Good luck with that," he stated, staring at him. "You're nothing but a pathetic excuse for a man who's too scared to come out and fight properly."

"Well, I couldn't do that to you now, could I?" he asked. "You think I don't see how you limp? You're nothing but a washed-up loser anyway."

And, with that, Kyron laughed, then continued to check the fence boards. One fell off while he was checking to see how secure it was. And yet again, the man came out with his rifle.

"Get away from my fence," he yelled, his voice deadly.

"Well, it's not your fence. It's her fence, and I'm trying to fix it, in case you hadn't noticed."

But the guy wasn't having anything to do with that thought process. "Get away from the fence."

"Or what?" he asked, daring him. "You'll shoot me because we're fixing our fence?"

"It's not your fence. It's *her* fence, and you're the problem," the neighbor yelled. "Now that you're associated with her, nobody'll have anything to do with you."

"Really?" he snorted, staring at him. "Or maybe you know something I don't, but I have no reason to think that is true."

The guy stared at him, then slowly raised his rifle. "You know what? I just don't even care," he snapped. "I can just deep six you, and nobody will know."

"You don't think that Miranda will notice?"

"She'll find another sucker," he replied in a dark tone. "You keep pissing me off like this, and soon you'll be whining like that kitten."

"That's a pretty major threat coming from you," he noted. "The cops should be here any moment."

"Why is that?" he asked. "The little pretty boy here can't handle anything on his own?"

"You're the one with the rifle," he pointed out. "Come out here and fight like a man."

"Oh no. I'm not stupid enough to fall for that shit. Believe me. If I decide to take you down, I won't even tell you about it," he explained. "You'll just disappear in the night."

"Well, you can try," Kyron stated, his voice dark. "But this is a scenario that doesn't have any happy ending."

"Not for you, not for her, and sure as hell not for all those vermin over there," he snapped. "Maybe I'll just start with popping the dogs." And, with that, he raised his rifle and pointed at Beth, beside Kyron. But she was already on full alert. As she raced toward the neighbor, Kyron picked up a piece of ice formed at the base of a fence post, and he threw it hard, hitting the neighbor on the shoulder, jolting him backward. Then he stared at him, raised the rifle and fired at him several times.

By then, Kyron had already tackled Beth, who couldn't get through the fence, and the two of them were huddled up against the wood. But Kyron also knew that wooden fence was no protection at all, once the bullets started flying. He realized just how much this man hated Miranda and how miserable he'd been making her life. This was no way for her to live. He looked down at Beth and recognized the sound deep in the back of her throat, although very low and almost silent, was borderline deadly.

"It's okay, girl," he said quietly. "It's okay." And he hoped it was okay, though he wasn't sure, because the situation was escalating down a pathway he did not like in any way, shape, or form. When he heard a door slam on the other side of the fence, he cautiously took a look through the fence slats and noted that the man had gone inside. He immediately phoned his brother and told him what had happened.

"Shit," Allen said. "Did you have to set him off?"

Kyron stared down at his phone. "Did you just say that *I* set him off?" he repeated, immediately frustrated and angry.

"No, I didn't mean it like that," his brother replied. "Damn it. It just seems like, since you came back to town, we've had nothing but trouble with him."

"No, actually she had already contacted the cops several times, but you guys didn't do anything."

"Because it wasn't that bad," he added.

"What do you think now?" he asked, beyond angry. "Is it bad enough? Or is it all on me because I came into town and got this guy pissed off at me. You could be right," he snapped, "but I'd like to think that that the local law enforcement gave a bigger shit about what was going on already, regardless of me being back in town. I get that you don't want me here. Believe me. I know. You didn't stick up for me when I was a kid, and you won't stand by me as an adult," he spat. "But don't you worry. I won't be bothering you again. Tell Sandra that I won't be back because of you and your parents." And, with that, he hung up.

He sat here against the fence, trying to figure out what his options were. If he were on a mission, and that asshole was the enemy, Kyron would have taken him out in a heartbeat, but he wasn't doing that line of work anymore, and this was not a war zone, even though this guy had turned it into one. But Kyron apparently couldn't expect anybody to come and help him. Obviously the cops would show up at some point to warn the neighbor again, maybe to even slap a fine on him, but that would not stop this guy.

Macintyre was out for blood now and unfortunately it wasn't just her blood, it was his and every animal on the property.

And with that thought, he realized that everybody needed to come in from the fields, yet how the hell would he do that? There just wasn't enough room for everybody in the house. And what about the horses, the llama, the goat?

Swearing, he walked over to the barn and checked on the animals there. So far, everybody was fine, but, if this guy decided to get even more violent, set everything on fire? That would be a whole different story. And what Kyron didn't want was for her to sell the property and have nothing left of the house to sell. He didn't even know if she had insurance to cover everything that could happen at her place as it was.

She needed out, and she needed to get into a much better situation. And, of course, his mind immediately leaped to his place. Making that decision, he headed out to his rental truck, took a look, and realized that he would need stock racks in order to move any of the larger animals. He wasn't even sure that the larger animals were part of this asshole's ire. And, as much as Kyron hated the idea of backing down, he knew he needed to do something to take this down a notch. If he couldn't go in and finish the damn thing, he needed to drop it down to where she wouldn't be in danger when just coming outside to feed the animals.

Just then he thought about Miles. He phoned his old friend and asked, "Hey, do you know anybody who moves livestock?"

"Yeah, I do. What's up?" Then Kyron quickly explained what was going on.

"Oh, is that Old Man Macintyre?" he asked. "That guy's crazy when he goes on a deep bender. Then he's fine for a while, until suddenly he goes on a bender again, and all hell breaks loose."

"Well, he's already shot at both Miranda and me more than once. Plus, he's shot at least one dog and one cat, which we've taken to the vet to save them. At this point, I wouldn't put it past him to burn down her place, all while he has a For

Sale sign up in his yard. Like he can't get rid of her and her animals quick enough. The man is crazy," Kyron noted. "So, I figured, if I could move the animals somewhere safe, it might calm him down."

"Wow, that's something I didn't expect to hear from you," he said, with a laugh. "Let me call my guy."

A few minutes later, Kyron got a phone call back from a stranger.

"Heard you need to move some livestock. What have you got?"

Heading back into the barn, Kyron stated, "A goat, a llama, and three horses in the field at the moment, plus lots of dogs, cats, and barn cats. I have a place to move them to, some acreage just out of town," he explained. "Don't know what Miles told you, but I'm quite worried about the crazy neighbor shooting at us and the animals."

"Yeah, I hear you," he replied. "Let me come have a look." About twenty minutes later, a vehicle pulled up, towing a large trailer. As the guy headed out to talk to Kyron, the neighbor stepped out and watched.

"Is he the one causing trouble?" the guy asked.

Kyron nodded. "Yeah, and we're not talking just a little bit of trouble but a lot of trouble."

"Well, it never does any good to get yourself into trouble with somebody like that," he noted. "That old man looks pretty damn crazy in the eyes."

"I know. It's apparently been going on for far too long, and the cops aren't doing squat."

"Well, if you care about the animals," he stated, "then you'll have to do something about it."

"Well, my first thought was to get them out of here into a better situation."

The man looked around and noted, "Looks like it's pretty cramped here anyway."

"I know. She's just listed the place for sale, so she can try to find something bigger. But I've got a place with forty acres just out of town," he explained.

"Yeah, forty acres would do it," the guy with the trailer said. "What do you want to move first?" As he walked around the barn and checked out the field, he added, "You know what? I can take pretty much most of these smaller animals at one go, if you want."

"Yeah, let's take everything from the barns and the bulk of the dogs," he replied. "I'm not sure what to do about the horses though."

"I can't take them all together anyway," the guy noted, "because I don't have enough compartments in the trailer. But we can move everything else, come back for the horses." And, with that, since most of the animals from the barn were fairly tame, he got everything loaded into the big trailer.

Kyron gave the guy the address, in case they got separated, and then loaded up as many dogs as he could fit in the rental truck, which ended up being nine, leaving both Beth and Grace behind. Kyron drove up to his property, with the trailer guy not far behind, and unloaded everybody into the one pasture that had a barn, then put all the dogs in the house.

Hating to leave them, but not really having any choice, he paid the driver and said, "This is for the first load. I'll need your help to get the horses and the llama out."

"Not a problem," he said. "You want to do that now?"

"You know what?" he noted. "We probably should." They headed back, and, as they pulled in, he pointed at the horses in the back field, adding, "Those are hers too."

At that, the truck driver nodded and agreed, "She definitely needs more space."

"Yeah, and she needs to get away from guys like this asshole." And, with that, they started to load the horses. When the cops showed up and asked what was going on, Kyron looked over at them and said, "Wow, you show up now that we're moving horses, but not because of the guy who's been shooting at us?"

"What guy?" one of the cops asked. "What are you talking about? Who is shooting?"

Kyron stared at him, dumbfounded. "Why are you here?'

"I'm here because we got a report that somebody was stealing horses and livestock."

"Well, that call probably came from the crazy neighbor right next door," he said, pointing at the man staring at him from the window. "I'm moving them because he just threatened to kill them all, so you may want to get the whole story before you put too much value in what he has to say," he explained. "And if you hadn't heard about all the rest of the bullshit going on here, it's probably not even worth your time."

"Now hang on a minute," the cop replied, getting angry at him. "I don't know what you're talking about, but we take theft of livestock very seriously."

Kyron stopped, looked at him, and asked, "Are you kidding me? This guy's been shooting at both people and animals here. He's shot at me. Twice. He's shot at the woman who owns all these animals, threatening to kill every one of them and us. He's already shot a dog and a cat, which we've taken to the local vet, but you're concerned because he says that we're stealing her livestock?"

The cop just looked confused. "Are you serious? He's been shooting at you guys?"

"Yeah, the fence back there is freshly peppered with his latest shots. And he put a bullet hole through my jacket. Just take a look." He turned to show the cop. "Believe me. He's half corked." It was obvious the cop didn't know what to do.

"Look. My brother is a cop," Kyron said. "He can bring you up-to-date. Call him." And, with that, the guy took one look at him in surprise and then stepped back and phoned him. When he came back, he said grudgingly, "Well, he did confirm your story, but I still don't have any proof these are your horses."

"They aren't mine. They belong to Miranda, and she's down at the vet's, getting treatment for the cat Macintyre shot earlier," he repeated, bringing up her phone number.

When she answered, she said, "I'm coming. I'm on my way home now."

"Yeah, but not fast enough," he snapped. "I've got the cops here, but you won't believe why."

"*Uh-oh*, what's going on?" When he told her what he was doing, she gasped, followed by silence.

"Yes, I should have asked you," he admitted, "but this crazy guy has now threatened to kill every animal on the place, right after he shot up the back fence, while Beth and I were on the other side of it." Kyron turned to face the cop, who was listening anyway. "Your fence is now riddled with bullet holes, and I already know the cops don't give a shit," Kyron added, glaring at the one in front of him. Then he turned around and told Miranda, "so I'm moving everything up to my place, so we could solve the problem from there. Besides, if the place is empty, it will be easier to sell."

"I don't even know what to say, but *thank you* is a huge

part of it."

"I know. I took an awful lot on myself, and I should have phoned you first," he said, reaching out to brush the hair off his face.

"I'm almost there," she stated. "Tell the cop that I've got paperwork to prove ownership."

Kyron put his phone away, turned to the cop. "She's almost here, and she's got paperwork for all these horses."

The cop looked relieved. "That's good, good to know."

"Yeah, of course it is," he said, with a head shake.

"Look, man. We don't know about a lot of these problems until people tell us."

"And then when we do tell you," Kyron interjected, "you don't do anything anyway. Obviously you guys don't give a shit, and this guy can shoot whoever he wants, until there's an actual death, is that how it works?" Kyron snapped. "At that point in time, I'd like to think you'd actually care, but I don't know. Even after talking to my own damn brother, I get the feeling you guys just get comfy up in your nice little offices and nobody gives a crap about what happens out here in the real world."

"That's not true," he said. "Honestly, it's not."

Kyron didn't even answer. As her vehicle raced toward them, he realized it was her. She hit the brakes hard, pulled up on the side of the road, then walked over to the trucker, took one look at the horses, reached out to pet them, and smile at them. "You guys will be just fine." As soon as they were loaded, confirming who was here, she turned to the driver.

"Looks like you'll have to make more than one trip just for the horses. If you know where you're going, go ahead and take off." And, with that, the truck driver nodded over at the cop, then hopped into the vehicle and drove away, leaving the cop standing there, his jaw wide open.

"Hey," he said, "I came here to investigate those horses being stolen."

"Well, they're not being stolen," she snapped, in a hard voice. "They are mine and are being moved for their own safety, after being threatened by my crazy gun-shooting neighbor, which I assume you've already been told about. If you'd like to step inside the house, I have all the paperwork there."

He nodded and followed her inside. At that, Kyron walked around and checked the fences. Once all the horses have been moved, there was still all the hay, which would be a pain in the ass to move, but they would need hay today, so he moved several bales and started throwing it into the back of his truck. Then he went back, remembering the pallet of dog food they had just moved as well. *Now we have to move it all again.* He groaned but started lifting and tossing. By the time the cop came to find Kyron, all the cop did was nod to him and took off.

Miranda came over and noted, "We don't have to move it all right now."

"No," he began, "but I also didn't want to leave too much of it behind in case your neighbor really goes off the rails."

"I can't believe there isn't anything we can do about it," she muttered.

"I'm afraid he'll just snap and be even more dangerous," he muttered.

"Maybe," she said, taking a long deep breath. "I don't even know what to do at this point with the old coot and all the problems he's creating."

"I'm sorry about all that. And I agree. Anything we did, no matter what, seems to enrage him because he's an angry asshole to begin with. My gut instinct was to just get out of here, but I wouldn't leave the animals behind to be slaughtered."

She gave him misty smile, then gave him a hug. "You did the right thing," she said and stepped out back and shook her head. "Wow, you got the goat and all the others already?"

"Unless I missed somebody," he said. "I wanted to move enough hay to get us through a couple days. We can come back tomorrow to get more and the same for the dog food."

She added, "I have a ton in the house to move too."

"And that's a whole different story," he noted. "It might be way faster if we could get a local moving company or even a couple kids to give you a hand."

She stopped and stared. "There's just so much to even pack up," she noted, the weight of it all suddenly slowing her down.

"Remember though. This time you're not alone." He reached out and touched her arm.

Smiling, she reached back and added, "And you're not either."

CHAPTER 12

BY THE TIME Kyron and Miranda got the necessities loaded up in his truck, he asked Miranda, "Look. Do you know how to get there by yourself?"

She nodded. "Although I might have trouble finding the driveway," she noted cautiously. "Why?"

"I'll take this load up and come back."

She nodded. "Go ahead, while I start loading up in my truck, and what about Grace?" she asked.

"We'll take her with us in our last load tonight," he stated. "So no animals get left behind." And, with that, he hopped in the vehicle and took off. She had to admit that it was really high-handed, moving everybody at the same time, but he'd taken action when action was needed, and there was an awful lot to respect about that. Then she started loading things into the back of her truck, more dog food, cat food, cat beds, cat cages, carrier cages—the list was endless. The neighbor stepped out, took one look and sneered.

"Moving out, are you? Good," he spat, "good riddance."

She was pissed off, but she knew better than to engage a crazy person with a gun. He was dangerous as hell, and she didn't want anything to do with him. But what she did allow herself the pleasure of was turning around and secretly giving him the finger. Then, with a smile, she headed back into the house and grabbed more stuff. She kept it up for another hour, and, before she realized it, she turned around, and Kyron was back. He smiled as he stepped inside the house and asked, "Hey, how's it going?"

"It's going," she huffed out. "At least I think it is. I don't know if I'm making any progress. It just seems like an endless job."

"It is in many ways," he agreed. "What about the neighbor? Any trouble?"

"Yeah, he came out once and told me good riddance."

"Good enough," Kyron said. "Let's see if we can get more of this stuff loaded, and then we'll call it a night. I'll take both dogs in my truck, after we're all loaded." And, just as they went to get more, an odd sound came from the back. He looked at her and then broke into a run. She raced behind him.

There was Beth standing at the back door, growling, her hackles up. And, in the backyard, near the house, the neighbor stood there, his rifle in his hand.

"That's my dog," he said, with a roar. "You goddamned thieves. You don't get to steal my dog." He raised the gun and fired at Kyron's feet. Making a running tackle, Kyron grabbed the rifle from his hands, threw it over the fence, then took his fists to him.

Miranda pulled him back. "Easy," she said, "we can't kill him."

Kyron swore, as he stepped back. "Are you sure?" he asked. He picked up the old man in a fireman's carry, then shoved him over the fence to the other side.

"Now stay the fuck on your side," he yelled. "We're doing our best to stay out of your life, so you stay off ours." The old man groaned, picked himself up, and walked slowly back to his house.

"I don't like the sounds of that at all."

"No, I don't either," he agreed, "but it's geared at us, not so much at the animals at least."

"That doesn't make me feel any better," she whispered.

"I know. Come on. Let's finish packing up," he said.

"We won't get anywhere near finished," she noted, feeling stressed.

"No, I know," he agreed.

She noticed that he was moving slowly and looking stiff and sore. "Are you okay?"

He stopped, took several slow deep breaths, and nodded. "Yeah, I'll be okay. I'm just really tired."

"Do you think he'll be able to press charges against you?"

"Well, that would be interesting," Kyron noted. "I'll bring in a lawyer if it comes down to it. He can't just stand there on your property—or his for that matter—and fire weapons at us. I take offense at that," he said in a hard voice.

Then he went back and grabbed more dog food. She watched, then started packing paperwork and other things that she might need for the animals. Bringing the rest of it outside and grabbing some clothes, she suddenly thought about food for her and Kyron because absolutely none was at his place. With that in mind, she headed to the kitchen and looked at the spaghetti sauce. "And I made such a great spaghetti sauce for dinner," she moaned.

"Well, we need food there anyway, so let's take it. He grabbed a few empty boxes that she had lying around. "Let's fill these with food. At least enough for the moment. We'll grab more later." She nodded, and together they went to town, packing up food from her kitchen.

One of the last things he did was carry out the big covered pot of spaghetti sauce and put it on the floorboard on her truck. They had as much as they could fit for this trip, so he headed back in to get Beth and Grace. He carried Grace out, even though she was struggling in his arms, and, when he laid her down in the back seat, he told Beth to hop up to be with her. The minute she did, Grace immediately calmed down. He smiled. "A blind dog. That'll be a new one for me."

"I can't even imagine," she replied. "Do we know that for sure?"

"No, we don't," he noted, "but, from what I'm seeing, that makes the most sense."

"We'll let Doug check it out to be sure, but I don't even know how he'll do that. It's not something I've ever dealt with. I haven't had a chance to even talk to him about it either," she added.

At that, he stopped and looked at her. "What happened with the kitten?"

"She needs stitches, and they're keeping her overnight," she replied, "mostly because everything in my world is such a nightmare."

"I'm sorry about that," he said.

"Yeah, you and me both," she replied. "I have to go to work tomorrow at my regular job too. The water pipe has been fixed and all the water mopped up."

He winced at that. "Well, at least I'll be at home to take care of the animals," he added, "so not to worry about that."

"No, maybe not," she agreed, "but my life is a mess right now. It was bad before, but right now, knowing that I'll be homeless, that won't make anything in my world happy."

He stopped, stared at her, and shook his head. "You won't be homeless. I get that this happened really fast, but we don't dare stick around here and have things continue to escalate. Let's deal with this problem regarding safety first, keeping all the animals safe, including us," he stated, "and the thing is, you'd already decided to sell, and your neighbor is just pushing it forward."

"I know," she admitted, "and you're right. It's something that needs to happen regardless of him. Though I still can't believe he's being such an asshole and that we're in danger of losing our lives and all the animals."

Kyron smiled, gently nudged her under the chin, and said, "Come on. Let's go." And, with the two vehicles in a convoy, they slowly headed back down the road.

KYRON WATCHED THE whole way to make sure that Miranda followed him, and she did, although she seemed to be going a little bit slower, but then she had a full load, and it wasn't tied down and all that stable. As they got closer to his place, he gave lots of warning for the turn with his signal blinking early and then pulled into his driveway. Remembering the hay and feed in the back, he backed up toward the side of the house, unloaded dog food onto the porch, then moved some hay out for the horses. He had no clue where water was located here and knew that would be a problem they would need to solve right away.

Swearing at that, he went around to the other side of the house, noting a very big water trough, but, with the freezing temperatures, he had no idea how that worked. Happily, a hose stuck through the deck, and, when he tested it, turning it on, to his surprise there was water, so he immediately filled the trough. With that taken care of and a smile on his face because something had actually worked, he unloaded the rest of his truck and then headed over to help with hers. When he got to where she was unloading food, he smiled. "I don't know about you, but I'm damn tired and looking forward to a hot meal."

She nodded. "I hear you there." The fatigue in her voice was extensive.

"You know what we didn't think about?" he asked quietly.

"What?"

"Bedding."

She winced. "Well, let's hope Granddad left something, at least for the night," she replied quietly. "Other than that, as long as I can get warm, I'll be fine."

He nodded. "I'm sure we'll find something here." Then finally, with the rest of the food unloaded, they headed in, and he locked up the trucks and made sure everybody outside was safe for the night. "Now I really have work to do on the place," he muttered.

"What do you mean?" she asked, as she put the spaghetti sauce on the stove and grabbed the big pot she had brought, filled it with water, and put it on to boil for the pasta.

"Well, the horses will need shelter," he explained. "You have barn cats, but my barn is not in very good shape. Plus we need a place to store feed. Once you start thinking about it, the list just goes on and on."

She stopped and looked at him worriedly. "I'm sorry. This is adding pressure to what could have been a much more leisurely project for you."

"Honestly, it's okay. It's giving me something to think about and a direction to go."

"I get that," she noted quietly, "but it is hard for me to

understand that you could just pick up and do what you did."

"I'm just so grateful that, in that moment, we had a place to bring them." Then he walked over, looped his arm around her neck, and gave her a gentle hug. "And you did great today."

She snorted. "I didn't do *great* at anything," she argued. "It's just been a bloody nightmare for far too long."

"Not everybody has a neighbor from hell," he murmured.

"Or cops who don't give a shit," she added, with a sigh.

"So one of the problems is that you're in violation of the city bylaws or something?"

"Of course I am," she stated. "What am I allowed? Four animals per property?" She shook her head. "Hence the need to try to get things a little more legit and, of course, move outside the city limits."

"Well, we'll go back tomorrow and clean out some more stuff," he reminded her. "Or I can, while you're at work."

She closed her eyes and winced at the reminder then nodded. "You think it's safe here?"

"Yes," he said, "I do."

"I actually wondered if we were being followed," she told him.

He stopped and stared at her. "When?"

"On the road. A couple times I slowed down to see if the vehicle would pass me, but it didn't. It just slowed down with me."

"But then with the winter roads," he suggested, "that makes sense for anybody out there in a way."

She nodded. "I was thinking of that too, so I don't really have a conclusive answer."

"But you're afraid it was your neighbor?"

"I don't know." She stared at Kyron, the nightmare still present in her gaze. "I really don't want to hear you say that out loud."

"Hiding it won't make it any easier," he noted thoughtfully. "I guess, for the moment, I'll sleep in the living room."

"Why?" she asked.

"Because I'll sleep lighter, knowing that there could be something going on later."

"I hope not," she said. "I really hope not."

"Me too, and we can hope for that, but we don't want to be caught unprepared, especially tonight. We're exhausted, and our reaction times are slow, and we have a lot of animals that aren't optimally arranged yet."

She winced at that. "Exactly," she admitted quietly. When the pasta was ready, she quickly served up dinner, which they made short work of. Putting down her fork, she looked at him and said, "I really need to crash."

"And you will." He nodded. "Let's take a quick glance upstairs and see what there are for sleeping options." And, once they'd checked it out better, for living here purposes, they found that the spare bedroom was still made up, although it was probably dusty as hell.

She said, "I don't care about dust. I'll survive either way. But, right now, I need to crash anywhere." And she dropped to the bed, atop all the dust, in all her clothes.

He could also see that she was damn close to tears, and he felt bad for his part in that. He walked out, left her alone, and headed downstairs.

Looking at the boxes of food in the kitchen that they couldn't put away because the cupboards were already full of things that were probably ancient, he felt his shoulders sag.

Then his phone rang, and he looked down to see it was Badger. "Well, your phone number is a sight for sore eyes," he answered quietly.

"What's going on up there?" Badger asked. "You sound terrible."

"It's quite the story. Do you have a lot of time?"

"Yeah, I do. What the hell is going on?"

And, with that, Kyron got a glass of water and proceeded to tell Badger the whole saga.

"Holy crap," he replied, "and the city is doing nothing about it?"

"No, they aren't, and that's just adding to the problem. For some reason they don't seem to see Macintyre as a viable threat."

"But that's BS."

"I know."

"And your brother, the cop, what about him?"

"He's no better than the rest. In fact, we had quite a dustup on the phone earlier," he explained. "I highly doubt he's even thinking about me, and, if he is, it's not good because I called him out."

"I'm sorry about that," Badger replied. "I had no idea we'd be sending you back into a war zone."

"I'm still just stunned that something like this could be happening right in the city with nobody to back her up," he moaned quietly.

"So, where are you now?"

"Years ago, I inherited a property here from my grandfather," he told Badger, "so I basically reopened it today, and we're hiding out here."

"What happens if this guy finds you?"

At that, Kyron winced. "He may already have. Miranda

was afraid we were being followed as we drove up."

"Crap," Badger said. "Do you want me to contact the local authorities?"

"Unless you know somebody you trust and who trusts you and who will believe you when you tell him that this is for real," he complained, "it won't do any good. We've already had more than our share of trouble, and I think we're just being labeled as troublemakers."

"Well, I'd rather see you labeled as troublemaker than dead," Badger said bluntly.

"And the War Dog's is doing fine, by the way," he shared.

"Good, I'm glad to hear that." There was a note of humor in his voice, as he added, "This isn't quite the way we expected this mission to go."

"No, I'm sure you didn't, but sometimes things are just more of a headache than anything imaginable in this weird wonderful world of ours."

"And you sound exhausted."

"Yeah, I need to crash, but I also need to stay awake."

"And that won't work," Badger noted. "Why don't you crash for a couple hours, and I'll call you back in about two and make sure you're awake again. Is it daylight there?"

"It is still for a little bit, yeah."

"So you've probably got a couple hours before anybody'll make their move."

"And, even at that, I can't guarantee it," he muttered.

"No, but, in the meantime, I'll see if I can find somebody we know and trust in your town. We did have another case close to there."

"Well, it sure as hell isn't my brother," Kyron snapped, "and you have no idea how it pains me to say it."

"Have a little faith. He's probably distracted. He's got a pregnant wife, thinks you're exaggerating maybe. I don't know. He's probably listening to the other guys in the force too."

"Well, that could be it, I suppose. It's not in his actual jurisdiction, and maybe he's thinking I'm asking for favors." Kyron snorted. "I'm not. I was just hoping for fair treatment, but apparently that doesn't happen here."

"Ease up and get some rest, while I'll see what I can do." And, with that, Badger rang off.

Kyron laid down on the couch and was asleep almost instantly. When the phone rang again, he woke up instantly, and Badger said, "This is your two-hour wake-up call."

"Good enough," Kyron replied, yawning. "I'll get up and take a look around and maybe do a little reconnaissance walk."

"Only if you have somebody with you," Badger noted. "Otherwise you're leaving yourself open as a target."

"I know," he admitted, "but I don't want this guy to come in here and burn us alive either."

At that, Badger sucked in his breath. "The fact that you're even thinking along that line freaks me out a little bit."

"I know," Kyron agreed, "but do I think this asshole is done? No way in hell. And the little bit of a beating he took at my hands is something he won't forget easily."

"And you just had to do it, didn't you?"

"Yeah, I sure did. Assholes peppering me with gunshots like that can't be allowed to continue," he clarified quietly, "and, in this case, it was long overdue. He was brazen enough to be on her property, shooting at Beth, then at me."

"I won't argue with you there," Badger murmured. "I

will call you again in two hours."

"What about you? Are you getting any sleep?"

"If somebody needs me, you know I'm there," he replied, his tone brisk. "You stay safe now." And again, he rang off.

CHAPTER 13

WHEN A HAND shook her awake, Miranda bolted upright and stared around in a panic.

"It's okay," Kyron said gently. "You were having what sounded like terrible nightmares."

She stared at him and then slowly sank back into place. "Yeah," she agreed. "I get those when I'm stressed out." She yawned. "What time is it?"

"Midnight," he replied.

"Is that all?" She was shocked enough that she reached for her phone and double-checked. "Wow. I was really out too."

"And you can go back to sleep again," he suggested. "I just didn't like the sound of the nightmares."

She smiled at him. "Once again you're back to that really nice guy persona," she said, with a smile. "Because, you know, nightmares happen."

"They do, but they don't have to happen all the time," he replied quietly.

"So, what about you? Have you had any sleep?"

"I slept for a few hours on the couch, after telling my boss everything that's been going on. He'll see if he can find somebody trustworthy within the local department to talk to."

"Yeah, is that even a possibility?" she asked, shaking her

head.

"He seems to think so. But me? I don't know at this point." He added, "I heard you crying from downstairs."

"I'm sorry," she said, feeling embarrassed. She looked up at him. "That's only slightly mortifying."

"Don't apologize. If you need to cry, you're fine," he replied. As he sat here, they steadily looked at each other.

She finally explained, "It's about an emotional release after all this crap, not that I don't want to be here. Did I tell you how much I appreciate this?"

"Yes," he confirmed, with a smile. "And no, I don't want anything for it. You've done plenty helping with Beth and Grace and letting me stay at your place. I feel bad for having taken the move on myself, without checking with you first."

"Well, I would have just diddled and dawdled, frozen with indecision, not knowing what to do," she admitted, with a frown. "That always makes me feel wholly ineffective. Especially when I see a man of action at work, who just makes a decision and goes forward."

"Stop worrying about it," he said. "It's all good."

"Says you, but I think I'll have to call in sick tomorrow," she noted. "Just way too much is going on in my world."

"Would that be a problem?"

"I don't know." She frowned. "Not likely, though it's always crazy busy and stressful. I've been there too long in a way because it's hard to leave," she explained, "but I should. I mean, it doesn't pay nearly enough, and yet it pays the basic bills. And now, with everything upside down, I don't know where I'm at."

"Well, a little bit of routine won't hurt you right now," he murmured. "Keep that in mind."

"No, you're absolutely right there," she agreed. "A routine would help actually," she stated, "but I'm so tired."

"Go back to sleep," he murmured. "Come on. Get back under the covers again."

"What will you do?"

"I'll go back downstairs and relax."

"But what about sleep?" she asked.

"Not tonight," he said. "I want to make sure that, if somebody was following you, it wasn't him."

She stared at him. "You know that's why I told you," she confessed, "because I was afraid it was him."

"Nobody likes getting the crap beaten out of them," he confirmed, "and, if he wants revenge, it could be exactly what he's looking for, a location to come in and whip my butt."

"But he won't though. He'll shoot you in the back, when you're not looking."

"And that could be," he noted quietly. "That really could happen with the crazy old coot, so I'll go down and keep an eye out." And, with that, he smiled and said, "Now go on back to sleep."

"How am I supposed to sleep after that conversation?" she complained.

He shrugged. "Because you have to go to work in the morning."

"No, I don't think so," she argued, but, as she laid back down on the bed, she thought about it. "The trouble is, I need the money."

"Yeah, I know," he agreed, "so one step at a time, and, either way, you need some sleep." And, with that, he headed downstairs.

She tried to relax, she really did, but when she heard an odd sound downstairs, she immediately sat up, and looked around. They had put Beth and Grace in one room locked up together. For the first time, she wondered if that was actually sensible. The neighbor had been shouting about them stealing his dog. And maybe Beth had been at the neighbor's place for a few days, after he'd found her or captured her or whatever, but he wasn't entitled to own this dog, and that was something he wouldn't be happy about either.

As she listened intently, her ears straining for any noise, she heard another weird sound, something like the single creak of a floorboard.

She rose to her feet and quietly reached the top of the stairs. It was a house that she didn't know, so how was she to discern the difference between the noises of an old house settling or trouble? That would drive her nuts all night.

Swearing to herself, she headed down to the first landing. Ahead of her on the ground floor was a shadow, a shadow with a long rifle raised, pointing at the living room couch, and just as she watched, the rifle fired, and then there was a laugh. With her heart in her throat, she softly headed back upstairs and opened the door to the dogs. They had put all the animals in various rooms for the night.

Beth was already there at the door, glaring at her in the darkness. Miranda whispered to her, "I don't know what to do, sweetheart, but, if he finds us, we're all dead," she noted. "You'll probably do better on your own, than being a sitting duck like this. But leave Grace behind, and I'll do my best to keep her safe." With that, she let Beth out and shut the door to leave Grace behind in the bedroom.

Now what she had to do was get downstairs and see if that asshole had actually shot Kyron. Her heart just ached at the thought that such a good man could have been shot down in the darkness like that. She couldn't imagine her crazy neighbor would have gotten the drop on Kyron, but she couldn't take a chance. Creeping back down to the first landing, she heard the man swear.

"Where the fuck are you? What the hell?"

She smiled, realizing that Kyron must have set him up. And now she was likely to be in the way. At that, the gunman raced toward the stairs, and she tripped, trying to turn around.

"There you are, you little bitch," he yelled, "but you won't be for long."

The sound of the rifle cocking came first, and, when the pain slammed into her leg, she cried out, grabbing for the railing, to hold herself up as she tried to climb higher up the stairs. He started up the stairs behind her, his gun raised, but just as he was about to shoot her a second time, a growl came from the top of stairs, and she looked up to see Beth standing there, her teeth bared, glaring at the man who stood behind her.

"Easy girl. He'll shoot you," she warned Beth. "Run, go on now, please run!"

The man behind her laughed. "Well, there she is, bitch number two," he snarled, as he raised the rifle and fired, but Beth was already in motion. As she sailed over Miranda's head, she landed right on the old man, the two of them going back down the stairs, the rifle firing harmlessly in the air. Almost immediately she heard Kyron's voice in the background, yelling at her. She couldn't even make out the words over the din caused by the growls, the shrieks, and the screams, not to mention the cacophony of barking from throughout the house. And she could not even begin to do anything about any of it.

As she struggled to move, the pain took over, and she felt the chills settling in. Almost as if in slow motion, she slid down, until she sat on the stairs, falling over ever-so-lightly.

Then everything went black.

KYRON SHOUTED COMMANDS at the dog, who was already in a bloody frenzy, momentarily confused about another potential target to go for. Kyron finally got Beth to listen, and she realized it was Kyron, her handler of sorts, pulling Beth away, shuddering and yelping, with blood pouring from her mouth. "Stay."

Kyron walked over to the old man on the ground, who was screaming and groaning. Kyron pulled out his phone, and, just as he went to dial 9-1-1, Badger called.

"I need an ambulance," he barked into the phone, "and I need somebody here who actually can handle this nightmare."

"I've got somebody coming," he replied. "Who's hurt?"

"The asshole neighbor who came into my house with a gun just shot Miranda," he stated, hovering over him, as he realized the old man was no longer able to do very much, so didn't pose a threat.

Moving quickly up the stairs, he assessed Miranda's condition. "She's taken a bullet to the upper thigh," he told Badger, "and is unconscious on the stairs."

"I've got both heading your way," Badger replied quietly. "The man coming to help is Jacob, Jacob Luis."

"I don't care who he is," he snapped, rubbing his face with his free hand. "She's so cold."

"Just sit tight and keep talking to her," Badger said.

"You know how important that is. You know all this, Kyron. Just let your training take over."

"If I'd have done that earlier, I'd have taken out this asshole on the first day," he snapped.

"How's the dog?"

He couldn't help but smile at Badger's very narrow focus. "Beth ripped into the old man."

"Ouch."

"Definitely, but, at the same time, Beth also saved Miranda's life because he would have fired a second shot."

"Hopefully that will help in this case," Badger noted.

"Well, I will fight tooth and nail if somebody decides that Beth has to be put down because she's dangerous," he snapped, his tone hard. "Beth is many things, but I don't consider her dangerous. She was forced into the role of protector, and she did her job. And, after what Miranda has been through with this asshole, with cops who didn't do anything about it? Believe me. I will spend every penny I have to make sure that we finally get some justice here."

"I'll back you on all that," Badger said calmly. "This dog has been through hell, and yet this isn't even the family who ditched her."

"No, but we'll finally get the story behind what happened," Kyron noted, "assuming the asshole lives."

Badger hesitated and asked, "Will he?"

"Yeah, more's the pity," Kyron acknowledged. "Unless he has a heart attack on the way or something."

"Though it would be a colossal hassle, it would be better in some ways if he didn't survive," Badger theorized, "because you guys could use some closure."

"Yeah, no good answer there," he noted. "I hear sirens now." He checked Miranda again for a pulse, then raced down the stairs, still on the phone to Badger. "Lots of flashing lights are coming down the driveway now." Then he saw that his brother was coming in too. "*Great.* … *Now* my brother decides to show up."

"He actually comes highly recommended," Badger noted, "but, given the circumstances, I chose not to call him."

"Well, I'm glad to hear that. I already told him that this Macintyre guy was a loose cannon who had fired at both of us, not to mention the animals, and Allen told me that the bullet hole in my jacket was insufficient proof."

"Sounds like there's an awful lot of history between you two."

"Yeah, and he just made a whole pile more."

"Maybe he needs to see the damage for himself this time," Badger urged. "Keep your cool and an open mind. Let me know what happens and if I can help." And, with that, he hung up.

As the police and paramedics came into the house, Kyron met them.

"I've got two down," he told them. "The one at the bottom of the stairs is a dog attack. And one up the stairs is a gunshot wound."

At that, his brother stepped up. "Who's been shot?" he asked sharply.

"Miranda," Kyron snapped, looking bitterly at his brother. "She is the woman I told you about. Her asshole neighbor is the one who's been chewed by the dog," he added.

"Is that dog dangerous?"

"No," he spat, his tone hard. "Unless you're coming in here with a gun raised, shooting the woman who saved the dog."

At that, one of the paramedics stepped in. "Listen, man. I'm not afraid of dogs, but somebody must have opened a door and let some out or something. An awful lot of animals are in here all of a sudden. Cats too. Can you help us out?"

"Oh, Jesus, sorry." He moved as many of the dogs as he could, and he quickly herded them and put them away again. He realized the cops probably went door to door, clearing the bottom floor, unwittingly releasing all the animals. He stepped out to find Miranda being loaded onto a gurney already.

"She'll be okay," the paramedic shared. "It's a through-and-through gunshot wound. The shock probably knocked her out, not to mention the loss of blood."

Kyron just nodded, as he stood here and watched as they loaded her up. "And what about him?"

"He'll live too," the other paramedic added, "although some of his injuries look pretty severe."

The old man glared at him. "I'll sue your ass."

"That's fine," Kyron said. "You'll have plenty of time to work on your case from prison. As far as I'm concerned, it's attempted murder, you asshole. You're looking at twenty years to life."

The old man's eyes widened.

"Not to mention stalking, breaking and entering, animal endangerment …"

"What the hell are you talking about?"

"You shot Miranda," Kyron yelled. "You deliberately came into my house, armed with a weapon to kill her. I won't have to worry about you suing me," he noted. "We'll take that house of yours right out from under you."

At that, Macintyre protested. "No, no, no, no, I didn't shoot anybody."

"Yeah, you did. You came close to shooting her yesterday, and you shot at me on at least three different occasions, once hitting my jacket, not that anybody else gave a shit about that," he snapped to the local cops.

"Yeah, and I would have taken you out if I could have," the asshole declared loudly. "I don't know what the hell you did that it hit your jacket and not you. That was a good shot."

"A good shot at my *back*, you coward." Kyron stared at him.

The old man grunted. "Who cares? You're young and strong. You beat me to a pulp as it is."

"After you trespassed onto her yard and started firing at the animals, then firing at me," Kyron snapped. "You're damn right I beat you to a pulp, and now I'll make sure your ass stays in the slammer for the rest of your life."

"I haven't got too much life left anyway," he said, coughing and spitting out blood.

"Maybe not," Kyron noted, "so we'll make sure we get the lawsuit filed fast, then collect on the damages you inflicted on her."

He stared at him. "You can't do that." Still protesting, he was taken out to the ambulance.

Kyron looked around at the cops milling about, then he asked, "Which one of you is Jacob Luis?"

One man's hand went up.

"You're the one who I want to talk to," he said. "The rest of you guys step outside." His brother immediately protested, but Kyron shook his head. "No. I gave you a chance to do the right thing. More than once. I'm not talking to you about this right now. Or probably ever." And, with that, he slammed the door in his brother's face.

Jacob looked at him. "Hurt feelings?"

"I went to him over being shot at by this asshole, even showed him the bullet hole in the *back* of my jacket, but he told me that anybody could have fired that shot."

Jacob frowned at that and nodded. "You also need to understand that Miranda has been investigated for too many animals many times."

"Yes, all as a result of this same neighbor complaining," Kyron replied. "But I'm not talking about that right now. That man came onto my property, entered my house, and he shot her."

"Don't worry," Luis said. "I hear there's a lot of history, but we can get to the bottom of it. Now do you want to start from the beginning?"

Kyron scrubbed at his face. "Yeah, but we don't have enough hours."

"You'll make time," he said. "Now sit."

By the time they were done, it was nearing four o'clock in the morning. Kyron stared at his watch and groaned. "I have about two hours before I need to deal with the animals."

"Well, I'll head home myself," Luis replied. Just then his phone rang. He listened intently, while Kyron barely paid any attention. Turning to Kyron, he stated, "Your girlfriend's okay. They've got the bleeding stopped and have her all cleaned up, and she's now sleeping comfortably. The other guy will live as well, but we'll keep him locked up."

"Well, if you don't," Kyron snapped, "and he comes back onto my property, I will put an end to this myself."

Jacob gave him a hard look. "I wouldn't let anybody else hear you say that."

"I don't give a fuck," he replied. "I'm done fooling

around, and I'll stand my ground with the police force in this town if you're all going to be assholes. The way Miranda's been treated is terrible," he spat, "but it'll be a different story with me."

Jacob nodded. "Don't worry. There'll be an investigation into that issue as well," he noted. Then he headed for his car, Kyron watching.

Another vehicle remained out there, and Kyron looked over to see his brother sitting in an oversized rocking chair on the porch. "What are you doing here?" Kyron snapped.

"I came to apologize," Allen replied. "Well, I came to help, but I stayed to apologize," he admitted. "Listen. I thought you were making a big deal out of nothing. I'm sorry."

"And you thought I manufactured evidence or something and shot up my own jacket?"

"I don't know what I thought," Allen admitted. "But sitting here, I just realized that you've moved back to the property Granddad gave to you, that I was never included in."

"Ah, *never included in. Right.* Do you think I don't know that your parents gave you the bulk of the cost of your down payment for your place?"

His brother's eyebrows shot up. "Oh, … yeah, I didn't know that you knew it was that big."

"I knew because Dad very quickly let me know it was a gift to you, his favorite son."

"Dad's an asshole," Allen said immediately.

"I'm surprised that you even recognize that."

"Look, Kyron. I'm not blind to who they are. I'm not blind to the fact that I'm their favorite or to the way they treated you," Allen admitted. "What I don't want is for that to poison things between us. We used to talk. We used to be friends."

"I don't know about being friends, back then or now," he said, leaning against the door. "What I can tell you is that I'm way too tired to be dealing with this shit."

"Yeah, so, while your defenses are down, maybe I can actually talk to you then," he said. "I get that you hate me for our childhood."

"I don't hate the childhood you had," he replied sharply, his arms crossed over his chest as he stared at his brother. "I had a shitty childhood."

"It was a shitty childhood, and I can't say that it was terribly fun being on the other side of that either."

"*Boo-hoo,*" Kyron replied. "What a horrid childhood you must have had, being the favored son."

Allen took a moment, then continued. "I'm sure it never even occurred to you, but it wasn't that easy knowing I was the favorite and watching them treat you like that. As for me, I was jealous because you had Granddad's interest. You were out here with him, and I knew there was no way in hell I would ever have that same relationship, so I kept looking after the one with our parents," he explained. "As a kid, I was just trying to survive."

"Got it," Kyron said. "You wanted your parents' *and* Granddad's total attention. Why? Because I couldn't have anyone in my life? Don't bother trying to explain. Honestly, I don't hold anything in the past against you. It wasn't your fault that you were the favorite, and why wouldn't you like it? You were coddled and spoiled. I was the hated one, but I had Granddad, and eventually that's all I needed. Granddad left me this place, and, since you've got your place from your parents, as far as I'm concerned, we're even."

"This is worth a hell of a lot more money," he said, with a raised eyebrow.

"Wow. See? Now that I can hold against you, the supposedly grown-up brother now. So it's all about the money? Are you mad that you chose your parents over Granddad, so you could have the bigger payday if you had chosen Granddad instead? Well, remember this. You'll get everything that your parents have to leave anyway."

"Maybe." He shrugged. "But I know they are looking forward to seeing you."

"*Right*," he snorted. "I canceled that farce of a dinner with you already. Now, with Miranda in the hospital, we definitely aren't coming. She's been up against enough negativity already from her own family, and I sure don't want to subject her to any more of that crap from my supposed family."

"Why would you think it would be negative?"

"Oh, I don't know," he snapped. "Mostly because how negative your parents are where I'm concerned."

Allen raised both hands and sighed. "Look. How about if we push it back for a couple weeks?"

"No."

"But that will give Miranda time to recover a bit."

"No, Allen. Deal with your wife. Tell her how you screwed all this up. Don't make it about me."

Allen shook his head. "You can see how you feel about it by then, but it would be nice if we could all meet together, under cordial circumstances. Kyron, they're getting older, and, while I won't promise they'll be any nicer," he explained, "maybe you could meet them and greet them as equals? If nothing is worth salvaging there with the parents, just walk away, but I would really appreciate it if you wouldn't walk away from me, my wife, and our child."

"I wasn't planning on it," Kyron began, raising one finger, "*until* I talked to you and realized that Miranda really wasn't getting the support or assistance due any citizen of this town, much less a woman I care a lot about. I won't intentionally hurt Sandra while she is vulnerable. But don't you dare ask me to worry about hurting Sandra's *feelings*, when you don't give a shit about Miranda getting *shot*."

"I'm not sure it was a case of nobody helping her, but maybe it wasn't taken seriously."

"*Nobody* helping her? No, *you* weren't helping her. That is BS, and you know it."

"Well, now I do, most definitely."

"After he shot her!" Kyron glared down at his brother. "God, is that the only way to get your attention?"

Allen bowed his head. "And I'm really sorry for what happened tonight."

"Not good enough. Too little, too late. That asshole Macintyre needs to be put away," Kyron muttered. "What if your son grows up and lives next door to a crazy gun-toting bully? Do you want him to be treated the same way you've treated me and Miranda? Do you want your own son to feel like second best when it comes to his father too?"

His brother winced at that. "I want to be a better father to my son than our father was to either of us." Allen swallowed loudly. "Honest, I would have done anything to have avoided this with Macintyre. It's absolutely BS that this was allowed to happen, and I know there'll be a hell of an investigation about it."

"Maybe." Kyron shook his head. "But will it be enough to avoid something like this in the future? Say, by the time your son owns his own home?"

"It will," Allen said, more firmly this time. "That's the thing. We need to look at what happened and why and do better. I can't leave here with you so mad at me."

"Yeah, you can." Kyron turned on his heel.

"Kyron," he called out again, "I'd like to be a better brother to you, while I learn to be a better father to my son." After a long moment of silence, Allen added, "And I think I need you to help me do both." He reached out his hand again, waiting for Kyron to take it.

"Don't know how many times we can do the whole *fresh start* thing," Kyron muttered, but he shook his brother's hand.

"One at a time," Allen said, with a wry grin. "Thank you, Kyron. Hopefully I'll be a fast learner." And, with that, he turned and walked away.

Kyron then turned and looked at Beth, who stood guard inside. He walked over, opened the door and bent down in front of her, and said, "It's okay, girl."

She licked his face, and her tail wagged. Trying to avoid dealing with the blood on her and all over the stairwell, he led her upstairs and opened the bedroom door, where she could go join Grace.

Then he walked over to the bed that Miranda had slept in and crashed. He didn't even get a full two hours' worth of sleep, but more than one hour would make a hell of a difference right now. Closing his eyes, he slept.

CHAPTER 14

MIRANDA OPENED HER eyes and stared, looking around her, seeing a dozing male on a chair beside her.

"If you're here looking after me," she murmured, "who's looking after the animals?"

His eyes opened, and he smiled at her. "Well, it's been two days," he explained, "and they're settling in nicely."

Her eyes widened. "Surely it hasn't been two days."

"Yeah," he repeated, "it has. You surfaced and slept, surfaced and slept, then pretty well just surfaced and slept again," he replied, with a smile. "As soon as you're cleared by the doc, I can get you home again."

"That would be nice," she muttered. "But wow, that was not exactly how I expected to get out of work for a day or two." Then she remembered. "What about Macintyre?"

"Well, he's an inmate right now. He's been charged with attempted murder and other counts, including breaking and entering, unlawful use of a weapon, discharging a weapon, attempting to injure, animal cruelty, making false reports to 9-1-1, and *blah, blah, blah, blah,*" he stated, with a wave of his hand. "The bottom line is that he's not getting out anytime soon."

"Well, thank God for that," she murmured. She moved cautiously and then nodded. "So, am I on some good drugs, or am I not too badly hurt?"

"Both probably. You aren't badly hurt, considering you were shot," he stated, "and plenty of good drugs, no doubt."

At that, she laughed. "Well, I really would like to go home and call my poor bosses ..."

"As long as you know that *home* is at my place," he replied. "And I spoke to Doug and Brian, whom Doug told me about, so you're clear for as long as you need."

"Huge news," she replied, "at least for the moment."

"You know what? I'm totally okay if you want to stay there for a long while," he admitted. "I really want to get to know you a hell of a lot better."

She laughed. "And here I thought we were in the course of doing that already."

"We were, and we got interrupted," he clarified, with an eye roll.

She smiled. "Sometimes we just have to take things as they come."

As it was, several days later, she was home, walking in the front door, greeted by all the animals, as Kyron tried desperately to keep them from jumping up on her bandaged leg. And, sure enough, by the time she made it to the couch, everybody was all around her, trying to get hugs and cuddles. When it calmed down enough, she smiled and looked at him. "Now this is a homecoming."

"It is, indeed," he agreed, with a smile. He immediately brought over a cup of tea and a sandwich.

"Wow, did you have this all ready?"

He nodded. "Yeah, I had everything prepped and ready in the kitchen, so that, when you came home, we could just sit down and eat."

"Sounds good to me." She picked up one half of the sandwich and started munching. "Is everybody settled in?"

He grinned. "Yep, the horses are happy. Everybody seems happy."

"What about the Realtors? Anything happening there?"

"I don't have any way of knowing," he noted. "You'll have to check your phone and your emails."

She nodded. "Well, I listed it with a second group of Realtors," she told him, "but I haven't even checked this one out. Honestly, I kind of forgot about it."

"Go figure. You get shot, and some things just aren't as important as before."

Smirking, she pulled out her phone. "Would you look at that?" She wiggled her phone at him. "Apparently I have an offer."

"You're kidding," he said.

"They told me that mine was a good property and should sell fast, but I don't know about this."

"It depends on what the offer is," he noted. "Does it say?"

She looked at him in surprise. "Oh, right. Actually there are *two* offers. Maybe more," she said. "I don't know. … A lot of emails are here. Maybe I should just give them a call."

"Maybe, or maybe you should rest and do it later."

"That sounds good too," she agreed, yawning, "although these may have a time frame."

"Yes, but look. You're already yawning."

"I am." She yawned again and nodded. "But this is really good news, and it would completely relieve my stress if I have legitimate offers that could go forward."

"That would be awesome," he noted. "So you do what you need to do. I'll go make more sandwiches." And, with that, he got up and went into the kitchen. She quickly phoned the real estate agent and discovered that three offers were pending. After they summarized the details for her, it was easy to pick the best one. The Realtors would send over the paperwork shortly.

When he returned to the living room, she smiled broadly. "Full asking price, plus ten thousand."

"Sounds good to me," he murmured. "Congratulations." He sat down beside her and passed her a second sandwich.

"I didn't think I was hungry," she said, taking a bite.

"Well, I am," Kyron admitted. "So, if you don't eat it, I will." Then he quickly munched through his own.

She looked over at him and smiled. "I'll need a nap soon."

"Naps are allowed," he noted. "You've got all day to relax. All week for that matter. Or all month, as far as I'm concerned."

"Yeah, I don't even know how long I have off from work," she stated. "I'll have to phone my bosses too."

"You can, but you could first just ask your doc how long you should be off that leg to allow it to heal, without ripping apart the stitches. Either way, you don't have to do that right now either."

"No, I don't," she agreed. As she finished eating, she looked at him and asked, "How about a hand going upstairs?"

"Absolutely," he said, then helped her stand up slowly. He carefully led her to the stairs, and, when she was halfway up and faltering, he scooped her up and said, "This will be easier. We should have just put you in the downstairs bedroom to begin with."

"No, this is fine," she said, yawning.

"I'll come back up and check on you in a little bit."

"Or you could just lie down with me for a while," she

suggested.

"I could do that too." He pulled back the blanket, gently placed her on the bed, then covered her up, and laid down beside her. When a bark came from the threshold to bedroom, she looked over and smiled. "Come here, Beth." And the dog raced over, giving her a huge welcome.

When a second bark sounded, Miranda softly called, "Come here, Grace. Come on." Grace took several tentative steps forward, with Beth back at her side, guiding her along. "She really is blind, isn't she?" Miranda asked Kyron, studying Grace's face and those blue eyes.

"Yeah, she is," Kyron confirmed.

Miranda gave both dogs a cuddle, and then they headed over and laid down at the end of the bed. "How long before she'll get to know where she's at?"

"She'll be doing fine real soon," Kyron said. "With Beth around, Grace is already going up and down the stairs."

"That's awesome," Miranda replied. She laid here quietly and then added, "My leg is a hell of a lot better."

He snorted. "A bullet went clear through your leg and out the other side. A lot of healing has to happen."

"And I've got painkillers," she stated, with a broad smile.

"Well, I'm glad to hear that. I don't want you hurting."

"I was wondering," she began, "what your plans are."

"Well, the plans are to get you back on your feet in due time, to help you look after the animals, and to figure out what I want to do with my life. In the meantime, fix some fence, you know, feed animals, feed you." Then he repeated, "And feed you again, and then feed the animals again."

She burst out laughing. "Okay, I got the message. Are you seriously okay with me staying here?"

"Absolutely," he said, "and we have lots to do still at

your place."

"I know." She groaned.

"But maybe we can hire someone to help get you moved out of there."

"I still have to find another place too."

"And"—he placed a finger against her lips—"you can stay right here, and we can figure all these things out."

"What are we supposed to figure out?" she asked, her eyes twinkling.

"How we feel about each other," he stated. "Everything is happening so damn fast."

"I know," she murmured. "So fast. I hadn't really expected that."

"Neither had I, but I'm totally okay to run with it," he admitted. "Nothing like almost losing you to prioritize things in my life quite nicely."

She smiled. "You didn't almost lose me."

"Yes, I did," he argued. "You got shot. I have been in enough war zones and seen enough people shot to realize that life is short and can be fragile. If I want to enjoy what time I have on this planet," he explained, "I need to get busy making the most of it."

"I like the sound of that too," she agreed, looping her arms around his neck. "Did I hear you tell my great-uncle that you were a Navy SEAL?"

He nodded. "Absolutely."

"So I guess you're good at figuring things out, huh?"

"Absolutely. Why?"

She pulled him down closer, kissed him gently. "So, if I wanted to take this to the next level …"

His eyebrows shot up. "We'll wait until you're fully healed," he murmured immediately.

"And if I don't want to wait?" He frowned, and she grinned at him. "See? I like that about you," she said. "You don't want to take advantage, and yet here you are, trying to figure out a way to make it work."

"Well, I could make it work," he stated, "but the chances of injuring you are still pretty high."

"I'm willing to take the risk."

"I'm not," he snapped.

"Yes, you are," she whispered, her hand sliding down his chest.

"We have lots of time."

"We do, but you know what? Like you just said, coming so close to death, it brings things back into perspective that I had forgotten."

"And what's that?"

"That I have to look after myself as well," she admitted. "Not just the animals, although they will always be a huge priority in my world. But I also need to look after me, and a part of me needs to feel alive, … right now," she whispered. "I need to feel whole and renewed."

"That's a low blow," he muttered, nuzzling her neck. "Because, damn, you know, with an injury like yours …"

"Nope, no excuses," she replied.

He rolled over, pulling her with him gently, both now at the edge of the bed.

As she came down onto his chest, she raised her eyebrows. "Oh."

"Well, this leaves it entirely in your ballpark," he stated, nodding toward her bandaged leg hanging off the bed. "If you think you can sit up, just using one leg?"

"Oh, I can sit up." She smirked, and sure enough she could, pushing off his chest with her hands, letting her injured leg dangle off the bed, her foot on the floor, just as he'd arranged it. She had to smile. "You know something? I think I can get used to having you around."

"Well, I hope so," he replied, "and I'm hoping you can get used to it for more than just a day or two."

"Oh, I'm pretty sure I can," she stated, as she lifted the T-shirt over her head. "Not only that, you're just really handy to have around."

He picked her up, sat her on the side of the bed and stripped her down to nothing but her socks. Then, as he stood before her, he stripped down too.

"Like you're *seriously* handy to have around," she noted in astonishment. Then stopped as she saw his prosthetic, as her gaze roamed onto the scars crisscrossing his belly. An odd one close to his chest. She reached out a finger and traced the one there. Her bottom lip trembled.

"Easy," he whispered. "I'm fine. It was bad at the time, but I've healed, and it's all good." He reached down and lifted up her chin. "Unless it bothers you."

She stiffened, glaring at him. "Yes, it bothers me. It bothers me that you were hurt. It bothers me that you went through so much trauma, and I wasn't there. It bothers me that the world is such a mess that you were forced to serve at all, and this is the reward you got."

He sat down beside her and pulled her into his arms and just held her. After a moment she leaned back and grinned up at him. "Of course it makes for an interesting body that I plan on taking lots of time to explore."

He laughed. "I'm glad to hear that because I really don't plan on going anywhere for quite a while."

"Good," she murmured. As she opened her arms, he laid back down on the bed, where she could once again get back into position. She stared at him. "Do you realize I've never actually had anybody let me be on top?"

"Why on earth not?" he asked in astonishment.

She shrugged. "I don't know. I guess to them maybe it was a control thing or dominance or just no imagination."

"You just haven't been with the right men," he replied instantly.

"Oh, I'll have to agree with you there," she noted. "They couldn't have been the right men because they weren't you."

He smiled, then pulled her down closer and whispered, "I think you're talking too much."

She realized his rather large erection was growing between the two of them. She gently wiggled against him and said, "You're right. I could definitely be thinking about something else right now."

He pulled her down and kissed her gently. "But remember—"

She placed a finger against his lips and said, "No, we're fine. I'm fine. I feel no pain right now." Then she kissed him gently. However, it turned into a growing passion, as all the locked-in emotions she'd been holding back were released. When she lifted her head again, his eyes had crossed.

"Okay," he muttered. "You really need to have your way with me now."

She burst out laughing. "I absolutely adore the fact that we can laugh at a time like this. I really appreciate that."

He pulled her down and kissed her again, and she realized that was another hint. Smiling, she kissed him deeper, her hands gently exploring his ribs, his belly, his hips. But, when she wrapped her hands around his erection, he groaned beneath her, his hips bucking up against her. She slid back and forth along his shaft, teasing him, teasing her until she couldn't stand it any longer. Then shuddering, she sat back up, and using her hands and her good leg, braced herself until she could slowly lower herself down. She finally reached the point where he was seated deep within her.

She threw her head back and asked, "Do you know how to ride?"

"Absolutely," he said. "Do you?"

"Let's see," she replied, her voice smoky.

"Then ride, sweetheart, ride for all you're worth."

And she did, taking them both through a crazy crest, before tossing them both over at the same time, and finally collapsed against his sweaty chest. "I'm so glad we did that."

"You and me both," he whispered. "Now would you please go to sleep?"

WHEN KYRON REPEATED the question, he realized Miranda was already sound asleep against him. Murmuring against her head, he slowly shifted, so she laid on the bed beside him, but she was on top of the blankets. He picked her up, pulled back the bedcovers with one arm, and softly laid her down, then climbed in beside her.

He smiled and whispered, "You are something." And, with that, he just held her close for a long time.

When Badger sent a text, asking if everything was okay, Kyron sent a heart emoji and added, **Everything's better than okay.**

When the question mark came back, Kyron softly chuckled, not wanting to wake up Miranda, and sent back a message saying, **Just something I hadn't expected. I'll explain later.** And he left it at that.

But he knew Badger would enjoy everything Kyron had to tell him about this K9 mission. As he looked down at the woman at his side, he realized that something he had never thought would happen actually had happened, and he was so damn happy about it. Life had never looked so good.

EPILOGUE

BADGER READ THE text and looked over at Kat. "Wow, look at that," he said, holding up his phone, showing the text message of the heart emoji.

"Ah, looks to me like we have another happy success story. It just blows me away that it's happening time and time again." She smiled, looking over at him.

"I know. So who do we have next?"

"You want me to look?" she asked.

"Yeah. Do you know anybody who needs rescuing?"

"I don't know about rescuing, but I have a case that's driving me crazy."

"What do you mean by a case?"

"Somebody who isn't adapting well to his prosthetics because he's pushing them too hard," she admitted.

"What's he doing?"

"Tons of outdoor hiking, survival-type stuff," she noted. "He's all over the board. He brought me back one of the latest titanium prosthetics that was damn near broken." Badger stared at her in shock. "Well, he's also big," she added, "and I guess I hadn't made quite enough allowances for that."

"How big?"

"Six feet six," she replied, "and I suspect, with both legs, he would be somewhere around two-sixty."

"Right." Badger nodded. "That's big. Does he like dogs?"

"I can ask him."

"Sure, ask away. What does he do for a living?"

"He's ex-navy," she stated. "Why?"

"Because I don't have anybody around here to recruit. We've pretty well tapped out all our resources, at least for the moment, though we always have new guys coming and going. But you know what? We do have another missing War Dog."

"I could ask anyway. He seems to keep himself so busy because he has nothing else to do."

"Does he know anything about dogs or about horses, cattle, or anything else like that?"

"Why?"

"Because it sounds like this War Dog was taken to a cow ranch in Kentucky," he explained.

"What happened to it?" she asked, astonished.

"Nobody knows. It just disappeared."

"Coyotes?"

"Not likely," he said.

"Is this dog injured?"

"No, it seemed to be healthy, but, according to everybody we've talked to, it just vanished."

"You don't sound like you believe that."

"Nope, I sure don't. Not if the dog was well treated."

"And, of course, that's the trick, isn't it?" she stated. "Not only do you have to find sincerely good people but you also have to find someone the dog bonds with."

"I'm thinking that, in this case, we have a problem because the wife died, and the dog was basically bonded to her."

"Of course, and now the dog is dealing with yet another loss."

"Exactly," Badger agreed. "I need somebody who'll give the dog an outdoor life."

"Well, maybe my client would be a good fit," she suggested. "I can ask him."

"What's his name?"

"Jake," she said. "No wait." She stopped and reconsidered that. "Jenner. It's Jenner."

"Not a problem," Badger said. "Give him a call." She grabbed her phone and called him. He sounded surprised to hear from her. "Have a question or two," she stated. "I know you're really active outdoors, but I just wondered if you ever had any experience with dogs."

"Of course," he said. "Why?"

"My husband has been dealing with some of these retired K9 War Dogs. I think I told you about that."

"Yeah, I heard something about it. So, what's up?"

"A dog in Kentucky went missing, and we were sitting here brainstorming, trying to find somebody willing to make a trip up there to take a look for the dog."

"Why Kentucky?" he asked, his voice hard.

"The dog may be at a cattle ranch there." She hesitated and asked, "Is that triggering something for you?"

"Yeah, … my ex-wife is there."

"Ah," Kat replied, "so I gather you're not the right person for this job."

"I don't know," he stated. "What's involved?"

"Well, no money for one thing," she noted. "I can tell you that."

"I don't need money," he said quietly.

"I know. It's one of the reasons why I thought about

you. We just need somebody to go see what happened to the dog. I mean, if it died or something, that's one thing. Or if it's been adopted by somebody else and is happy, that's all good. But if it's suffering out there somewhere, we need it brought into a better situation. You mentioned your ex-wife. What kind of scenario did you leave behind?"

"She didn't like military life and chose somebody else instead," he noted quietly.

"Ouch, I'm sorry."

"Yeah, me too," he said. "I haven't spoken to her since."

"Maybe it's time to make peace?"

He hesitated. "Maybe, … not exactly what I was thinking I would be doing."

"No, but how do you feel about a dog in need?"

"That," he replied, "I would do in a heartbeat."

"That makes you the right man for the job then," she stated. "I'll pass you over to Badger now. And by the way," she said, before she handed the phone over, "What is your wife's name?"

"Laura," he said. "Why?"

"*Huh*, that's a nice name."

"She's a nice woman, or at least she was."

"Are you sure she remarried?"

"I don't know," he replied, "but she divorced me pretty damn fast."

"Maybe she just needed to know that you would come home one day."

"Well, I did, and she wasn't expecting it. Or maybe she was afraid I'd come home in pieces, like I did," he admitted, his voice even harder.

"Pieces that you've been working really hard at putting back together," she added.

"Yeah, but, as you know, nothing is perfect about any of it."

"Nothing is perfect in life at all," she reminded him. "It's all about progress."

"Well, if I can help a dog, I'm happy to," he said. "Besides, it'll stop me from going crazy. I'm kind of growing tired of all the hikes."

"That doesn't sound normal for you."

"No, I know," he admitted. "I guess maybe I'm just missing something in life."

"Yeah," she agreed, her voice soft as she whispered, "You're missing Laura."

"Doesn't matter if I'm missing her or not," he snapped. "She made a choice, and it didn't include me."

"Maybe you need to go see *why* she made that choice," she added, her intuition kicking in.

"Maybe," he admitted. "If nothing else, it'll be good to call it quits, to look at my past, and to move forward again," he noted. "For that reason alone, I should probably do this. I'll do it because I need to," he added, "but I'll enjoy it because I get to help an animal. That makes it worthwhile to me."

And with that, she said, "Good enough, now here is Badger."

This concludes Book 15 of The K9 Files: Kyron.

Read about Jenner: The K9 Files, Book 16

THE K9 FILES: JENNER (BOOK #16)

Welcome to the all new K9 Files series reconnecting readers with the unforgettable men from SEALs of Steel in a new series of action packed, page turning romantic suspense that fans have come to expect from USA TODAY Bestselling author Dale Mayer. Pssst… you'll meet other favorite characters from SEALs of Honor and Heroes for Hire too!

Heading to Ashland, Kentucky, where his ex-wife's family lives, is not in Jenner's plans anytime soon. But, given a War Dog is potentially in trouble, well, Jenner will even face his past. Arriving at a small bed-and-breakfast, he meets a woman more interesting than anyone he'd met in a long time. His job to find this missing dog seems like a long shot, until he learns about the B&B neighbor's son and his pack of dogs, who have been scaring Kellie …

Kellie loves her bed-and-breakfast establishment, as much as she loves meeting new people, particularly when she doesn't have a great relationship with many of the locals, who judged her harshly for a past mistake. Determined to enjoy life regardless, she tries to move on but finds it hard to leave her past behind. And now there's her neighbor …

Having Jenner around makes Kellie feel more secure and gives her hope that maybe good people still exist in this world. Yet, before they can truly move forward, there is a canine issue, … and a neighbor with something else on his mind …

Find Book 16 here!

To find out more visit Dale Mayer's website.

http://smarturl.it/DMSJenner

Author's Note

Thank you for reading Kyron: The K9 Files, Book 15! If you enjoyed the book, please take a moment and leave a short review.

Dear reader,

I love to hear from readers, and you can contact me at my website: www.dalemayer.com or at my Facebook author page. To be informed of new releases and special offers, sign up for my newsletter or follow me on BookBub. And if you are interested in joining Dale Mayer's Reader Group, here is the Facebook sign up page.
https://smarturl.it/DaleMayerFBGroup

Cheers,
Dale Mayer

Get THREE Free Books Now!

Have you met the SEALS of Honor?

SEALs of Honor Books 1, 2, and 3. Follow the stories of brave, badass warriors who serve their country with honor and love their women to the limits of life and death.

Read Mason, Hawk, and Dane right now for FREE.

Go here and tell me where to send them!
http://smarturl.it/EthanBofB

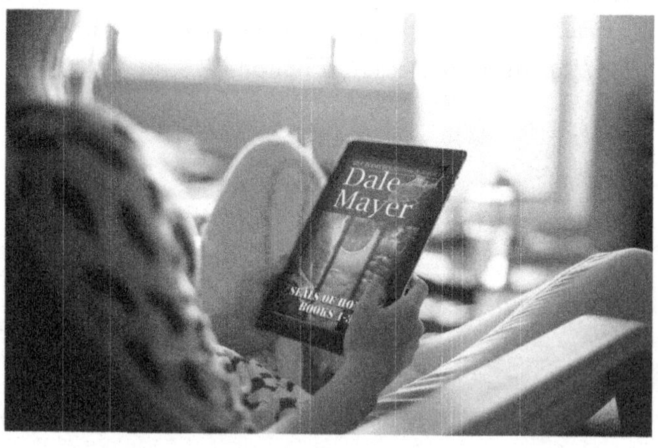

About the Author

Dale Mayer is a *USA Today* best-selling author, best known for her SEALs military romances, her Psychic Visions series, and her Lovely Lethal Garden cozy series. Her contemporary romances are raw and full of passion and emotion (Broken But … Mending series). Her thrillers will keep you guessing (By Death series), and her romantic comedies will keep you giggling (*It's a Dog's Life*, a stand-alone novella; and the Broken Protocols series, starring Charming Marvin, the cat).

Dale honors the stories that come to her—and some of them are crazy and break all the rules and cross multiple genres!

To go with her fiction, she also writes nonfiction in many different fields, with books available on résumé writing, companion gardening, and the US mortgage system. She has recently published her Career Essentials series. All her books are available in print and ebook format.

Connect with Dale Mayer Online

Dale's Website – www.dalemayer.com

Twitter – @DaleMayer

Facebook – facebook.com/DaleMayer.author

BookBub – bookbub.com/authors/dale-mayer

Also by Dale Mayer

Published Adult Books:

Bullard's Battle

Ryland's Reach, Book 1
Cain's Cross, Book 2
Eton's Escape, Book 3
Garret's Gambit, Book 4
Kano's Keep, Book 5
Fallon's Flaw, Book 6
Quinn's Quest, Book 7
Bullard's Beauty, Book 8
Bullard's Best, Book 9

Terkel's Team

Damon's Deal, Book 1

Kate Morgan

Simon Says… Hide, Book 1
Simon Says… Jump, Book 2
Simon Says… Ride, Book 3
Simon Says… Scream, Book 4

Hathaway House

Aaron, Book 1
Brock, Book 2
Cole, Book 3

Denton, Book 4
Elliot, Book 5
Finn, Book 6
Gregory, Book 7
Heath, Book 8
Iain, Book 9
Jaden, Book 10
Keith, Book 11
Lance, Book 12
Melissa, Book 13
Nash, Book 14
Owen, Book 15
Percy, Book 16
Hathaway House, Books 1–3
Hathaway House, Books 4–6
Hathaway House, Books 7–9

The K9 Files

Ethan, Book 1
Pierce, Book 2
Zane, Book 3
Blaze, Book 4
Lucas, Book 5
Parker, Book 6
Carter, Book 7
Weston, Book 8
Greyson, Book 9
Rowan, Book 10
Caleb, Book 11
Kurt, Book 12
Tucker, Book 13
Harley, Book 14

Kyron, Book 15
Jenner, Book 16
The K9 Files, Books 1–2
The K9 Files, Books 3–4
The K9 Files, Books 5–6
The K9 Files, Books 7–8
The K9 Files, Books 9–10
The K9 Files, Books 11–12

Lovely Lethal Gardens

Arsenic in the Azaleas, Book 1
Bones in the Begonias, Book 2
Corpse in the Carnations, Book 3
Daggers in the Dahlias, Book 4
Evidence in the Echinacea, Book 5
Footprints in the Ferns, Book 6
Gun in the Gardenias, Book 7
Handcuffs in the Heather, Book 8
Ice Pick in the Ivy, Book 9
Jewels in the Juniper, Book 10
Killer in the Kiwis, Book 11
Lifeless in the Lilies, Book 12
Murder in the Marigolds, Book 13
Nabbed in the Nasturtiums, Book 14
Offed in the Orchids, Book 15
Poison in the Pansies, Book 16
Lovely Lethal Gardens, Books 1–2
Lovely Lethal Gardens, Books 3–4
Lovely Lethal Gardens, Books 5–6
Lovely Lethal Gardens, Books 7–8
Lovely Lethal Gardens, Books 9–10

Psychic Vision Series

Tuesday's Child
Hide 'n Go Seek
Maddy's Floor
Garden of Sorrow
Knock Knock…
Rare Find
Eyes to the Soul
Now You See Her
Shattered
Into the Abyss
Seeds of Malice
Eye of the Falcon
Itsy-Bitsy Spider
Unmasked
Deep Beneath
From the Ashes
Stroke of Death
Ice Maiden
Snap, Crackle…
What If…
Talking Bones
Psychic Visions Books 1–3
Psychic Visions Books 4–6
Psychic Visions Books 7–9

By Death Series

Touched by Death
Haunted by Death
Chilled by Death
By Death Books 1–3

Broken Protocols – Romantic Comedy Series

Cat's Meow
Cat's Pajamas
Cat's Cradle
Cat's Claus
Broken Protocols 1-4

Broken and… Mending

Skin
Scars
Scales (of Justice)
Broken but… Mending 1-3

Glory

Genesis
Tori
Celeste
Glory Trilogy

Biker Blues

Morgan: Biker Blues, Volume 1
Cash: Biker Blues, Volume 2

SEALs of Honor

Mason: SEALs of Honor, Book 1
Hawk: SEALs of Honor, Book 2
Dane: SEALs of Honor, Book 3
Swede: SEALs of Honor, Book 4
Shadow: SEALs of Honor, Book 5
Cooper: SEALs of Honor, Book 6
Markus: SEALs of Honor, Book 7
Evan: SEALs of Honor, Book 8

Mason's Wish: SEALs of Honor, Book 9
Chase: SEALs of Honor, Book 10
Brett: SEALs of Honor, Book 11
Devlin: SEALs of Honor, Book 12
Easton: SEALs of Honor, Book 13
Ryder: SEALs of Honor, Book 14
Macklin: SEALs of Honor, Book 15
Corey: SEALs of Honor, Book 16
Warrick: SEALs of Honor, Book 17
Tanner: SEALs of Honor, Book 18
Jackson: SEALs of Honor, Book 19
Kanen: SEALs of Honor, Book 20
Nelson: SEALs of Honor, Book 21
Taylor: SEALs of Honor, Book 22
Colton: SEALs of Honor, Book 23
Troy: SEALs of Honor, Book 24
Axel: SEALs of Honor, Book 25
Baylor: SEALs of Honor, Book 26
Hudson: SEALs of Honor, Book 27
Lachlan: SEALs of Honor, Book 28
SEALs of Honor, Books 1–3
SEALs of Honor, Books 4–6
SEALs of Honor, Books 7–10
SEALs of Honor, Books 11–13
SEALs of Honor, Books 14–16
SEALs of Honor, Books 17–19
SEALs of Honor, Books 20–22
SEALs of Honor, Books 23–25

Heroes for Hire

Levi's Legend: Heroes for Hire, Book 1
Stone's Surrender: Heroes for Hire, Book 2

Merk's Mistake: Heroes for Hire, Book 3
Rhodes's Reward: Heroes for Hire, Book 4
Flynn's Firecracker: Heroes for Hire, Book 5
Logan's Light: Heroes for Hire, Book 6
Harrison's Heart: Heroes for Hire, Book 7
Saul's Sweetheart: Heroes for Hire, Book 8
Dakota's Delight: Heroes for Hire, Book 9
Tyson's Treasure: Heroes for Hire, Book 10
Jace's Jewel: Heroes for Hire, Book 11
Rory's Rose: Heroes for Hire, Book 12
Brandon's Bliss: Heroes for Hire, Book 13
Liam's Lily: Heroes for Hire, Book 14
North's Nikki: Heroes for Hire, Book 15
Anders's Angel: Heroes for Hire, Book 16
Reyes's Raina: Heroes for Hire, Book 17
Dezi's Diamond: Heroes for Hire, Book 18
Vince's Vixen: Heroes for Hire, Book 19
Ice's Icing: Heroes for Hire, Book 20
Johan's Joy: Heroes for Hire, Book 21
Galen's Gemma: Heroes for Hire, Book 22
Zack's Zest: Heroes for Hire, Book 23
Bonaparte's Belle: Heroes for Hire, Book 24
Noah's Nemesis: Heroes for Hire, Book 25
Tomas's Trials: Heroes for Hire, Book 26
Heroes for Hire, Books 1–3
Heroes for Hire, Books 4–6
Heroes for Hire, Books 7–9
Heroes for Hire, Books 10–12
Heroes for Hire, Books 13–15
Heroes for Hire, Books 16–18
Heroes for Hire, Books 19–21
Heroes for Hire, Books 22–24

SEALs of Steel

Badger: SEALs of Steel, Book 1
Erick: SEALs of Steel, Book 2
Cade: SEALs of Steel, Book 3
Talon: SEALs of Steel, Book 4
Laszlo: SEALs of Steel, Book 5
Geir: SEALs of Steel, Book 6
Jager: SEALs of Steel, Book 7
The Final Reveal: SEALs of Steel, Book 8
SEALs of Steel, Books 1–4
SEALs of Steel, Books 5–8
SEALs of Steel, Books 1–8

The Mavericks

Kerrick, Book 1
Griffin, Book 2
Jax, Book 3
Beau, Book 4
Asher, Book 5
Ryker, Book 6
Miles, Book 7
Nico, Book 8
Keane, Book 9
Lennox, Book 10
Gavin, Book 11
Shane, Book 12
Diesel, Book 13
Jerricho, Book 14
Killian, Book 15
Hatch, Book 16
Corbin, Book 17
The Mavericks, Books 1–2

The Mavericks, Books 3–4
The Mavericks, Books 5–6
The Mavericks, Books 7–8
The Mavericks, Books 9–10
The Mavericks, Books 11–12

Collections

Dare to Be You…
Dare to Love…
Dare to be Strong…
RomanceX3

Standalone Novellas

It's a Dog's Life
Riana's Revenge
Second Chances

Published Young Adult Books:

Family Blood Ties Series

Vampire in Denial
Vampire in Distress
Vampire in Design
Vampire in Deceit
Vampire in Defiance
Vampire in Conflict
Vampire in Chaos
Vampire in Crisis
Vampire in Control
Vampire in Charge
Family Blood Ties Set 1–3
Family Blood Ties Set 1–5

Family Blood Ties Set 4–6
Family Blood Ties Set 7–9
Sian's Solution, A Family Blood Ties Series Prequel Novelette

Design series

Dangerous Designs
Deadly Designs
Darkest Designs
Design Series Trilogy

Standalone

In Cassie's Corner
Gem Stone (a Gemma Stone Mystery)
Time Thieves

Published Non-Fiction Books:

Career Essentials

Career Essentials: The Résumé
Career Essentials: The Cover Letter
Career Essentials: The Interview
Career Essentials: 3 in 1

Made in the USA
Middletown, DE
28 August 2022